THIS C
PLENTY O

M000211173

She was a clean-limbed, lemon fluff blonde standing there, waiting for a taxi. Gordon Banner was a lonely out-of-towner who happened to be driving by. The ominous threat of rain, plus a shortage of empty cabs, made the pick-up easy…

Before long, he found himself inside her apartment. Flung upon the bed was the still warm body of the clean-limbed, lemon fluff blonde. She'd been strangled—strangled while he waited outside her door for her to change out of her ripped dress. Thus did Gordon Banner become the prime suspect in the murder of a girl he had known only a few short minutes.

Swiftly paced and filled with raw, gritty, suspense, "The Deadly Pick-up" ranks among renown mystery author Milton K. Ozaki's most spine-tingling tales.

FOR A COMPLETE SECOND NOVEL, TURN TO PAGE 123

POLICE LINEUP:

GORDON BANNER
When you're brand new in town you don't expect to fall in with a corpse, but that's what happened to this flour salesman.

SARAH LIVINGSTON
Her dad had been a detective; now she wanted to be one, too. But it was tough being a woman in a man's racket.

PETER PONZIO
As cheap gangsters went, he was a pretty smooth operator and not easily ruffled—until the cops found a corpse in his backyard.

MILLIE ROYCE
She was a sweet kid who happened to fall in with bad company. The more desperate she became, the deeper she seemed to fall.

CARLO VENTUTTI
He was old, wizened, and confined to a wheelchair—but that didn't stop him from having the biggest drug racket in the city.

LIEUTENANT FIELDING
This tough cop had been in the police game for a long time and pretty much knew all the angles.

LILA LIVINGSTON
She had a body that would stop a truck and the brains to go along with it, but it turned out to be a deadly combination.

TONY GRECO
There was no question about his sexuality. The only real questions were how crooked he was and how far he'd go.

THE DEADLY PICK-UP

By
MILTON K. OZAKI

ARMCHAIR FICTION
PO Box 4369, Medford, Oregon 97504

*The original text of this novel was first
published by Graphic Books*

Armchair Edition, Copyright 2015 by Gregory Luce
All Rights Reserved

*For more information about Armchair Books and products, visit our
website at…*

www.armchairfiction.com

Or email us at…

armchairfiction@yahoo.com

CHAPTER ONE

SHE WAS STANDING on the edge of the curb in the middle of a block and I spotted her while I was still a good eighth of a mile away. She was a good-looking young babe with long yellow hair that hung in a breezy lemon fluff about her neck and shoulders and when she caught my eye, she was gesturing frantically at a taxi. The taxi was loaded, apparently, for it sailed right past her. I was too far away to hear the names she hurled after it, but I could see her lips chewing at angry words and I noticed that she stamped a neatly shod foot against the pavement with considerable spirit.

I grinned, slowed my sedan, and tried to get a better look at her. She was indeed young and startlingly pretty. The wolf inside me had been dozing tranquilly, but it awakened suddenly and began to howl. Braking the sedan, I swung it toward the curb. The line of cars behind me began to honk raucously, but my mind was on the blonde in the svelte pink dress, the one who was tapping a neat black pump against the curb and exhibiting a nice expanse of leg. I ignored the horns.

As I approached, she turned her head and eyed my car, speculatively at first and then with relief. The frown around her pretty eyes smoothed out and her bright red lips curved in a quick dazzling smile. At the same instant, a friendly gust of wind came in off the lake and paused to pluck at her dress, molding it to her body in a way that left very little to the imagination. The wolf got up on his hind legs and shrieked hungrily. I stopped my car and opened the door.

"Hello," she said, sounding very friendly. "Going anywhere near Jackson and Wells?" Her eyes were clear and blue and she had a smile that would have melted stainless steel.

"Climb in," I told her, making a conscious effort to keep from licking my lips. "I'm new in the city, but I'll certainly try to find it."

"I wouldn't want you to go out of your way—"

I grinned. "Why not? I really wasn't going anywhere in particular."

"Well—" She looked up and down the street, as if to make certain that no other means of transportation were available and I noticed that she was hugging a small package against her hip. "I'd certainly appreciate a lift. I'm late for an appointment and it looks like it's going to start raining any minute."

"It sure does," I agreed. "I've been just driving around seeing the town and I'll be glad to take you wherever you want to go."

"It's awfully nice of you—" As she slid into the car, a fold of the pink dress caught on the inside handle of the door and there was a sharp tearing sound. "Oh!" she gasped. "My dress!"

The tear was a long jagged one extending nearly to her hip and revealing the pale blue of a lacy nylon slip beneath her dress. "That darned handle!" I exclaimed. "Gosh, I'm awfully sorry! It was put on backwards, I think. You'll have to—"

"Oh, what am I going to do?" she moaned. "I simply can't go downtown like this!"

"Honestly, I'm awfully sorry! I'll pay for the dress, of course, and—"

"Don't be silly!" She folded the edges of the tear together and tried to smooth the skirt down over her shapely knees. "It was as much my fault as yours and I can mend it easily. But I've simply got to get downtown this afternoon—and I can't go like this! What in the world am I going to do?"

"Do you live near here?"

"Just around the block. But—"

"Well, why don't I drive you there and wait while you change? It won't take you more than a few minutes to slip into something else, will it?"

"Oh, I couldn't impose on you to—"

"Why not?" I asked. "I'm not going any place in particular and it's really my fault that your dress got torn. That handle—"

"You're sure you wouldn't mind waiting a minute or two?"

"Of course not. I'll be glad to. Incidentally, my name is Banner, Gordon Banner."

"I'm Lila Livingston." She frowned and bit her lip, then said, "I don't know what you're thinking, Mr. Banner, but when I saw you coming, I was nearly desperate. That's why I—well—that's why I let you—"

"Pick you up?" I supplied, grinning at her.

"Yes." She nodded and managed another dazzling smile. "I have to get to the club as soon as possible and you looked like a nice guy, so—"

"You don't have to apologize," I told her. "Which way do I go?"

"Turn right at the next corner and circle the block. It's a two-story brick building on the right-hand side."

I swung the sedan around the block and brought it to a stop in front of the building she indicated and turned off the ignition.

"You're sure you want to wait?" she asked anxiously.

"Of course." I pointed at a couple of splotches of water on the windshield. "See, it's starting to rain already. You'd never find a cab."

"Well—I'll hurry."

She snapped the door open and, holding the torn dress together with one hand, she slid off the seat and out of the car. I watched her slim nylon-clad legs dash up the walk to the building, then I grinned at myself in the rearview mirror and lit a cigarette. Mentally, I stroked the wolf and advised him to be patient for a while. Chicago was going to be a nice place to work. Imagine meeting a girl like that on my first day in the city! I'd not only learned her name and where she lived, but I was reasonably certain that she was unmarried. Furthermore, I was about to make her feel obligated to me.

Whoops.

I noticed that she had left the package on the seat beside me. I prodded it with a finger, then weighed it in my hand. It was solid, fairly heavy and sealed at each end and down the middle with large blobs of red wax. I dropped it back on the seat, stroked the wolf behind his ears a few times to pacify him, and treated my lungs to some more of the tangy perfume that still lingered in the car.

Here's some autobiography: I'm big in the shoulders, medium-tall and have 33 years under my belt, most of them spent in northern Wisconsin in the area around Fond du Lac. I'm soft-spoken, fond of banana cream pie, and play a darned good game of two-bit-limit draw poker. Some of my friends say that I'm inclined to talk too much. That's a lie.

A salesman has to talk or starve and I happen to have a stomach with a great fondness for food. The Tacoma Flour Company thinks I'm a good salesman; at least they decided I was being wasted in the wilds of Wisconsin and transferred me to their Chicago office. Matrimonially, I'm wide open. Like most guys my age, I've been up and down the gamut of blondes, redheads and brunettes several times, but I never found one I couldn't shake loose. Either I got damned sick of them or they decided there were greener pastures elsewhere. I don't think it's because of my face either. I have all the normal equipment and more than my share of brown semi-wavy hair, which is more than a lot of so-called "eligible" men have. Maybe it's my attitude. I've been looking for a girl who combined the attributes of a cook, courtesan, and Miss America, preferably with the features of Arlene Dahl and I haven't run across anyone even remotely capable of getting beyond the qualifying rounds.

But Chicago girls are different. The blonde looked as though she had possibilities. She might even be able to cook. Lila Livingston—a pretty name. I rolled it around on my tongue a few times to get used to it, then smashed my cigarette and lit another. I began to make devious and ulterior plans.

Ten minutes passed.

Fifteen minutes.

The rain was falling in a steady drizzle and the windshield had become a slab of writhing rivulets. I tried to visualize her pulling the torn dress over her blonde head and slipping her arms into another. She said she'd do a quick change. It shouldn't take more than a couple of minutes, but perhaps she'd decided to repair the pink dress. No, I decided, she'd been in too much of a hurry. She sounded quite definite when she said she'd change into something else. So what the devil was keeping her so long?

Twenty minutes. Twenty-five.

It couldn't take that long to change a dress, cartoons and comics to the contrary. Something was wrong. The thought made me straighten in the seat and crush out my cigarette. I knew suddenly that something was very wrong. I started to get out of the car. Bumping against the package, I picked it up and tossed it on the back seat. Then I got out, slammed the door, locked it, and ran through the rain toward the building.

Her name was printed beneath the bell of apartment 2-B.

I jabbed a finger against the bell button and held it there for several seconds. I waited a moment, then jabbed it again. Why didn't she answer the bell? She was certainly in her apartment. There was a possibility that the bell was out of order, of course, but it didn't seem likely.

I was standing there, frowning at the small round black button of the bell when an elderly man opened the door and entered the vestibule. He glanced at me, nodded, took a key from his pocket, and unlocked the inner door. I smiled and nodded and held the door open for him. We entered together and the door closed softly behind us. The stairs were wide and thickly carpeted. He went first, taking his time and moaning a little as though the effort bothered his arthritis. I followed impatiently. At the second floor, I spotted the door of 2-B and strolled toward it. The elderly man glanced back, nodded again, and limped toward the door of the adjoining apartment. I waited until he opened the door and went in, then I banged my knuckles against the door of 2-B. The seconds crept by like tired soldiers—and nothing happened.

I noticed that the key slit of the tumbler lock was at an angle indicating that the tumblers had not been restored to neutral. I took a dime from my pocket, pressed the edge of it into the key slit, and turned it slightly. The lock clicked back as I had known it would. I listened a moment, then pushed gently on the door. It swung open. With a quick glance down the corridor, I stepped inside.

"Miss Livingston?" I called softly.

The apartment was beautifully furnished. Sunlight through the Venetian blinds illuminated a large living room containing a wide sofa, upholstered chairs, a combination radio-phonograph, and a magazine-littered coffee table. An archway to the left caught my eye.

Louder I called, "Miss Livingston!"

With an odd cold feeling at the base of my spine, I walked toward the archway. I found myself in an alcove. A sort of closet was to my left, its contents concealed by a maroon drape on runners. Straight ahead, a half open door revealed a bathroom. Another door was to my right. I hesitated a moment, then turned its knob and pushed it open. I stood there looking into a large bedroom. Clad in the sheer, lace-edged, pale blue slip that I had glimpsed through the tear in the pink dress, Lila Livingston was stretched limply across the bed. Her slim neck was strained back at an awkward angle and the white of her skin was marred by ugly purplish blotches.

I didn't need to touch her to know she was dead. She had been strangled. Someone had strangled her, then lifted her slim, beautiful body and tossed it on the bed. My stomach writhed and turned over. Then something crashed against the back of my head and blackness rushed into my eyes and swallowed me...

CHAPTER TWO

GREAT WAVES were splashing into my face. I was swimming, struggling, trying to fight the water that gurgled in my nose. Then an iceberg slid over my face and I was freezing. I groaned, tried to claw my way up, tried to find air amidst the water that was drowning me. Gradually, I began to realize that hands were on my shoulders, pressing me down and that the only part of me that was wet was my face. Someone had me in a vise-like grip and was deliberately trying to suffocate me. Then a voice penetrated my mind. It was a low voice, faintly irritated, faintly sympathetic. It kept saying: "Lie still, can't you? I'm trying to help you. Can't you lie still?"

I stopped struggling for a moment and tried to see where the voice was coming from. My eyes refused to open. I could feel them trembling as the muscles wrenched at them, but I couldn't see a thing.

"That's better," the voice said. It was a female voice, I decided, and for a moment I thought of my mother. But she was in Fond du Lac, several hundred miles away. While I was struggling dazedly with this fact, the voice said, "Just a couple more moments. Lie still for just a couple more moments."

Fingers moved firmly about my body, tracing the placement of bones, then they ascended and touched my head. I yelped and tried to roll away from them. They were insistent. A hand caught my shoulder and pressed me down and the fingers explored a painful area behind my right ear. A kaleidoscope of colors exploded behind my eyes and a scream surged toward my lips. With all my strength, I jerked my head away from the bedeviling hand.

"You're all right," the voice soothed. "You were hit rather hard, but the skin isn't broken. There's nothing seriously wrong with you." The darkness and wetness disappeared suddenly, when a cold wet rag was taken off of my face. "How do you feel?"

"Rrrr!" I groaned.

My head felt as though there was a red-hot pile driver inside it trying to work its way out. I rolled over on my stomach, got my elbows on the floor, and began to struggle up. I got onto my knees, then a hand grabbed one of my arms and helped me the rest of the way to my feet. I stood there, swaying dizzily. The hands guided me to a chair. I sat down, held my throbbing head with both hands, and stared giddily about the reeling room. Things began to come into focus.

Across from me, sitting in the center of a maroon studio couch was a girl. She had a lot of red hair, which was piled up on top of her head and held in place with several small gold combs. She was dressed in a severely tailored dark blue suit. Her face was rather pretty. It was almost oval in shape and featured a pert chip of a nose, a red mouth, delicately arched brows, and wide green eyes. The green eyes were watching me intently and as casually as though she were holding a book or a napkin. She was balancing a large blue-black automatic in her right hand, the big eye of the gun was pointing at my chest.

"Well, what's your story?" she demanded. As she spoke, her hand moved a trifle and the gun pointed at my stomach.

"Hey," I gasped, "is that thing loaded?"

"There's one way to find out," she said casually, "but I don't recommend it. I'd advise you to start talking—and fast."

The scene in the bedroom came rushing back like a bad dream and the devil at the controls of the pile driver set it pounding inside my head again. "Lila!" I groaned. "Good God! She's—she's—"

"She's dead," the girl commented matter-of-factly. "I know that. What happened?"

"I don't know. I was waiting for her. I waited nearly a half hour, but she didn't come down. She was just supposed to change her dress and—" The pile driver rammed into the area behind my ear. "Ouch! My head!"

"Someone sapped you," the girl admitted. "It'll hurt for awhile, but you'll be all right in a few hours. Now, say that again. You waited nearly a half hour for her—then what?"

"I was in my car, out in front, waiting for her. You see, I—she—picked me up. It was just starting to rain and there weren't any cabs. I offered to drive her wherever she wanted to go, but she tore her dress getting into my car and I brought her back here so she could change." The words came out slowly and painfully. "I waited nearly a half hour, but she didn't come down and I began to get worried. So I—I came up to see what was the matter."

"How'd you get in?"

"While I was ringing her bell, one of the other tenants came in and I came in with him."

"How did you get in here?" Her foot tapped the floor. I noticed that the foot was shod in neat business-like brown oxfords and that it was surmounted by a very attractive leg. "Was the door unlocked?"

"Well—to tell the truth, it wasn't."

"Then how did you get in?" The green eyes flickered. "Did Lila open it for you?"

"No..." I blurted the word. "I knocked and when she didn't answer, I noticed that whoever had unlocked it last had removed the key without turning it all the way back. I pushed a dime into the slit and forced the tumblers around."

"Bright boy." The comment was faintly sarcastic. "Where was Lila?"

"She was in there." I nodded toward the bedroom and immediately regretted it. The pile driver started banging away like fury. "I saw that she was dead—and then something hit me. That's all I remember."

"You didn't see anybody?"

"No. Only the old geezer who lives down the hall. He's the one who opened the door downstairs. He came up just ahead of me."

"Did he see you come in here?"

"I suppose so."

"That's bad." She sat there holding the gun and frowning at the wall behind my head. Abruptly, she laid the gun on the studio couch and stood up. "You say she tore her dress?"

"Yes. It was a pink dress. She must have taken it off, because all she had on—"

"Just like a man," she commented, striding toward the archway. "You made sure that you saw that much, didn't you?" She went into the bedroom and returned in a moment with the pink dress. "Is this the one?" she asked, holding it up.

"Yes." I started to nod but caught myself just in time. "That's the one she tore while getting into my car. It caught on the door handle and—"

"It certainly is torn," she agreed. "Where'd you say you met her?"

"On Lake Shore Drive. She was trying to flag a cab and I was just driving around, getting acquainted with the city and—"

A cynical smile tugged at her lips. "I know. You saw her and she saw you. Before you knew it, you were falling into each others' arms. That's the way Lila operated. She attracted men the way some people attract mosquitoes." She made the statement drily and when I didn't say anything, she added, "I'm her sister. Sarah Livingston is the name." I must have looked surprised, for with a quick grimace, she said, "I know we don't look or act much alike. Lila got all the sex appeal, and God gave me all the brains. Lila didn't have sense enough to come in out of the rain."

"Good Lord, don't you realize that she's—"

"Sure, she's dead—and I'm her sister. But I have no intention of becoming emotional or irrational about it. Frankly, there was very little love lost between us. She went her way and while I didn't approve, I didn't interfere, because it wasn't any of my business. She was always selfish and greedy and lazy and the only person's feelings she ever considered were her own. I'm not surprised that someone killed her." The green eyes snapped as she talked. "You didn't kill her, did you, Mr. Banner?"

I jumped a little. "No, of course not! But how—how did you know—?"

"Your name?" A smile softened her face for a moment. "I know a lot about you. You're Gordon Banner, you've been living and working in Fond du Lac, Wisconsin, you're five-eight, weigh 175. Caucasian race, 33 years old, single and about to report to the Chicago office of the Tacoma Flour Company where, beginning next week, you'll be employed in their sales department at a salary of $350 a month."

"For Pete's sake!" Unconsciously, I reached up and patted the pocket of my suit coat where I carried my wallet.

"Don't worry. I looked through your wallet and read a couple of the letters in your pocket, but I didn't steal any of your money. Lila might have, but I didn't. It's all there, all $191 of it."

"I didn't think—"

"Oh, yes, you did. Let's be frank and honest, Mr. Banner. I like to keep things neat and rational and in their places. I don't think you killed Lila. I know how Lila affects men, and I believe that you saw her on the street, just like you say, and that she decided it'd be cheaper to ride with you than in a taxi."

"That wasn't it at all!" I protested. "There weren't any cabs and she had an appointment—"

"That isn't the way Lila thought of it," she interrupted. "I know how her mind worked. As far as she was concerned, men were simply public utilities. She used them and took advantage of them whenever it suited her convenience and apparently you happened along at the right time. Then she tore her dress. Lila gave more thought to the way she looked than to anything else in her life. I can't imagine her wearing it downtown in this condition. So she came up here and started to change. But someone else was already here, or they came in while she was changing—and they strangled her. When you came up, that someone was still here. The closet, right behind that drape, gave them a good place to hide."

"That's where they were," I agreed. "Seeing her like that made me feel a little sick. I was backing out of the room when—blank."

"I figured that. Whoever it was gave you a terrific blow on the head. You're lucky your skull isn't fractured. It's beginning to feel better, isn't it?"

"Not much. But never mind me. What are we going to do about Lila?"

"I'm thinking about that. You see, Mr. Banner, this is a serious situation. I came here to get a purse that Lila borrowed from me last week. I know you were unconscious when I arrived and I know you didn't give yourself that crack on the head. I'm a private detective and I'm not easy to fool."

"A detective?"

"Don't look so astonished. You find women everywhere these days and my father happened to run one of the best agencies in the country during his lifetime." She straightened a little as she said it, as though there were an invisible chip on her shoulder, and the pile of red hair on her head looked as though it were getting ready to burst into flame.

"But—a detective!" I exclaimed. "Well isn't that rather dangerous for an attractive young girl like—"

"Flattery will get you nothing," she interrupted coldly. "I'm twenty-eight years old and proud of it. As I was saying, I'm not easily fooled. That's why I believe that story of yours. But there are other people who are going to think differently. The police, for instance."

"The police?"

"Certainly. Lila was murdered, don't forget. When the police find her poor dead body stretched out on that bed, a lot of wheels are going to start turning and the man who saw you come in here will be interviewed. Even if he doesn't give them a good description of you, there's the danger that you put your fingerprints on something, that someone saw her get into your car and dozens of little things like that. You may not realize it, but you're in the beginning of a very bad spot."

"But I didn't even know her! I just—"

"I believe you, Mr. Banner, because I know Lila. I think everything happened exactly as you said. But the police won't. They'll take one look at the superficial facts and decide that she picked you up and brought you here. Then they're going to look at the torn dress and decide that you started something that she didn't want to finish. By the time it gets to the newspapers, you'll be Suspect Number One in a sex murder. They'll print big pictures of Lila and they'll say that you ripped her dress off and—well, I'll leave the rest of the details to your imagination."

I stared disbelievingly at her. "You mean they'll say I tried to..." I couldn't finish it.

"That's exactly what I do mean." A business-like tone came into her voice. "Fortunately, I found you and I believe you—and I'm a licensed private detective. If you were my client, I'd be inclined to forget the normal routine and give you a break."

"What's the normal routine?"

"I ought to phone the cops without delay and turn you over to them."

I moistened my lips. "And if I retain you—"

"In that case, we'll get out of here and the Livingston Agency will start looking for the murderer. I'm the Livingston Agency, of course, and my fee would be $25 per day plus expenses."

I sighed. "You aren't leaving me a great deal of choice."

She moved her shoulders casually. "Lila never did anything for me while she was living. The least she can do now that she's dead is supply me with a case so I can keep the agency's rent paid."

"How much would I have to pay you?"

"Well, let's see." The green eyes narrowed a little as though she were trying to read fine print on the wall behind me. "You've got $191 and you don't start work until next week. Suppose you give me $75 now—that'll pay for three days and I ought to have things pretty well in hand by then. I can collect the rest after you've drawn a check from Tacoma Flour."

"This is blackmail."

"On the contrary. You're in trouble, trouble of your own making, and I'm offering to help you out of it. If you weren't a chaser and hadn't tried to pick—"

"But I didn't kill her!" I interrupted hotly. "You don't really think I hit myself on the head, do you? When you got here—"

"I told you that I believe your fantastic story—but only because I know Lila. The police didn't know her and they won't believe a word you say."

"But you're just a girl! If I have to hire a private detective, it might be better for me to get a—"

"My sex has nothing to do with this." She snapped the words at me, then turned and walked purposefully toward the telephone. "As long as you're going to be stupid, I may as well phone the police. I thought I was doing you a favor."

"Wait a minute." I caught her arm. "I'm just trying to get things straight in my own mind. It might be dangerous for a girl like you to get involved in this sort of a case. Lila was murdered. You might—"

"I understand my position," she said coldly, jerking her arm away from my hand. "The point is, do you understand yours?"

The trouble was I did. Actually, I was less worried about the police than I was about details getting into the newspapers and reaching the ears of the officials of the Tacoma Flour Company. They certainly couldn't react favorably to a new employee who went home with a strange blonde as soon as he hit the big city and got himself in the news as a suspected sex murderer.

"I'm afraid I do," I admitted reluctantly. I took $75 from my wallet and handed the bills to her.

She pushed them carelessly into the pocket of her suit jacket and, in business-like tones, asked, "Exactly what time was it when you met her?"

"It was a little after three." Automatically, I looked at my wristwatch, then held it to my ear. It was ticking. "It isn't really after five now, is it?"

"Yes. You were unconscious quite a while, long enough to give the murderer a good chance to look for whatever he wanted." Her green eyes narrowed a little. "I wonder if he found it, whatever it was."

"You think he was—looking for something?"

"Of course. You saw the bedroom, didn't you?"

"I saw her on the bed, that's all."

"Well, maybe the search hadn't gotten as far as the bedroom when you arrived. It's a mess. Drawers emptied on the floor, everything turned upside down. They were definitely looking for something and it must have been something valuable—or they wouldn't have murdered her to get it." Her lips bent in a wry sort of smile. "That's another reason why I went through your pockets. I had to be sure you didn't have it."

The telephone rang. We both started nervously and, instinctively, I reached a hand toward the instrument.

"Don't answer it!" Sarah Livingston said sharply. "Let it ring."

I jerked my hand back. The phone rang six times, its shrill peal jangling through my aching head like a whirling knife and then it was silent.

"We've got to get out of here," Sarah Livingston decided. She picked up the gun and put it in her purse. Then she went into the bedroom. When she came back, she surveyed the living room critically and moved quietly toward the door. "We'll go downstairs together," she said, "and we'll get into your car and drive to my apartment. It's only a few blocks from here. Then we'll decide what we're going to do." She turned the knob and opened the door a few inches. "Do you want me to help you down the stairs?"

"No," I assured her. "I'll make it all right."

We went down the stairs and out of the building without meeting anyone. I unlocked the door of my sedan, waited until she got in, then walked around to the other side. I was about to start the car when I remembered the package. It was still on the back seat, so I leaned over, got it, and handed it to her.

"Lila was carrying this when I met her," I explained.

Sarah Livingston raised her eyebrows a little, weighed the package in her hand, but made no move to open it.

"You're her sister," I said. "See what's in it."

"I don't know if I should."

"It may be what they were looking for," I pointed out. "Go ahead, open it."

She hesitated, then untied the string and tore the seals. A moment later, she stripped away the heavy wrapping paper. I sucked in my breath and gaped incredulously. From the opened package tumbled six packets of crisp new paper currency. Each packet was bound with a narrow band of paper on which was printed the name of a bank and the numerals, $10,000.

"Good Lord!" I gasped. "Sixty thousand dollars!"

CHAPTER THREE

THIS IS what they were looking for," Sarah Livingston said softly, fingering one of the packets. "Lila had all this money—and someone knew it."

"But—sixty thousand dollars!" I exclaimed. "What was she doing with that much money?"

"That's what I'd like to know," Sarah said. She rimed the edges of the bills. "She was taking it someplace. I wonder where."

"She asked me to drive her to Jackson and Wells, where ever that is, and she mentioned something about a club."

"Pete Ponzio." Sarah mentioned the name as though there were a bad taste in her mouth. "Yes, she might have been taking it to Ponzio's place. He runs a joint called the Flask Club where a lot of characters hang out, the sort of characters Lila found fascinating." With deft fingers, she aligned the packets of currency and hastily rewrapped them in the paper. "We'll have to get rid of this as soon as possible."

"What do you mean, get rid of it?"

"Put it in some place safe, it was probably stolen."

"Stolen?"

"Of course. You didn't think Lila earned it, did you?" Sarah emitted a feminine snort. "Knowing Lila, I wouldn't be surprised to learn that one of her playmates had robbed a bank and given her part of the loot to keep." She frowned suddenly. "Lila would have done anything for that amount of money. I wonder if she was pulling a double-cross on someone and trying to skip out of town with this?"

"She told me she had an appointment at the club. If she'd planned to leave town, it seems to me she'd have had some luggage with her."

"Not necessarily. She may have been in too much of a hurry to pack anything. Besides, she could have bought anything she needed."

"Including a new dress," I reminded her.

"That's right." Sarah shook her head. "It sounds sort of silly. Why rush off—and then go back to change clothes? Lila wasn't dumb. She wouldn't do anything as stupid as that."

I was staring at the package. "I don't see why she left it in the car with me," I said slowly. "That was sort of careless, wasn't it? She'd never seen me before, didn't even know who I was, yet she—"

"Say, that is screwy! I'd almost forgotten that. I can't imagine anything upsetting Lila enough to make her run off and leave a fortune in cash in a stranger's hands. Gosh, I wonder—" Quickly, she reopened the package and removed a crisp green bill from one of the packets. She bent her red head over it and studied it intently. "No wonder!" she exclaimed softly. "It's as phony as a yellow pousse-café!"

"Phony? You mean counterfeit?"

"Exactly. Take a look."

I took the bill and eyed it critically. I hadn't seen many $100 bills, of course, but it looked genuine enough. I held it up to the light. Small red and blue threads were visible in the paper. "You're wrong," I said. "There are silk threads in the paper and only real money has—"

"They're fake," Sarah said positively. "They were probably drawn on with a fine pen and colored inks. The real test is in the quality of the engraving. Look at Franklin's face. There are broken lines in his cheeks and the shadows around his eyes and nose are kind of muddy. The government would have discarded a plate that was as worn or as sloppily engraved as that. See them?"

"No."

"Look, right here." She sketched over Franklin's puffy cheek with a long fingernail. "See how broken those lines are? Either the etcher's tool slipped accidentally or the lines were corroded with acid."

She was close beside me and as she bent over the bill, a tendril of her hair brushed against my nose. It had a clean mild fragrance, which tickled my nostrils and made them dilate pleasurably. "Oh," I said. "You mean *those* lines." I laid my head gently against hers.

Instantly, she jerked away and gave me a scathing look.

"Lila was the floozy of the family," she snapped. "Let's not have any of that."

"Any of what?" I tried to look blank.

"You know what I mean. Just keep your mind on a high plane, as I intend to keep mine. You're merely a client of the Livingston Agency and the only reason I'm sitting in your car with you is because it happens to be expedient, for purely business purposes, for me to do so. The kind of service I give doesn't include intimacies with the cash customers."

"Say, you've got me all wrong, Miss Livingston——"

"Okay, so I've got you wrong. Just don't let any of that head-to-head stuff happen again." She tossed her hair spiritedly, then pointed at the bill in my hand. "We were talking about counterfeit money, remember? Do you see the flaws?"

"Yes, but I'd never have noticed them if you hadn't called them to my attention—and I don't think anybody else would either." I folded the bill and put it into my pocket. "This is the nearest I've ever come to owning a $100 bill. I'm going to keep it as a souvenir."

"Don't you dare! It's against Federal law to possess counterfeit money and——"

"No one will miss it and I certainly don't intend to go around showing it to people."

"Then——"

"I'm going to keep it," I said firmly. "Period."

"Well—all right, but if you get caught, I don't know anything about it. Understand?"

"Sure."

She wrapped and tied the package again and tossed it on the rear seat of the sedan. "That's as good a place as any for it at the moment," she commented. "Too bad it isn't genuine. We could split it and both retire."

"Maybe that was Lila's idea."

She was silent a moment. "Drive north for a few blocks and see if you can find a drugstore," she said finally. "For sisters, Lila and I weren't very thick, but the least I can do is notify the authorities and see that she's buried properly. It probably isn't smart to make an anonymous phone call, but the police have to be alerted and I can't think of any other way of doing it. I don't want the murderer to get too much of a head start."

"Why not?"

"I want him caught, of course."

"You do?"

"Certainly."

I drove north as she requested and thoughts drenched my mind like gusts of icy rain. For the first time in my life, I realized I was in a hell of a jam—and I was scared. I parked suddenly and turned off the ignition.

"Look," I said. "Maybe you're a trained investigator and all that, but I don't like the idea of phoning the police, particularly from a neighborhood drugstore. We should have phoned from the apartment and stayed there and told them the truth. As it is, they'll find that rag you used on my face. I've heard they can analyze things like that and work out a description of the person it was used upon, especially if there happens to be any sweat or soil or hair on it. If they do and if they find out we were there and didn't call, then we'll really be in hot water."

She shrugged. "We can't go back now."

"Why not?"

"Because you said she was killed between three and three-thirty, while you were still sitting in your car. It's five-thirty now. We'd never be able to explain that two hour lapse."

"Why don't we go back and pretend that we just discovered her?" I suggested. "That would explain our fingerprints in case they find any. I could say that you fainted when you saw the body and that I used the washcloth on you."

"I've never fainted in my life!"

"You could pretend, couldn't you? It'd certainly be safer than going into a neighborhood store, using the phone and gambling that the clerk won't remember you."

"Maybe you're right," she admitted. "What if they examine your car and find the phony dough?"

"We could stick some stamps on it, address it to General Delivery and drop it in a mailbox."

"No." She shook her head decisively. "It'd be just like some fool postal clerk to get nosey and peek into it. We'll leave it at my apartment. Turn right, go one block east, then turn right again. It's that large apartment hotel on the west side of the street."

When we reached the building. I halted the car. Taking the package, she ran inside and came out almost immediately.

"That was fast," I said.

"I left it with the manager."

Neither of us spoke during the drive back to Lila's apartment building. With considerable relief, I saw that the street was as quiet and deserted as it had been when we left. No squad cars, no sirens, no blue uniforms in sight at all. Taking a deep breath, I parked and got out of the car. Sarah in a strained voice murmured, "It's good they haven't found her yet!"

"I hope we're doing the right thing," I said fervently.

"We are," she replied. She sounded more confident than she looked. "Remember, Mr. Banner, you're a friend of mine from out of town and I'm taking you to meet my sister. You've never seen her. That's all you've got to remember. You've never seen her and you don't know anything about her."

"Okay," I said. I grunted, then added, "And I wish to hell I hadn't."

"You aren't the first man who has felt that way, I assure you," she said grimly. "You might keep that fact in front of your mind. Lila probably deserved what she got, but we're both going to be shocked and I'm going to faint."

She unlocked the downstairs door with a key that she took from her purse and we went up the carpeted stairs together. We met no one. The door of 2-B was closed and the corridor was silent and deserted. We stopped in front of the door, stared into each other's eyes briefly, then Sarah slid her key into the lock and clicked it back. Remembering Lila's white blotched throat, I felt my stomach twist into knots as we entered the apartment. Sarah with a warning hiss shut the door and turned on a lamp beside the sofa. Everything seemed to be exactly as we left it. I don't know why I felt surprised, but I did.

"All right," Sarah said impatiently. "Let's get this over with." She walked toward the phone and picked up the receiver.

"Hey!" I said. "You're in the middle of a swoon. How can you do any telephoning?"

She dropped the instrument as though it had scorched her hand. "I must be upset," she admitted, coloring a little. "You're right, of course. I should have thought of that. You'll have to phone them."

"What's the number?"

"You're a stranger in town. You wouldn't know the number. Just dial up the operator and ask her for police headquarters."

I spun the dial and when a throaty-voiced operator answered, I said, "I want the police." The line went silent, then it click-clicked and a brisk male voice growled, "Central headquarters." I didn't have any trouble sounding excited. My voice trembled naturally as I said, "I want to report a murder. Please send someone to…" I gave the address. "…as soon as possible." I hung up quickly before he could start asking questions.

"Fine," Sarah said approvingly. "You sounded just right, nervous and not too smart. They ought to rush right over."

I ignored the jibe. "Where'd you put the washcloth?" I asked. "It ought to be wet when they get here."

"I think I threw it in the bathroom." She turned and went through the archway. "I'll get it."

I heard a light switch dick, then a muffled scream tore through the quiet of the apartment. My heart jumped eight inches and rammed against my larynx. I ran toward the archway and reached it in time to collide with her as she came rushing out of the bedroom. Her face was as white as steamed rice and her green eyes were dark with fear.

"It's gone!" Sarah cried in a voice shrill with consternation. "Lila's body—it's gone!"

CHAPTER FOUR

I DIDN'T BELIEVE her. Grabbing her shoulders, I thrust her aside and strode past her into the bedroom. Incredulously, I stared at the bed. The spread was rumpled showing where Lila Livingston's body had rested—but the body had disappeared. Frantically my eyes searched the room, then I dropped onto my knees and peered under the bed. Dust and dark shadows—and nothing else. I ran to the closet, tore aside the drape, and plunged my arms between the hangers loaded with dresses and suits. The scent of Lila's clothes clogged my nostrils and I jerked my arms away—empty. The bathroom! I pushed the door open and pawed the wall, trying to find the light switch. When I found it, finally, my heart was beating like a tom-tom. Light glared into my eyes revealing nothing except the usual bare, white fixtures. Incredulity became fear and fear became horror. Lila's body had actually vanished—and the police were on their way!

Sarah looked as though she had lost her vital organs. Her lips trembled speechlessly and she seemed a mere wraith of her former self. I squeezed her shoulders between my hands and shook her. "What the hell could have happened?" I demanded. "Try to think. The cops are coming. They'll be here any minute!"

She shook her head.

"We've got to think of something!"

A very small moan escaped her.

"Sarah!" I shook her so hard her teeth rattled.

"I'm sorry—" she whispered. She clenched her hands, holding them stiffly against her sides and her whole body trembled. Then color began to return to her face. "The back door," she murmured hoarsely. "We can go out the back and—"

"No," I said. "We can't run. That would only make them more suspicious. We've got to stay here. We've got to stick it out. For God's sake, Sarah, try to get a grip on yourself. Our only chance is to bluff them!"

"W-what d-do you m-mean?"

"Listen." I squeezed her shoulders and shook her a little to emphasize each word. "We didn't call them. We won't know what they're talking about. We've been sitting here all alone and we haven't seen Lila. They can look around if they want to. They won't find anything and eventually they'll get the idea that they misunderstood the address or that some practical joker sent them on a wild goose chase. Get the idea?"

"Yes." She swallowed and her lips tightened with decision. "That's a wonderful idea, Mr. Bann—"

"Gordon," I corrected. "We're old friends; otherwise we wouldn't be sitting here like this."

"Yes, Gordon." She jerked her head. "I'll straighten the bedroom a little. We'll have to pretend that we're—" Her eyes became hard and thoughtful for a second, then she swallowed again and continued, "We'll pretend that we're very good friends, and that we were waiting for Lila and—"

"Sure, sure," I interrupted. "Hurry and get things picked up. They'll be here in a second!"

We rushed into the bedroom. While I scooped things up with my arms and crammed them into drawers, Sarah smoothed the bedspread, patted the pillows and rearranged the hangers in the closet. When we finished, I was moist with perspiration and Sarah looked as though she'd just finished doing a job of washing and ironing. I surveyed the room critically. It looked halfway tidy. It might pass inspection. Hell, it *had* to pass inspection!

"They're coming..." Sarah whispered tensely.

Heavy feet were ascending the stairs. "Quick," I gasped, "the sofa..."

We sank onto its cushions just as a heavy hand banged peremptorily on the door. I threw my arms around her, pulled her roughly against me, and covered her lips with mine. She struggled furiously and her green eyes blazed at me like fluorescent stones, but I held her tightly and did a good job of smearing her lipstick. When I released her, she said, "Oh" in a thoroughly disgusted whisper and jerked away from me as though I had a flaming case of measles.

"I think someone is at the door, honey," I said loudly, waving my hands and shaking my head warningly.

"Oh!" she said again. Then comprehension hit her. The sparks in her eyes subsided suddenly and in a nearly normal tone she managed to say, "I'll see who it is." She walked to the door and opened it, unconsciously tucking a stray strand of her red hair into place with one hand as she did so.

"Police," a gruff voice announced. "We got a report that somebody's been murdered here."

"Murdered!" Her voice sounded as though it had been dipped in sleigh-bells. "Are you kidding?"

"This is the address they gave and this is apartment 2-B, ain't it?"

"Yes, but—"

He pushed past her, a tall thin cop in plainclothes followed by two burly uniformed assistants. "You don't mind if we look around, do you?" I had my handkerchief out and was wiping lipstick from my mouth. He looked at me hard and one of his eyebrows did a little jiggle, but he didn't crack a smile. "This your apartment, Miss?"

"It's my sister's," Sarah told him. "I'm Sarah Livingston and this is Mr. Banner. We were, well, waiting for my sister to come home."

"I'm Lieutenant Fielding. Homicide Bureau. You say you didn't phone headquarters?"

"Of course not!" Sarah's mouth gaped prettily. "You don't really mean that—"

"Yeah. What's in there?" He tipped his head toward the archway.

"A bedroom and a bathroom."

"Take a look, boys," Fielding directed. He stood in the center of the room, hands deep in the pockets of his suit jacket and stared somberly at us. "You look sort of familiar, Miss Livingston," he said finally. "Where have I seen you before?"

"I operate the Livingston Agency," Sarah said, coloring faintly. "You may have seen me around the—"

"Oh, so you're that female private eye." Fielding rolled his lips, eyed me appreciatively, and nodded. He grinned. "Business is kind of slow, eh?"

"On the contrary!" Sarah snapped. "Business is very good."

"That so?" Fielding looked at me again and lifted his eyebrows. "You a client, Mr. Banner—or is she keeping you under observation?"

"I'm one of her most ardent admirers, Lieutenant."

Fielding shrugged and eyed Sarah with frank approval. "Well, can't blame you for that."

The two cops came out of the bedroom. "Nix," one of them said. The other one shook his head and spread his hands.

Fielding grunted, went to the phone, and dialed a number. "Lieutenant Fielding," he said into the phone. "You sure you got that address right?" He listened a moment. "It's a phony then.

We're here and there's no sign of a body… Yeah… Okay." He hung up. "Sorry, folks." He walked to the door and opened it. "Come on, boys." With a short jerk of his head, he nodded to us and went out. The door closed after them.

"Whew!" I said gratefully, sinking back on the sofa. Sarah ran to the windows and peered through the slats of the Venetian blinds.

"They're downstairs," she announced. "One of them is looking at your car."

"Fine," I muttered. "What'd I do, park too near a fire hydrant?"

"It's all right. They're getting into their squad car. They're going away."

"They'll be back," I said. "She's dead and someone will find her body somewhere and then they'll remember about the call and they'll come back." I groaned. "What a mess!"

"You were swell, Mr. Banner." She turned from the window and came toward the sofa. "I'm afraid I underestimated you. For a man fresh from the country, you certainly have a lot of imagination." Her eyes studied me a bit thoughtfully, then she said, "Did you plan that little scene extemporaneously or did you just let yourself go?"

"Sheer inspiration," I told her. "It seemed a natural thing to do."

"Well, it worked out all right, thank heavens, but for a minute I thought I had a maniac on my hands. Just don't get the idea that you've established a precedent or something."

"You're the most egotistical female I've ever met."

"Egotistical?"

"You heard me. What makes you think I'm anxious to paw you? That's the second time you've accused me of making a pass, and the idea hadn't even occurred to me. I'll bet you've got calluses on your knees from looking under your bed every night."

"Why, the idea!"

"Instead of keeping your mind on business like you keep telling me to do, you're knocking yourself out trying to avoid a seduction that isn't even threatened." I went on with some heat. "For heaven's sake, if you're going to be a detective, why don't you act like one—and not like a woman who's sexually starved."

"Mr. Banner! I won't—"

"You probably resented your sister because men liked her and because she didn't go around with a chip on her shoulder all the time. Why not be realistic and face the facts? You're old enough to be married and have kids—and you're not. Instead, you're chasing around trying to convince people that you're a flint-skinned detective," I snorted. "I noticed that Lieutenant Fielding wasn't very impressed."

Her hand whistled through the air, aimed at my cheek. I ducked, caught her arm as it sailed past, and jerked her toward me. With a frightened squeal, she landed in my lap. I locked her arms behind her and pinioned her flailing legs.

"Relax, damn it!" I growled. "We're in trouble. We can play these kid games some other time."

"Let me go!"

"Not until you start acting like an adult."

"You're hurting me!"

"You're hurting yourself. Just relax. I can't think while you're twisting around like an animated corkscrew."

"Please! Let me—"

"Shut up."

I leaned back, holding her stiff protesting body against me and closed my eyes. Her breasts pulsated against my chest and her thick hair lay in a tangled mass against my face, but I forced my mind away from them and tried to think. Gradually, she stopped struggling and some of the stiffness went out of her. Her head dropped back and laid against my shoulder. I knew her eyes were open and that she was watching me, but I kept my eyes closed.

"I'm sorry," she murmured after awhile.

"Forget it," I growled.

"I'll behave."

"Sure." I released her hands and cradled my arm about her. She didn't try to get up. I took my other hand away from her legs. She sighed and rested her head against my shoulder. I moved my nose back and forth, stroking a strand of hair with it. "We've got to find Lila's body," I said slowly.

"Why?" She moved faintly, adjusting her curves to mine.

"Because the longer it's missing, the more deeply we'll be involved when it does turn up. The police department probably keeps a permanent record of calls received, and Fielding impressed me as the kind of guy who'd remember the color of my eyes ten years from now. As soon as he stumbles over her body, he'll connect things—and guess what'll happen to us."

"But the situation has changed, now." She sat up and raked her fingers through her hair. "Don't you see? The cops came here and inspected the premises. We were here and they got the impression that we'd been here all afternoon having a cozy little party all by ourselves. Whoever took her body did us a favor. The police will never connect us with her murder now!"

"You're sure?"

"Of course. We've alibied each other. You didn't tell them who had been murdered, so they won't be looking for anyone's body in particular. And when Lila's body is found, it'll simply be a coincidence. They'll think that we were here, waiting for her to come home—and she was somewhere else, getting herself killed."

"In that case, you can give me my seventy-five bucks back."

"What?" Her eyes had been relaxed and friendly, but now they snapped wide and became alive with consternation. Her shoes slapped the floor as she slid off my lap.

"If the cops aren't going to suspect me, I don't need a detective at twenty-five bucks a day." I wiggled my fingers. "Come on. Kick back."

Green fires flickered. "Why, you cheap—"

I grinned. "Look who's talking. You wouldn't keep a fee you didn't earn, would you?" I pointed at her purse. "Open up, honey. Give me back my hard-earned money."

"But—but—"

"No buts about it. You practically sandbagged it out of me and I want it back."

"But I've already spent it..."

"Like hell. Come on, cough up, Sarah. After all, it's—"

"But I did spend it!" she wailed. "When we stopped at my apartment, I left that package with the manager and—and I owed some rent, so I gave him the $75, too!"

"How do you like that?" I asked the wall behind her.

"One minute she's a little platinum-plated saint and the next minute she's a kept woman. She's got me paying her rent."

"I am not a kept woman!" Sarah shrilled. An octave higher and her voice would have been beyond range of the human ear. "You've no right to say—"

"The hell I haven't. It was my dough and you used it to pay your rent. That's the same as if I paid it. If that doesn't make you a kept woman, I'd like to know what—"

She stamped her foot and swung at me. I don't remember getting to my feet, but I guess I did, because when the door clicked open I was standing with my back to it and trying to avoid a flurry of feminine haymakers, which she was furiously attempting to pin on my chin. She stopped in mid-blow suddenly, thrust her head forward like a turkey swallowing a grain of corn and apprehension flooded her eyes. The apprehension swirled there for a split second, then it changed swiftly to an expression of flat stark terror.

I bent at the knees and started to whirl around. I was too late, much too late. Before I even glimpsed the newcomer, a black ball rolled into my eyes and the floor reached up for me.

CHAPTER FIVE

A COLD SPIDER of dread wriggled at the back of my neck when I regained consciousness. Clawing at the floor, I turned over and sat up. I regretted it immediately. The back of my head jumped spastically like a caterpillar on a hot stove and my cranial cavity seethed with thick volatile chili juice. My eyes were all right though. They peered around somewhat anxiously and identified my surroundings. I was still in Lila Livingston's apartment—and I was alone. The redhead was gone. My memory of Lila and what had happened to her became uglier than ever. Feeling as though there were a couple of clenched fists in my stomach, I got up and lurched on rubbery legs to the doorway of the bedroom. I forced myself to look at the bed.

It was neat and smooth and unoccupied.

For a moment, relief surged through me, then I leaped against the jamb and stared blankly at the deserted room. What the hell had happened to Sarah? I pushed the question around in my mind with a mental finger, but thinking was like trying to bounce a rubber ball in a puddle of wet sticky mud. After awhile, shaking my head groggily, I moved into the bathroom. She wasn't there either, of course, but the white glistening fixtures were. I filled the washbasin and sloshed cold water over my face, then ran wet fingers through my hair. I felt as gay and feverish and as desperate and inadequate as a lover in a tuberculosis ward.

I went back to the living room. The carpet was scuffed a little, but that might have occurred earlier. I studied the room trying to find evidence of a struggle, but the only telltale sign was Sarah's square black leather purse. It still lay on the sofa where she had dropped it when we came in. I felt reasonably certain that had she not been rushed out of the apartment involuntarily, she would have remembered to take it with her. I picked it up and fingered it indecisively. Through the soft leather, I could feel her gun. Somehow it brought reality and the necessity for action back to me with a rush. Opening the purse, I dumped its contents onto the sofa.

Besides the gun, there was the usual assortment of feminine knick-knacks and emergency beauty aids plus a key ring, a small notebook and a wallet. The wallet bulged with identification cards—and not much else; there were three bills in the money compartment and less than a dollar in silver in the change pocket. She hadn't been kidding when she said she was broke. The notebook was pretty well filled with scrawled names, telephone numbers, and cryptic jottings in a shorthand of her own invention, some of it obviously having to do with a personal budget and an expense account. None of it made much sense and it certainly didn't have anything to do with the problem at hand. Keeping the keys and the gun, which I put in my own pocket, I crammed everything else back into the purse and dropped it on the sofa.

I left the building without meeting anyone and got into my car. I had no difficulty finding Sarah's apartment building again and without any scruples whatsoever, I went in, rode the self-service elevator to the fifth floor, and experimented with her keys until I found one that fitted her door. When the lock clicked back, I pushed the door open, then walked in and snapped on the lights.

The first thing that struck me was the complete dissimilarity between Sarah's apartment and Lila's. Lila's was lush, lovely, bright, spacious—and had an aura of modernity and money. Sarah's was a mere cramped kitchenette, clean and homey, filled with worn furniture and a suggestion of bustle and use.

I closed the door quietly and locked it. On a nearby table, a brown paper-wrapped package lay, topped by a slip of white paper. I recognized the package as the one Lila had left in my car. Stepping quickly toward it, I picked up the slip of white paper. It was a receipt, made out in the name of a rental agency and signed by the building manager, for $75.00 "on account of rent due." Sarah hadn't been lying. She had given my money to the manager of the building and apparently he'd brought the package and receipt up to her apartment for her. "On account of rent due." I stared at the words. They meant that the $75 was only part of what she owed. The kid had really been having it tough.

Stifling the pang of sympathy that rose in me, I searched the apartment quickly. The whole job took only a few minutes and all I learned from some printed cards, which I found in the top drawer of her dresser, was that her office was in the 500 block on North Dearborn Street. I unlocked the door, gave the room a final glance, then picked up the package and tucked it under my arm, leaving the receipt on the table. Then I turned out the lights, stepped into the corridor, and went hurriedly downstairs.

Obviously, the package of fake money was both an asset and a liability. It was an asset because Lila had had it and it was, therefore, a possible clue to her killer; it was a liability because the possession of counterfeit money is a crime and because, if either Sarah or I was found with it, we might find ourselves haunted by cops and tied definitely to the killing. I wanted to keep it—and I had to get rid of it. The problem stumped me for a few minutes, but then a simple solution suggested itself to me: Let the U. S. Post Office Department take care of it for a while.

Sitting in my car, I wrote my name and the address of the Devonshire Hotel in the upper left-hand corner of the package and then, in large block letters, I addressed it to Mrs. Alexandrovich Papadickolus at 4709 East Chicago Avenue. While driving around the city, I'd caught onto the street numbering system and I figured that the address was at least five miles offshore, where the waters of Lake Michigan would be pretty deep. Unless the Chicago post office was run even worse than those in Wisconsin, the package would drift around for a couple of days and then it'd come back to me at the Devonshire marked "No Such Address" or "Addressee Unknown."

At a drugstore, I bought a dollar's worth of stamps and plastered them across the top of the package. Then I found a mailbox with a large chute and dropped it in. As soon as it clunked into the mailbox, I felt as though a stone block had been lifted from my lungs. I headed for North Dearborn Street.

The office of the Livingston Agency turned out to be located in a large decrepit brick building which was virtually deserted when I arrived. A gnarled old elevator operator watched disinterestedly while I scrawled my name in an after-hours registry, then he creaked up to the eleventh floor with me and slid back the door of the cage. I jingled Sarah's keys importantly and strode down a bare tiled corridor to a glass door, which proclaimed in chipped black letters: THE LIVINGSTON AGENCY—Investigations Throughout the World. Behind me, I heard the elevator door slam and the cage begin its creaking descent. I found the right key and pushed the door back.

A hole-in-the-wall cubicle greeted my eyes as the lights came on. Its furnishings consisted of a much worn desk, a battered typewriter on a wheeled tin stand, several straight-backed chairs, and a scarred wooden filing cabinet. Behind the desk, a large framed photograph of a burly glowering man hung on the wall. At first I thought it was a portrait of President Taft, then something about the nose and eyes struck a chord of memory and I realized that I was confronting a likeness of Sarah's father, the founder of the Livingston Agency. I decided that her mother must have been a beautiful woman.

Closing the door, I pushed the typewriter aside and sat down behind the desk. There was a receipt book, showing very little use of late, in the top drawer and the other drawers were crammed with stationery, billing forms, cryptic notes in Sarah's odd scribble, lists of accounts receivable—and bills, bills, bills. One of the latter, carrying the current month's dating, was marked "Your Immediate

Attention Requested" and showed that $90 for three months rental of office space was due and payable. I was shaking my head over it when the door was flung open abruptly and a dapper character in a powder-blue suit strolled in.

"This is the Livingston Agency, I believe?" he asked in a high voice that left very little doubt as to whether he was selling hair ribbons or wearing them.

"That's right," I said.

"And you're Mr. Livingston?" he continued, in the happy fatuous tone of a card player who doesn't know what trumps are but who thinks he knows an ace when he sees one.

"No, no. I'm not Mr. Livingston," I told him. "Mr. Livingston is dead."

"Oh…" His mind stopped completely for a second, then it began to whirl again. "But you're a detective, aren't you, because this is the Livingston Agency and—"

"This is the Livingston Agency," I interrupted, anxious to get rid of him. "Miss Sarah Livingston, the owner, is out, however. It's nearly seven o'clock, you know, and the office closes—"

"Oh, that's all right!" He waved one hand limply as though attempting to dry it on the stale air and then adjusted the sharp creases of his trousers so they wouldn't cut his knees when he sat down. Quite daintily, he backed into a chair. "I can tell you all about it and you can tell Miss Livingston. After all, you're a detective, too, aren't you?"

"Well—" I hesitated. "Miss Livingston and I have been doing some work together, if that's what you mean."

"Of course! I just knew it. You look like a detective, you know." He beamed like a light eager for darkness and his eyebrows did a fancy dance. "I have a feeling for such things. I really have. As soon as—"

"I'm sorry, Mr.—"

"Oh, excuse me! I'm Danny Horan. I don't suppose your name is Livingston, is it?" Words seemed to run out of him like the last pint of water in a bathtub.

"No, no…my name is Banner, Mr. Horan. And I'm afraid you've—"

"Delighted to know you, Mr. Banner. I've read a lot about detectives, but you're the first one I've met personally. I should have come to you sooner, of course, but I thought I could find her—" He colored slightly and flicked at his lips with a pink tongue. "I mean, I thought I could find him by myself, but I can't and I simply have to find him before it's too late. I'm sure you can—"

I felt like throwing him out, but he obviously was a potential client and the drawer full of unpaid bills in Sarah's desk was still vividly in my mind. I'm heterosexual as hell, but after all, it was none of my business what sort of people Sarah trafficked with and I realized that the fee, if any, might be a godsend to her. With that in mind, I sat back and let him chatter away.

"I can't tell you what he does or where he lives or anything like that, but I'm almost certain that he lives or works somewhere near here," he went on, rubbing his forehead with an arm as though he had something sticky on his fingers. "One of my friends saw him on Grand Avenue just the other day and he said he had a little dog on a leash. A Pomeranian, I think; you know, one of those very little dogs with fluffy brown hair and—"

"This fellow you want us to find," I interrupted. "Does he have a name?"

"Certainly. His name is Tony Greco," He colored again. "He calls himself Katherine, sometimes." The thin shoulders jerked delicately. "He may be using either name, you know."

"What does he look like?"

"Well, he's quite handsome, I'd say. He has lovely brown hair, parted on the left side and it's quite wavy—"

"Brown hair." I wrote the words on a pad. "What else?"

"He's about my height and weight, has blue eyes, and a small perfectly straight nose like a chip of—"

He chattered through a vivid description, becoming almost poetic in places. I took notes and waited for him to calm down a little, then I asked, "Where'd you meet him?"

"At a private party about a month ago. He slipped away before I could get his address and I've been simply furious with myself ever since! I've asked everyone about him, but no one will tell me a thing. I must find him, though. You can, can't you?"

"All we can do is try." A thought occurred to me. "You say you met this Greco at a private party. Why can't you ask this friend, the one who had the party, who and where Greco is?"

"Oh, I couldn't do that! Sybil—I mean Frank—would be terribly angry if he thought I was interested in Tony. You mustn't connect me with him in any way. It would make things frightfully difficult for me." He frowned like a female wrestler confronting a fresh opponent. "Besides, I don't think Frank knows where Tony is. Tony came with someone else and I'm sure Frank wasn't interested in him. You'll have to leave Frank out of this, Mr. Banner, completely out."

"How about the friend who saw him on the street the other day?"

"He doesn't know a thing. I'm sure he told me everything he knew."

"Well, whereabouts on Grand Avenue did he see him?"

"Near Rush Street. He said Tony had a little dog on a leash and was just walking along—"

"How was he dressed?"

"He didn't say. He recognized him though. He definitely recognized him."

A little more conversation like that and I'd be a candidate for one of those funny jackets with the tie-around sleeves. I decided to get rid of him. "We'll do the best we can," I said briskly. "I suppose you know our rates?"

"No, but I'm willing to pay anything if you'll only find him for me quickly."

"We charge $25 a day plus expenses," I told him, remembering the way Sarah had nicked me for $75, "and it may take us several days to get a lead on him."

"Will it be all right if I give you $100 now?"

"That'll be fine."

While he thumbed delicately through a flat ostrich wallet, I got out the receipt book and filled in one of the blank forms. I signed it "Sarah Livingston, per G. B." and slid it across the desk in exchange for the crisp green $100 bill that he produced.

"You'd better give me your address," I told him. "Miss Livingston will want to keep you informed of progress on the case."

He mentioned an address that meant nothing to me and I wrote it down on the same sheet on which I'd jotted the description of Tony Greco. After another emotional expression of the necessity for haste and a less emotional reiteration of confidence in the Livingston Agency, he arose, laid a cool limp hand in mine for a moment, and sauntered out the door.

I wiped my hand against my thigh and stared at the $100 bill. The engraved face of Benjamin Franklin stared back at me. A thought rattled in my mind like a marble in a tin can. Picking up the bill, I examined it carefully. Then I got out the $100 bill I'd taken from Lila's package and kept as a souvenir. They felt and looked identical; in fact, I couldn't see a damned bit of difference between them except for the serial numbers, of course.

"Either he slipped me a fake bill," I decided, "or they're both genuine..."

CHAPTER SIX

THOUGHTS CAME and went in my mind like guests arriving by mistake at the wrong funeral. The way things stacked up, Lila was dead and Sarah had been abducted. The package of money, fake or otherwise, was at the hub of things. Lila appeared to have been killed because of it and Sarah may have been abducted on the off chance that she knew where it was. A thought chilled me: *Suppose they tortured her and forced her to admit that the package was in her apartment? It might mean her life—and I'd consigned it to the mails, tossed it into the postal system where it'd be pushed and carried around for two or three days!*

There was no chance of interrupting the postal process and getting the package back either. The post office would be closed and I was a stranger in town. Besides, once a letter or a package goes down a mail chute it's virtually impossible to get it back without an act of God. I know that for certain, because once I'd mailed a couple of letters and then discovered that I'd made a mistake and gotten their contents switched. I'd camped beside the mailbox, pleaded with the collector when he arrived, described the letters in minute detail, and offered him all sorts of identification, but he'd taken them off to the post office anyway and I'd had a devil of a time getting things straightened out. There was no chance of getting the package back; it was in Uncle Sam's hands for a couple of days, at least.

The thing to do, then, as long as I was already involved in things, was to find Sarah and affect her release. The trouble was, I hadn't seen my assailant and had no idea who had abducted her. Lila had mentioned going to a club and Sarah had said someone named Pete Ponzio ran a joint called the Flask Club in the vicinity of Jackson and Wells. It wasn't much of a lead, but following it might be better than sitting on my hands.

I locked the Livingston Agency's office and went down to my car.

It was 8:20 when I entered the Flask Club and wormed my way past a long crowded bar where four white jacketed bartenders were performing feats of alcoholic interest. At the rear was a huge room littered with closely spaced tables and chairs. The walls looked as though a whirlwind had flung huge gusts of newspapers against it and plastered them there, permanently imbedding their headlines in the calcimine. A dark-haired red-mouthed girl in black slacks and tight white blouse swung toward me and led the way to a tiny table against a wall. She leaned against my shoulder, giving me a whiff of her body odor and a glimpse of the deep V between her breasts while she lit a stub of candle, which projected from a wax dappled Ehrlenmeyer flask set between the salt and pepper shakers. That rite duly performed to her satisfaction, she straightened and asked, "What'll ya have?"

"Something to eat," I told her.

"Okay. I'll get a menu. Drink?"

"You might bring me an Old Fashioned."

"Sure thing."

She drifted away and I noticed that a pale blonde girl in a strapless white dress was sitting alone at a nearby table and watching me with questioning eyes. When I looked at her, she smiled in a friendly manner, rose and came toward me.

"Hello," she said in a low voice, pulling back a chair and sitting down. "Will you buy me a drink?" She was a cute kid, not more than twenty—if that—and she seemed oddly apprehensive and eager to please. "Sure," I said. "What'll you have?"

"What are you having?"

"An Old Fashioned."

She smiled again and I noticed that she had small, even, very white teeth. "I haven't had one of those in a long time."

"You mean you want an Old Fashioned?" I must have lifted my eyebrows a little.

"Yes, please. You don't mind, do you?"

"Of course not. But I thought you girls always drank straight shots—tea, you know, or vermouth—so you could drum up business faster."

She had a pleasant, tinkly laugh. "Oh, I'm not a B-girl. Is that what you thought I was?"

"Certainly. You mean you aren't?"

"Hardly." Her laugh tinkled again.

"What do you do here, then?"

"I'm Millie Royce, The Girl with the Voice. Didn't you see the signs outside?"

"Afraid not. You're a singer, then?"

"That's what it says on the billboards, but sometimes I have my doubts. Anyway, most of the drunks who come in here wouldn't know a contralto from a hole in the ground. I sing with the combo. The boys are taking a rest break. When they get back, you'll be able to hear me do my stuff, providing the mike doesn't go on the fritz." She wrinkled her nose. "Half the time there's so much noise in here that I don't know whether anybody can hear me singing or not."

The waitress came back with a menu and an Old Fashioned. I told her to give the drink to Millie Royce and to bring me another. She nodded and sailed off in the direction of the bar. "Care for something to eat?" I asked.

"No, thanks. I don't cadge from the customers very often, but you looked like a nice guy and I needed a drink."

"Not even a sandwich?"

"No, really." Her white teeth gleamed in the candlelight. "Later, maybe, if you're still around and in the mood."

"That's a deal." I glanced over the menu and decided on a steak sandwich with french fries, salad bowl, and coffee. When the waitress brought my drink, I gave her the order and sat back to sip the Old Fashioned.

Millie Royce looked at me over the edge of her glass and asked, "Do you come here very often?"

"This is the first time. I'm new in Chicago."

"Where are you from?"

"Wisconsin."

"No fooling?" Her blue eyes widened. "Whereabouts?"

"Fond du Lac."

"Why, I was raised in Ripon!"

"Ripon?" I grinned. "That's a suburb of Fond du Lac."

"Almost," she agreed. "We used to drive the 20 miles to Fond du Lac two or three times a week to go to shows and things. What are you doing in Chicago?"

"New job," I told her. "Incidentally, my name's Gordon Banner."

"Howdy, Mr. Banner." She set her glass down carefully and watched in silence while the waitress arranged my sandwich, salad, and coffee in front of me. When the waitress left, she said in a different tone of voice. "I'd get fired if the boss heard me say this, but you seem like a nice guy. Just between us country cousins, this is a good joint for a boy fresh from Wisconsin to stay away from."

"What's wrong with it?"

"It's strictly for suckers. You know, people who are in town for a convention or something and don't care how much they spend as long as they have what they think is a big time. Maybe that's the sort of thing you want, but if you're working and expect to save any money—well, you won't save anything if you come here often."

"The prices seem reasonable enough. I noticed that drinks are only—"

"Oh, sure." Impatience tinged her voice a little. "Drinks are sixty cents and the food is pretty good, but they're just to get you in and keep you here awhile. The main show is upstairs and sooner or later most of the suckers make a trip there. There's a whole lot of rooms—gambling, girls, things like that. It's early and the evening hasn't started yet or you'd see what I mean." She turned her head, then nodded toward a couple of girls in evening dresses and highly lacquered coiffures who were threading their way through the crowd at the bar. "Here come a couple of the girls now. In an hour there'll be a dozen of them floating around, weeding out the fat wallets from the flaties."

"So that's Pete Ponzio's racket," I said softly. "I suppose Lila Livingston was one of the girls."

"Lila—" Her eyes went wide with apprehension and her hand tightened on her glass. "What do you know about Lila? I thought you said—"

"I happened to meet her briefly this afternoon."

"Is that why you came here, to see her?"

"No," I shook my head and studied her for a moment before adding, "Lila's dead."

"Dead!"

"Someone killed her."

She sat there, staring blankly at me, until I thought she'd lost her voice. When her lips moved, I could barely hear the words. "Are you sure?" she whispered. "Lila's really dead?"

I nodded. "Take my word for it. I saw her."

She raised her glass suddenly and drained it. Color began to seep back into her face. "You aren't—a detective, are you?" she asked.

"No. I was telling you the truth when I said I'd just come to Chicago from Fond du Lac on a new job. I'm a salesman for the Tacoma Flour Company. You must have heard of them."

"Yes. Of course," She moistened her lips. "I don't think anyone here knows about it. About Lila, I mean. You say someone killed her?"

"She was strangled. What was she, a ringer for the house?"

"Well, yes and no. She acted as a sort of hostess part of the time and the rest of the time she just made herself useful doing things for the boss."

"What sort of things?"

"Gosh, I don't know. You know how girls talk. I've heard some of them say that she and Pete Ponzio were closer than scrambled eggs, but I can't say that she ever acted like it. I suppose we were all jealous of her in a catty sort of way, because she got the cream of everything and we have to drudge for what we earn. It isn't fun to sweat over a hot mike for $75 a week and see another girl make that much in one evening because the boss steers the best suckers her way."

"Judging by what you say, Lila wasn't very popular with her co-workers."

"We didn't dislike her. I'd say most of the girls were envious more than anything." She shook her head. "And to think that she's dead now. I guess that proves something, but I can't think what."

"Would you like another drink?"

"I haven't time. The boys will be coming back in a minute or two and I'll have to climb onto the bandstand." Her eyes became questioning. "Do you intend to stay awhile, or—?"

"I thought I'd have a talk with Mr. Ponzio. Is he around?"

"I haven't seen him yet this evening. Do you know him?"

"No, but I thought he might be expecting Lila and I wanted to tell him what happened. I think she was on her way here this afternoon when she was killed. What sort of a guy is he?"

Millie frowned faintly. "Well, he's small and rather thin and has thick grey hair. He's around forty-five I guess, maybe a little older. I don't know much about him because I've only been working here a few months, but according to the other girls, he's strictly business, if you know what I mean."

"No playing around?"

"Nothing to speak of. He's got a wife and three or four kids, I think, and when he isn't supervising things around here, he's home with his family."

"A little while ago you said he and Lila were palsy-walsy."

"Not that way. Around the joint here, Lila did pretty much as she pleased. In fact, part of the time she acted as though she owned the place, but I don't think there was anything else between them. Ponzio's the sort of guy who doesn't believe in getting too friendly with the paid help."

"Ever see Lila's sister around here?"

"I didn't know she had one."

A fat greasy-faced slob with slick black hair and small bright eyes came through the bar crowd and pushed his way between the tables toward the bandstand on the other side of the room. He was followed by three slighter males, all dark-skinned and well pomaded. The four were dressed in identical brown Harmel sports suits with flowery Hawaiian shirts. With an almost visible groan, the leader got a pudgy leg onto the bandstand and pulled himself up.

"Looks like it's time for you to dust off your larynx," I told her.

She glanced around, then sighed. "You were never so right. Thanks for the drink, Mr. Banner."

"I'll see you again," I promised.

She smiled and fluttered a hand as she arose. "I'll be looking for you. Bye now."

I watched her walk, slim and graceful, toward the bandstand and take her place on a chair near the mike. As soon as she was seated, the fat boy grabbed the chromium column of the mike as though he were going to Indian wrestle with it and flashed a toothy grin in the general direction of his audience. "Welcome, welcome, welcome," he slurred into the mike, giving the words a fake Latin-American emphasis. "For our first number we bring to you the tango. It is for your dancing pleasure." With a low bow, he turned, jerked his arms and a piano, accordion, and guitar crashed into a loud jangly rhythm.

The boys smoothed out as they got into the number and I found myself enjoying the savage swing of their music. The fat boy slapped a mean bass and in spite of his looks, was quite a musician. When they swung into the third number of the set, a spotlight came on above the mike and Millie Royce stood up, simulated a little dance step as she moved toward it, and came in on cue for the chorus. Her voice was stronger than I expected and had a warm little-girl quality that I found strangely stirring. The words she sang were Spanish and didn't mean anything to me, but the look she gave me over the heads of the other diners had meaning enough.

She was just finishing the number when I saw her eyes move toward a small slender grey-haired man in a dark blue suit who was standing near a rear door. She smiled in his direction and didn't miss a note, but her eyes seemed to harden and I noticed that her hands tightened at her sides like knots in a tautening rope. When the song ended, he turned abruptly and went through the door.

I finished my coffee, signaled the waitress, and paid my check. Then I got up and strode toward the rear door.

CHAPTER SEVEN

GOING THROUGH the door was like stepping from Skid Row to Lake Shore Drive. The newspaper-plastered walls ended abruptly and became a delicate coral pastel, which blended with the dark grey carpeting of a corridor. The closing of the door cut off the pounding jangle of the combo, which was embarked on another Latin-American number, and silence wrapped itself around me like an eager mistress. Even the scent of acrid cigarettes, sour beer, and old martinis vanished, being replaced with an aroma far more delicate, interesting—and expensive.

I located the source of the aroma at the foot of a flight of stairs that led to the second floor. She was a large, full-breasted girl in a tight-fitting red dress and she was sitting on the bottom step with a shapely leg poked out at an ungainly angle. When she heard me, she gave the seam of the stocking a final twitch, aligning it with an invisible point somewhere beneath her lap and lifted her dark head. Her brown eyes added and subtracted me rapidly and became filled with a hunger as wide as the world and as old as thought. In a throaty hopeful voice, she asked, "You looking for me, honey?"

"Mr. Ponzio came back this way," I said. "Did you notice where he went?"

The brightness went out of her eyes. "Upstairs," she said in a bored tone. She twitched her hips over to the side of the stairs so I could pass and stuck out her other leg.

"Whereabouts upstairs?" I asked.

"How the hell would I know?" she flared. "I don't get paid to keep track of him." Ignoring me pointedly, she began plucking at the seam of the other stocking.

I stepped past her and went swiftly upstairs. The walls of the second floor corridor were paneled with a tapestried wallpaper and punctured at regular intervals with solid-looking doors. I turned left toward what I figured was the front of the building and proceeded down the corridor until I reached its end. The door that confronted me bore a neat metal sign: PRIVATE. I rapped my knuckles against it.

The door opened with unexpected swiftness and a huge man with a face the color of a jaundiced oyster growled, "Yeah?"

"I'm looking for Mr. Ponzio," I said. "Do you know where he is?"

"Who're you?"

"My name is Banner, Gordon Banner," I told him, stepping back a little to avoid his breath. "If Mr. Ponzio—"

"He's busy. Beat it!" The door started to close.

Behind him, a voice asked sharply; "Who is it?"

"Aw, some jerk—"

My shoulder rammed the door and it snapped back, surprising him even more than it did me. As a salesman I'd frequently resorted to the old shoe-in-the-door ruse during my younger days, but this was the first time instinctive resentment had gotten the better of me and impelled me to violent rebuttal. With an oath, he grabbed at the door and his thin lips curled back over his large teeth like a snake about to annihilate a rabbit. But I was on my way in. Before he had control of the door and his reflexes, I had plunged past him into the room, straight into the arms of another big guy who spun me around, laid a fist against my jaw, and booted me into a wall.

Stars showered over me as my head met the wall and I felt my body go limp. I slid into a heap on the floor. Then, in an exploding rocket of dancing lights and shuttered movement, the stars melted and the scene whirled back into focus. I was in a large luxuriously furnished office. Ponzio's thin face was peering at me over a desk. The door was shut. The two big guys were standing over me, raveling and unraveling their hands and glowering like angry twins. Obviously, my presence was as popular as a mouse's in a harem.

"Who is he?" Ponzio snapped in an ominous tone.

"I think it's the guy who was with her," Oyster Face growled.

"You *think* he was with her!" Ponzio said icily. "Don't you know?"

"Yeah, he's the one," the other big guy growled. "He and she were fighting about something."

"You fools!" Ponzio said in quiet fury. "You blundering fools!"

"He was out cold," Oyster Face protested. "Honest, boss, he didn't even know what happened to him! He couldn't have followed us here. Chick frisked him and he didn't have nothing on him, so—"

"Shut up!" Ponzio snapped. He got up and came around the desk.

In an aching largo of movement, I pulled myself together and got to my feet. The room spun around, then steadied and for the first time I became conscious of another presence—Sarah. She was bound to a chair on the other side of the room and as my eyes found her, her arms and legs writhed beneath the ropes and the gag across her mouth bubbled where her teeth were chewing at it. Her suit was torn, her make-up was streaked with tears, and her green eyes were glaring balefully. I could see that she felt as completely hopeless as a kid who's just discovered there really isn't a Santa Claus.

"How'd you get here?" Ponzio demanded.

"Lila said," I began. The words hurt my lips and I licked at them with my tongue before continuing.

"What do you know about Lila?" He threw the words at me like a preacher getting ready to sweat out a tough congregation.

"She's dead," I managed to mutter.

"So..." The way Ponzio said the word was full of meaning. "Frisk him," he ordered.

Four hands reached eagerly for me, slapped at my body, jerked my pockets inside out. My wallet, papers, gun, keys, and money were transferred to Ponzio. He laid the gun and keys on his desk and pursed lips over my wallet. The two $100 bills interested him briefly, then he put them back into the wallet, tossed it on desk, strode around, and sat down. He stared at Sarah. "Is this the man you told me about?" he demanded.

Sarah jerked her head. Her eyes avoided mine.

Ponzio grunted and swung around toward me. "Talk," he suggested. He lit a cigarette and sucked on it, narrowing his eyes a little as though it was an anesthetic.

I wasn't ready to assign my body to the medical students and I couldn't see much sense in inviting any more bruised tissue and strained muscle, so I told him about picking up Lila, the tearing of her dress, how she had mentioned being on her way to the club and what had happened when I'd gone up to her apartment. When I finished, he blew a ragged gust of smoke at me and asked, "What happened to the dough?"

"What dough?"

"Don't give me that. You know damn well what dough."

I glanced at Sarah but her face was averted. Thoughts were skittering about in my mind like sheep in a storm, all going nowhere. Taking a deep breath I said, "You mean the $60,000 in fake bills?"

"I mean the hundred thousand—and there was nothing fake about them."

I shook my head. "We're talking about two different things then. Lila had a package when I met her, a package that she left in my car while she went up to her apartment to change her dress. Sarah and I opened it after we found she was dead and there were six packets of fake $100 bills in it."

"For chrissake," Ponzio snorted. "Who'd be dumb enough to make fake C-notes? It's hard enough to pass fake tens!"

"You mean it was real money?"

"Certainly."

"Well, anyway, there wasn't $100,000 of it. There were only six packets and each contained $10,000. Multiply it yourself."

Ponzio started to swear softly, then he snapped, "Where is that package now?"

An idea had been pawing at my mind like a nagging mendicant. I grinned at him a lot more confidently than I felt. "Why should I tell you?" I asked. "The money wasn't yours, was it?"

"It's my money," Ponzio informed me coldly, "and I intend to get it. Where is it?"

"It's in a very safe place."

"Where?"

"Look, Mr. Ponzio," I said, trying to keep my voice from trembling, "you can strong-arm some people and make them run off at the mouth, but there are some you can't. I'm one of the latter. I've admitted that I know where the money is. I'll also admit that I think Lila was on her way here with it and that she intended to turn it over to you. But Lila was murdered—by you or by one of your men, for all I know—and I'll be damned if I'm going to be forced into a one-way bargain. That isn't why I came here."

"I'll give you ten grand—for the whole hundred thousand."

"I told you there's only $60,000. Sarah must have told you the same thing. Why should we lie about it?"

"The pay-off was a hundred grand. That's what Lila should have had in the package."

"Well, it wasn't there. Sarah and I opened the package together. Ask her."

"We've already discussed it." Ponzio smiled thinly. "All right, Mr. Banner. Where is the sixty grand?"

"It still looks like a one-way deal to me."

"The dough belongs to me."

"Suppose you go and look for it then."

His eyes locked with mine and I could feel him assessing the pros and cons. Behind me, the big guy murmured, "Lemme work him over, boss."

Ponzio ignored him. "Perhaps you're right," he said in a brisk, business-like tone. "A good turn deserves compensation. I'll pay you five per cent commission. Tell me where the sixty grand is and three of it is yours."

"That isn't what I want."

"Four grand then. That's—"

"It isn't money I want."

Ponzio's eyes soared like flushed ducks. "Well?"

"I want you to release Lila's sister."

Ponzio frowned and Sarah sat straight up, still and listening, like a collie that has heard its master's footstep. "Do I understand you correctly?" he asked slowly. "If I promise to release this young lady," he nodded toward Sarah, "you'll give me the sixty grand?"

"No," I corrected. "If you release her, I'll tell you where the money is. Notice that I said *if you release her.* In other words, release her and after I'm certain that you haven't tried a trick play, I'll tell you where the money is."

"You don't trust me?" His eyebrows soared again.

"Not that far."

"But you expect me to trust you."

"Not entirely. Don't forget, I'll still be here. I'm asking you to release her, not me." I grinned. "There isn't much sense in your keeping her anyway, because she couldn't tell you where the package is even if she wanted to. The last time she saw it, it was on its way up to her apartment. But I moved it. You've everything to gain and nothing to lose by releasing her."

Ponzio made up his mind. Jerking his head at one of the big guys, he snapped, "Untie her."

With a snap-knife that he took from a pocket, one of the guys cut the ropes. Sarah, looking like a religious martyr just before the bundles of sticks are lit, got stiffly to her feet and tore the gag away from her mouth. Her chin was stained with lipstick and her lips looked a bit bruised and swollen. "Gordon—" she gasped. "Please don't—"

"Get out of here," I told her. "I can take care of myself. When you're safe outside, telephone back here. I won't tell him anything until I get your call."

"But—" She stood motionless, indecisive, with her hands clasping and unclasping in front of her like separate automatic things. "What if—"

"I'll be all right," I said firmly. "Go downstairs and telephone back. I'll see you later."

She started to say something, thought better of it and nodded meekly. She walked to the door and opened it. I sighed as it closed behind her. Oyster Face grunted disgustedly, then lapsed into an uncomfortable silence when Ponzio stared at him. The other big guy shrugged and flung himself into a chair behind me. Ponzio, quite disconcertingly, kept watching me as though my nose were an independent organism likely to do tricks.

The minutes crayfished along until, abruptly, the phone on Ponzio's desk emitted a soft buzz. Lifting the receiver, he said, "Yes?" He listened a moment, then handed the instrument to me.

Sarah's voice sounding nervous and distrait stroked at my ear. "Gordon'? I'm in a drugstore on Clark Street. Do you want me to call the police'? You can't—"

"No," I said, "don't call the police. It wouldn't be fair. I'll see you later."

"But—"

"Please trust me, Sarah. I know what I'm doing; at least I think I do." Before she could protest further, I laid the receiver on its cradle. "All right," I said to Ponzio, "here's the rest of the story," I told him what I had done with the package of money.

When I finished, his face paled as though I'd punched a hole in a vital organ. "You tricked me," he snapped. "By heavens—"

"On the contrary," I interrupted. "I said I'd tell you where the money is and that's exactly what I've done. You'll have to wait a day or two before you can get it, but it'll be returned to the Devonshire and one of your men can pick it up. That's better than not getting it at all, isn't it?"

"How do I know that you actually mailed it?"

"You don't," I admitted brazenly, "but a man in your business has to be a pretty good judge of character. If you thought I was inclined to be a liar, you wouldn't have released Sarah Livingston."

Ponzio regarded me narrowly. "You're pretty confident," he commented. "What do you expect me to do with you?"

"I don't know," I countered, "but I know what I'd do if I were you."

"What?"

"Well, if I—"

The phone buzzed, interrupting my reply, and Ponzio lifted the receiver impatiently. "Yes?" he clipped. His face went blank. *"What?"* Incredulity carved its way across his thin face and in G-sharp minor, he whispered, "Who is this?" Apparently he didn't get an answer, for he began clicking the do-jigger on the phone and demanding, "Hello? Hello?" When he dropped the receiver, his face was the mottled grey of a slice of liver sausage.

"What's the matter, boss?" the guy named Chick asked, half rising from his chair.

"Lila!" Ponzio croaked hoarsely. "The cops just found her body out in back of my house!"

CHAPTER EIGHT

VENTUTTI!" Ponzio exploded. "It's that damn Carlo Ventutti!"

"Who's Ventutti?" I asked.

The sound of my voice affected him like an unexpected gust of rainy wind. His face hardened and grasping the edge of his desk, he leaned toward me and rasped. "Get out of here. Get the hell out of here!"

I didn't need a second invitation. I got out.

On my way downstairs, I met a spicy scented blonde who was leaning intimately and heavily on the arm of a grinning fatso in a rumpled business suit. They were interested in affairs of their own and paid no attention to me. Entering the dining room, I noticed that a subtle change had occurred. The bar was doing business, but it wasn't so crowded. Most of the serious happiness-seekers had shifted to tables and many small blondes and large bottles were in evidence. Millie Royce elided the notes of a song as she caught sight of me and an expression of relief seemed to brighten her pretty face for a moment. I smiled at her and nodded and kept right on walking. When I came out onto the concrete of Jackson Boulevard, I felt like a *mal de mer* victim reaching dry land after a trans-Atlantic crossing.

According to my watch it was 9:27. It felt later. I got into my car, drove around to Dearborn Street, then headed north to the building where the office of the Livingston Agency was located. The door was locked but I leaned on the night bell until the old elevator operator poked his head out of his car and came and unlocked the door for me.

"Did Miss Livingston come in a few minutes ago?" I asked.

He scratched his ear as though I'd asked his opinion on a matter of political importance, then grudgingly admitted that she had. I signed the register and had him pilot me up to the eleventh floor. When I opened the office door and walked in, Sarah was chewing on the end of a pencil and frowning perplexedly at the receipt book open on her desk.

"Busy like a little bee," I commented.

"Gordon!" Her face lit up with relief. "Gosh, you really did get away!" She poked at a strand of hair, which had been hanging listlessly over one ear. "I've been so worried. I didn't know whether you meant what you said about not calling the police."

"I told you I'd be all right." I grinned and sat down across from her. "The fat's in the fire now though. The cops have found Lila."

"No!"

"Yes, indeed. Ponzio got the tip while I was there. It seems someone planted her in his backyard."

"In Ponzio's backyard?" She sounded as though I'd announced the atom bombing of Boston.

"That's what I gathered. Ponzio seems to think someone named Carlo Ventutti is responsible. Any idea who Ventutti is?"

"Gosh yes." Her green eyes widened still farther and her red lips hung open. "Ventutti—why, he's one of the big bosses. He runs the dope racket, I think."

"I was afraid he was somebody like that. It might be a good idea for me to go back to Fond du Lac."

"Why?"

"What do you think is going to happen when that cop—what was his name, Fielding, starts putting two and two together? As soon as he hears her name and learns where she lived, a bell is going to start ringing and it'll be ringing for us."

"They can't prove anything. They—"

"No, but neither can we. Not only that. On the other side of the fence, there'll be Ventutti and Ponzio, both of whom from what little I know of them impress me as unfriendly types. We'll be in the center of a vicious crossfire. Maybe you don't mind becoming an uninsurable risk, but I do."

Sarah's eyes snapped green sparks. "You were brave enough this evening! You burst into Ponzio's office like a little hero. I was proud of you."

"I was proud of myself."

"Well…"

"Let's face it, Sarah. With a looker like Lila to work on, the newspapers will make a big play out of the case. If she were an old hag, they might run a few inches on page seven and then forget about her. But she wasn't an old hag. They'll dig up every picture of her they can find and they'll plaster them all over their front pages. You ought to know what that'll mean. Even if the cops would like to ignore it, they'll have to knock themselves out trying to find a scapegoat and you and I are the first ones that'll come to their attention. Once they start digging, we'll be on our way down the drain like last night's dishwater."

"I'm not afraid. We know that we didn't have anything to do with—"

I sighed. "Your legs are better looking than mine, Sarah. I don't want to sit in front of a jury. They might not be impressed by what I've got."

"Gawd!" Sarah said, looking as feminine as a barber pole. "I never thought you were yellow."

"I'm merely being rational and using foresight. I want to get out of this mess while the getting is good." I took out my wallet and tossed one of the $100 bills onto the desk. "Here's some money I collected for the Agency." I explained my session with Danny Horan and made a few verbal additions to the description of Tony Greco. "I felt like kicking the pretty boy out," I concluded, "but it looked to me like you needed the business. I hope the fee I quoted is all right."

"Yes, but couldn't he tell you anymore about him than that?"

"He was seen near Grand and Rush streets with a pup on a leash. How much more of a lead does a detective need?"

"But, good Lord, Gordon, that district is simply filthy with dogs!" Sarah exclaimed, looking really concerned. "You aren't even sure whether it was a Pekinese or a Pomeranian according to what you said the first time. There're probably hundreds of little brownish pups in that neighborhood."

"But not all of them with a pretty wavy-haired boy on the other end of the chain," I pointed out. "For a hundred bucks, you can chase around and ask questions, can't you? I would if it were my rent which wasn't paid."

"You know, Gordon," Sarah said thoughtfully, "in some ways you're a lot smarter than I am. You talked Ponzio into letting us both go. You're shrewd. You know how to analyze things. You've got a talent for—"

"Hey, what's the matter? Have you gone nuts?"

"No, I'm just facing facts. Several times I've almost made a serious error in judgment, but you've spotted it and rescued me. You've helped me a lot, Gordon, and..." Her voice seemed to catch a little and her lashes batted the air. "...I don't know what I'm going to do without you. You've been lucky to me, sort of, too. And you understand all these characters. How am I going to find a—a man like that when I don't even know what he's liable to be like?"

"Oh, for Pete's sake," I said. "You needn't put on a sob act."

"It's not a s-sob act!" A tear rolled down one cheek. "I d-don't know what t-to d-do!"

"I thought you said you were a detective?"

"I h-haven't had a c-case for m-months. N-nobody w-wants to trust a w-woman..." Her tears gained momentum.

"Shut up shop then," I suggested. "You don't have to run a detective agency, do you?"

"It's all my f-father left m-me and he w-wanted me to keep it g-going," She dabbed at her eyes. "I c-can't even s-sell it because there isn't anything t-to sell."

"Well, hell," I said, feeling as uncomfortable as a liquor dealer at an AA picnic. "A good-looking girl like you can always get a job. I can imagine how you feel about your father and the agency and things like that, but sentiment is one thing and making a living is another. I don't see that you have much choice."

"I know it's s-silly, b-but I have a f-feeling that—" A sob blurred her voice then receded. "—that if y-you helped m-me I'd be able t-to get s-started—" She laid her arms on the desk and hid her face in them. Her shoulders trembled as though a breeze was playing beneath her blouse.

It takes a strong man to swim against the current of a woman's tears. Feeling like a heel, I went around the desk and put my arm around her shoulders. "There's nothing to cry about," I soothed. "You know I'd help you if I could."

"You c-could b-but you d-don't want to!"

"There isn't anything I can do, Sarah. You know there isn't. I don't know anything about gangsters and other sordid types."

"You're a s-salesman. L-Look—how you g-got me a c-client!"

"He walked in and practically forced the money on me. If you had been here, you'd probably have nicked him for twice as much as I did."

"If I'd b-been here, he'd have w-walked out!"

"The inference I get isn't nice." I tightened my arm a little and held her against me. I could feel the warmth of her body through the blouse and the sensation was oddly pleasant. When she lifted her head and leaned it against me, I stroked her arm. Her nose burrowed against my shirt and by a process not quite clear to me, she was suddenly in my arms and her lips were clinging wetly to mine.

"I'll help you, honey," I heard myself say. "I was just kidding when I said I was going back to Fond du Lac. What kind of a jerk do you think I am, anyway? I'll stick around until you're so sick of seeing me that you'll try to hide when I rap on the door."

"I won't get s-sick of s-seeing you-oh, Gordon, darling."

"Maybe you will. I'm a pretty ordinary guy and I talk too much and—"

"Don't say things like that."

Her lips sought mine again, melting the last remnants of whatever doubts I may have had. We were still locked in each others' arms when the door opened and Lieutenant Fielding strode in.

CHAPTER NINE

FIELDING'S EYEBROWS went up and the corners of his mouth deepened into scornful parentheses. "Well, well," he said, giving the words a faint shading of sarcasm, "I seem to keep interrupting you two love-birds. Sorry."

Sarah, her face the vivid red of a sun-ripened persimmon, sprang away from me and flounced into the chair behind her desk. I remained where I was, feeling like a school kid who'd been caught in the cloakroom with a sweet little girl. Fielding, with what sounded like a sniff, sat down and pushed his hands into the pockets of his jacket. He stared at Sarah and rolled his lips.

"What do you want, Lieutenant?" Sarah asked, finding her voice.

"That's a fair question," Fielding replied. "What do I want? Well, right now I want you and your boyfriend to come for a ride with me."

"A ride?" Sarah managed to sound surprised. "Where?"

"County morgue." His eyes remained fastened on her face. "We found your sister."

"My sister?" Color fled from Sarah's face and I felt my breath thicken. "You mean—Lila?"

"How many sisters have you got?" Fielding asked.

"What—what happened to her?"

"Someone strangled her."

"Strangled her!" Sarah's tone was perfect. I decided I'd underestimated her. She looked shocked and horrified and completely taken by surprise. I hoped she wouldn't ham the act by overplaying it. "When?"

"We don't know," Fielding admitted. "It happened sometime this afternoon probably, but we didn't find her until an hour or so ago. You're her nearest relative, aren't you?"

"Yes." Sarah shook her head dazedly. "Poor Lila. Strangled..."

"Yeah," Fielding's eyes narrowed almost imperceptibly. "Funny coincidence, isn't it?" he asked quietly.

"What do you mean?"

"She was killed sometime this afternoon. A guy called headquarters a couple of hours after it must have happened and reported a murder at her apartment. But when we got there, you and your boyfriend are playing hugger-mugger—and no body. Guess where we found her."

"I haven't the faintest idea."

"Well, we can talk about that later. Right now, I want you to ride over to the morgue with me and take care of a few formalities." Fielding got to his feet and sauntered toward the door, waiting for us to follow.

Sarah rose stiffly and went to the hanger where the jacket of her suit dangled. She removed it, poked her arms into the sleeves, and buttoned it slowly. Picking up her purse, she squeezed it under one arm and turned off the lights. I went ahead and rang for the elevator.

Fielding drove his squad car swiftly and with easy competence. I didn't feel like talking and neither did he or Sarah. When he stopped, Sarah got out and waited on the sidewalk, huddled in the jacket of her suit as though braving a wintry wind. I took her arm and we entered the building together.

"This way," Fielding said gruffly. He clattered ahead of us down a flight of tiled stairs and opened a door. The pungent stink of formalin stabbed at my nostrils and Sarah's fingers dug into my arm. Fielding gestured to an attendant who led us into a large chilly room, the walls of which were paneled like the face of a huge filing cabinet. "You know the one we want," Fielding told the attendant. "The girl."

The attendant tugged at a handle and a long stretcher-like drawer came out of a wall revealing a sheet-covered form. He pulled away the sheet. Sarah whimpered and I sucked in my breath sharply. Lila's slender lovely body, white and limp and as bare as the day she had been born, lay before us.

"Is it your sister?" Fielding asked after a moment.

Sarah nodded. "Yes," she whispered.

"Mark it identified," he told the attendant. While the attendant, looking bored, made a note on a paper tag that was fastened to a toe of Lila's left foot, Fielding pursed his lips and blew soundlessly through them. Shrugging, he walked around to the other side of the body and gently lifted the blonde hair away from her face. "Notice these bruises," he said quietly. He pointed at the series of blotches about her neck. "She was strangled by a person capable of exerting considerable strength. There are curved lacerations above each of the bruises," his finger indicated several tiny marks that looked like small blue pencil scratches, put there by the fingernails of her killer. That means that whoever killed her had fairly long nails, a woman possibly."

As though he expected no comment, he went on, "Now here's something interesting. Notice that purplish tinge of the lower part of her body? That's known as post mortem lividity. After death the blood has a tendency to settle and, in her case, it indicates that she was lying down flat on her back, for quite a while immediately after death. But that isn't the way we found her." Fielding lifted his eyes and stared at Sarah. "When we found her, she was propped up against a tree with her hands folded in her lap. An odd touch, don't you think?"

Sarah released my arm and turned away. I said, "Is this the way she was when you found her, Lieutenant?"

"She was wearing a nylon slip," Fielding said. "A blue lacy nylon slip. Why?"

"I just wondered."

"Did you know her?"

"No."

"Too bad," Fielding commented. Without explaining the remark, he returned his eyes to the body. He stared at her full proud breasts a moment, then frowning, he said, "Your sister wasn't married, was she, Miss Livingston?"

"No," Sarah replied.

'That's something else then," Fielding said moodily. He pointed at a series of faint creases along the side of Lila's abdomen. "See those marks? They're stria. They show that her abdomen had been distended at one time, the way it is when a woman carries a child. After delivery the skin contracts again but there telltale marks remain. She had a child at one time. At least, she was pregnant and the pregnancy was a nearly full-term one. There's no way of proving that the child lived, but the coroner says that it looks like a normal delivery occurred. Do you know anything about that?"

Sarah, looking as shocked as a girl who has just been told the facts of life, shook her head. "Oh, no!" she gasped. "Not Lila!"

"I understand she was pretty popular. Those things have a habit of happening, with or without benefit of clergy." With a shrug, Fielding lifted the sheet and pulled it carefully over the body. "Well, that's about it. I needed your identification particularly. I'll drive you back to your office."

We made the trip back to North Dearborn Street in utter silence. Fielding didn't speak again until we were seated in the office of the Livingston Agency. Then in a chilly voice, the kind a Jesuit might use in advising a pimply adolescent that Holy Orders were not for him, Fielding said, "Your sister was picked up out on Belle Plaine Avenue in Pete Ponzio's backyard. We know she wasn't killed there. We also know that she was killed several hours before her body was found. It looks to me like she was killed in her own apartment and dumped out north as a warning to Ponzio."

When Sarah remained silent, I asked, "Why would anyone do that?"

"She worked for him. I think she was mixed up in some of his rackets."

"What sort of rackets?"

"The kinds that make money, the only kind Ponzio is interested in. Since the heat went on in Chicago, the gamblers have been having a tough time and they've been looking for other fields. I have a hunch Ponzio—like some of the other big-timers—was trying to cut in on the dope peddling faction. That means that he was sticking out his neck and inviting Carlo Ventutti to chop it off." Fielding smiled thinly. "Not his own neck, of course. The smart boys don't do that."

"Ventutti," I said. "Who's Ventutti?"

"You must be new in Chicago."

"I am. I came here just yesterday from Fond du Lac, Wisconsin."

"Going to be here for awhile?"

"I'm a salesman for the Tacoma Flour Company. They transferred me to their Chicago office. Unless they decide it's the wrong move, I'll be living here from now on."

Fielding nodded as though everything was clear. "Well, Ventutti is a big name hereabouts. I'd advise you to steer clear of him. He graduated from the old Capone liquor rackets into gambling and assorted vice. A few years ago he shifted his activities to dope and the rumor now is that he's running things locally for the Eastern mob. I'm a homicide man, but I've sort of kept a finger on things because the rackets breed murder and I like to know what's going on." His tone didn't change but it seemed to become harder and chillier as he added, "That's why I'd like to know where the Livingston Agency fits into this caper." His eyes fastened on Sarah. "What are you up to, Miss Livingston?"

Sarah pressed her lips tightly together, then asked, "What do you mean? I didn't know Lila was—"

"I'm not talking about your sister right now," Fielding interrupted. "I'm talking about you, about the agency you're running. What have you got to do with Ventutti?"

"Nothing," Sarah said flatly. "I've read about him in the papers, that's all."

"What was one of his boys doing here this evening then?" Fielding demanded.

"I don't know what you're talking about!"

"Danny Horan," Fielding said coldly. "According to the register downstairs, he came up to your office this evening and spent a half hour here. It won't do you any good to lie. It's written down there in black and white."

I laughed. "You mean that pretty boy was one of Ventutti's boys?"

Fielding's eyes shifted to me. "That's exactly what I do mean."

"Miss Livingston didn't see him," I explained. "I was in the office waiting for her and he came in and said he wanted to hire a detective to locate a fellow named Tony Greco to whom he'd apparently taken a fancy. I had no idea who he was. I always thought gangsters were big tough brawny men with hair on their chests."

"Not all of them," Fielding said. "Greco. You say he wanted to contact someone named Tony Greco?"

"That's what he said." I reached over and got the pad on which I'd written Greco's description. I read it to him. "I gathered that Greco was of a breed similar to his. He admitted that Greco sometimes uses the name Katherine."

Fielding frowned. "He's a new one on me. I know a lot of his types, but none named Greco. The female tag, of course, isn't unusual; a lot of them use girls' names when they're sporting around. I haven't much use for any of them, but Danny Horan makes me want to puke. He goes around bragging about what a lousy facsimile of a man he is."

"That's the impression I got. I understood that he was carrying a torch for this Greco. I didn't know whether Miss Livingston would take the case or not, but he was insistent so I accepted a retainer from him in her name."

"You're sure that's all he wanted?" Fielding arched one eyebrow.

"Positive. He didn't mention Ventutti. Even if he had, I wouldn't have known who he was talking about." I grinned. "I probably wouldn't have believed him. For my money, he looked like the female lead in a rough game of Ring around the Rosie."

"A lot of people make that mistake," Fielding commented, his mind obviously on other matters. "Horan is solid with the Ventutti mob. He's in on the dope deal and that's for sure." He straightened in his chair. "I'd advise you to give him back his money, Miss Livingston. When you start working for characters like that, one thing is liable to lead to another. I still think it's damn odd that he picked your agency."

"Why not?" Sarah flared. "The Livingston Agency is well known and has as good a reputation as any firm of—"

"It used to be well known," Fielding interrupted. "The word around town is that your agency has been going downhill. That isn't what I meant though. I was thinking about your sister's murder. Don't forget, she was strangled and then dumped in Ponzio's backyard. That has all the earmarks of a pointed warning and seems to point to Ventutti. A few hours later, at about the time the police are getting on the case, one of Ventutti's boys strolls in out of the blue and retains you to do a job for him. There's no obvious connection, but it strikes me as a peculiar set of facts."

Sarah was opening her mouth to retort when the phone rang. Before she could answer it, Fielding reached over and picked up the receiver. "Yes?" he said. "Yeah, this is Fielding." He listened for several minutes. "Okay," he said finally. "I'm finished here. I'll come on in." He listened again. "Right. Be with you in a few minutes." He replaced the receiver.

Getting to his feet, he said, "It looks like we've gotten a break. One of our men has picked up a guy who says he saw your sister getting into a car on Lake Shore Drive this afternoon."

CHAPTER TEN

FOR SEVERAL MINUTES after Fielding left, Sarah and I stared into each other's eyes, neither of us capable of speech. I was the first to break the silence. "It's only a matter of hours now," I said hopelessly. "I don't know who could have seen her get into my car, but whoever it was will be certain to remember my Wisconsin plates. Fielding will know that it was me."

"Good Lord!" Sarah gasped. "I hadn't thought of that. What in the world can we do?"

"Not very much," I told her. "They probably haven't canvassed the apartment building yet. When they do, they'll get my description from the old guy who let me in. That'll cinch things as far as the cops are concerned."

She tightened her jaw. "We know you didn't do it," she said firmly. "If necessary, I'll swear that I was with you all the time."

"You'll be putting a noose around your own neck and you're in enough trouble as it is. It looks to me as though I've only got one out."

"You mean—?"

I nodded. "I've got to find the killer. Unless I can do that, and in a hurry, I'll be out for a long time."

"I'll help, of course."

She looked so brave and beautiful and determined that I had to laugh. "That makes me feel better," I said. "With the Livingston Agency on my side, the killer won't have a chance."

"You needn't laugh," she said, tossing her red head. "Dad taught me a few tricks. I can shoot and I can—"

"Sure, sure, honey," I said, putting an arm around her, "and you're beautiful and I love you, but you heard what Fielding said: This isn't the sort of mess for a girl to get into." I tried to kiss her, but she turned her head and avoided my lips.

"We haven't time for such things now, Gordon. We'd better find out what Lila was mixed up in and who could have killed her."

I sighed and released her. "You're right, Sarah. The sooner I get started the better, too. You'd better go on home and go to bed."

"Where are you going?"

"I don't know," I admitted. "But to begin with, I'm going to check on Danny Horan and try to find out where Carlo Ventutti spent the afternoon."

We argued for a few minutes, but she promised, finally, to go straight home and stay there. I kissed her thoroughly and went down to my car. I drove around the block, parked in the shadow of a building, and unscrewed the Wisconsin plates from the sedan. Throwing them into the trunk compartment, I got in again and drove slowly north. I turned in at the first parking lot I came to and abandoned my car.

A taxi cruising north stopped with a crash of gears when I waved my arms at it. I climbed in and slammed the door shut. "Where to?" the cabbie asked, twisting a stubbled chin around.

"I'm a stranger in town," I told him. "Know any place where I might find some excitement?"

"What kind of excitement?" He asked the question wearily, as though he were tired of the words.

"Oh, something out of the ordinary. Are there any pretty boy joints in town?"

His flat nostrils flared. "You kidding?" He measured me with experienced eyes. "What you wanta go to that kinda place for?"

"I thought it might be fun to see what goes on. I've heard a lot about places like that."

He shrugged. "Well, you're the boss. There's a joint on Clark near Division that's kinda like that. You wanta try it?"

"You're sure it's that kind of spot?"

"All I know is what I hear, Mister. Personally, I don't go in for that kinda' stuff."

"All right, take me there."

The taxi leaped ahead and rattled swiftly north. It stopped in front of a place festooned with green and red neon tubing above which a sign blazed: QUEENIE'S DEN. "This is it, Mister," the cabbie announced. "If you don't find what you want, there's another one just like it up the street a bit."

"Thanks." I gave him a dollar bill, waved away the change, and got out.

There was nothing fancy about Queenie's Den except the clientele. A long mahogany bar stretched down the far side of the room. Opposite the bar there were a half dozen square tables, each covered with a red-checkered cloth and surrounded by wooden chairs. At the rear, a gaudy jukebox reigned over a small dancing area dimly lighted by small yellow bulbs in paper lanterns. When I entered, there were several dozen people, male as well as female I noticed, crowded along the bar, a few at the tables and ten or twelve slowly-moving couples at the rear.

I strolled to the far end of the bar and leaned an elbow on it. Danny Horan, as far as I could see, wasn't present. The bartender, a huge big-chested man in a white shirt and black bow tie, nodded to indicate that my presence had been noted and served a frosted drink to a slim blonde lad who wore a beautifully pleated gray sports jacket. He murmured something to the lad, was rewarded with a gay laugh, collected for the drink, deposited the money in a chrome-trimmed register, then strode my way. I noticed that he had large muscular arms, around one of which an intricate green dragon was tattooed at the bicep.

"What'll you have, honey?" he asked in a treble voice.

Involuntarily I did a double take. "How about a Scotch-on-the-Rocks?" I asked, stifling my surprise.

Smiling sweetly, he said in the same girlish voice, "Is White Horse all right?"

"White Horse will be fine."

He made the drink expertly and set it in front of me. I laid a dollar on the mahogany. His hips undulated as he strode to the register and rang up the sale, then he returned and slid a fifty-cent piece beside my glass. "Thanks awfully," he murmured. "Would you like some popcorn?"

"Not right now. Has Katherine been in tonight?"

He frowned delicately with his eyebrows. "Katherine? I don't believe I know—"

"Katherine Greco."

"Oh, her!" He seemed relieved, like a woman who's discovered that the movement she felt on her leg really wasn't a stocking running. "No, she hasn't been in."

A dark-suited fellow who was standing down the bar a few feet turned a bland supercilious face toward me and smiled tentatively. I stared blankly at him and with a slight shrug, he returned his attention to the curly-haired boy beside him. Feeling as out of place as an uplift on a six-year old, I sipped the Scotch and listened to the high-pitched eddies of conversation around me.

"And believe it or not, she thought statutory rape meant doing bad things to statues!" a cute boy in a plaid suit shrilled. His companions nearly shrieked with laughter.

I had nearly finished my drink and was debating the wisdom of investing in another when a thin-faced youth in light slacks and a brown suede jacket strolled in. On a short leash, he led a frisky cocker spaniel. He went up to the bar holding tightly to the leash and waved a graceful hand at the bartender. Queenie set down the drink he had been preparing and rushed toward him. A low conversation ensued, during which a small roll of money was passed from the bartender to the newcomer. Suede Jacket slipped the money into his pocket, whistled to the cocker and when the pup stood up on his hind legs and pawed at his slacks, he patted it affectionately for a few moments. Something passed from Suede Jacket to the bartender and disappeared into the pocket of Queenie's shirt. They whispered together again, then Suede Jacket giggled softly, nodded, and tugged the cocker in my direction. With the dog capering at his heels, he moved up to the bar beside me and laid a slim effeminate hand next to mine. I noticed that one finger was encircled by a heavy, beautifully carved silver ring in which a large slab of green jade gleamed dully.

"Queenie says you're looking for Katherine," he murmured in a low falsetto.

"That's right," I said, wondering if I ought to put some tremolo into my own voice.

"She's staying home tonight," he informed me, tapping the ring against the edge of the bar. "Are you a friend of hers?"

"I met her at Sibyl's," I said cautiously.

"Oh..." He seemed to be waiting expectantly. "Well—" He moved his narrow shoulders and glanced toward the door. "If there's anything you want..."

"I'd like to see her. Could you give me her phone number or address?"

He started to freeze before the question had entirely passed my lips. With a frightened shriek, he flung the leash away and pounded his fists against the bar. The cocker, released, made a beeline for the door and darted between the startled legs of an arriving foursome. "He's a spy!" Suede Jacket shrilled. "Queenie, he's a spy!"

The cry pierced the flurries of conversation and killed them as suddenly as though the waves of high frequency sound had paralyzed all tongues within its range. Queenie, who had been spouting a Manhattan into a glass from a chrome shaker, dropped glass and shaker behind the bar with a shattering crash and swung toward us. A midget baseball bat appeared as if by magic in one of his hands and flattening his other hand against the top of the mahogany, he hurdled the bar as gracefully as a ballet dancer sailing over a papier-mâché bush. He landed on his toes. Flexed his legs and flung himself toward me, waving the bat ominously. He was not alone. The shriek had penetrated all corners of the joint and two solid phalanxes of shouting angry-faced members of the third sex were converging on me, one from the front and one from the rear. I was too surprised to run, too startled to move.

Queenie reached me first. He twirled the bat and lowered it at me like a housewife pouncing on a fly, emitting a shrill scream of fury as he did so. The bat struck my shoulder and pain flamed through my left side like liquid lava. The pain accomplished one thing: It made my mind snap awake to the fact that this was reality, not a dream, and my reflexes began to react to the danger that threatened to engulf me. Sarah's gun was in my pocket, but I had no chance to reach for it. Before I could move a muscle, I was at the center of a biting, scratching, pummeling mob, each member of which was eager for my blood.

Sharp nails clawed at my face and hands tore at my clothes. I slugged and kicked and kneed them, but their numbers appeared to multiply instead of diminish and they kept pressing into me like a corps of bargain shoppers around a slashed-price counter. Cursing, I crashed an elbow into a hate-crazed face, buried a fist into a narrow chest, rammed a knee into a flat belly, and plunged my other fist into a twisted mouth. They screamed and fell and wriggled away but others took their places. And Queenie's bat rose and fell persistently, swatting at my head and shoulders.

I was making slow, almost futile progress toward the door, leaving a shrill melee of third-railers in my wake, when someone screamed, "Cops!" I was blind with anger and deaf with sickening fury; the word meant nothing to me. But it penetrated their bloodthirsty yells and Queenie began screeching orders. The assaulting legions scattered suddenly, making clear a path to the door. I plunged forward, still pumping my arms in wild vicious jabs at anyone within reach and half fell, half stumbled through the doorway onto the sidewalk.

A squad car was unloading a quartette of burly cops at the curb. As I slid groggily to my knees, one of them ran forward and caught me.

CHAPTER ELEVEN

HE GRABBED my arms and pulled me roughly to my feet. "What the hell's going on?" he demanded.

"The sons of bitches!" I gasped. "They jumped me!"

"Go on in and clean 'em out," he told his companions. "He says they jumped him." To me he said, "You all right now?"

I rubbed the side of my face gingerly. "I guess so. I'm lucky to get out alive, it seems. I don't know what the hell happened. I had one drink and was standing at the bar minding my own business when one of them started pointing at me and yelling. Before I knew it, the bartender was swatting at me with a bat and everybody in the place was trying to claw my eyes out."

He grunted. "You must have made a pass at the wrong person."

"A pass? For chrissake, do you mean—"

"Yeah, we got trouble all the time at this dump. Nothing but pretty boys hang out there. They're jealous as hell, too. You try to talk to any of them?"

"Just to the bartender. I had one drink like I said and was just standing there sort of listening to things, you know, when a kid with a dog came over and started talking to me. I didn't say a dozen words to him when it started. There wasn't—"

The cop grinned. "His boyfriend musta been around and saw you chinning with him. He thought you were trying to cut in on his territory. You want to sign a complaint?"

"Well…" I looked at my clothes ruefully, "they certainly wrecked my suit, but maybe it's my own fault for not having sense enough to stay out of there. I'm from out of town and had a little time to waste and I—"

"You'd better skip it," the cop advised. "Just between you and me, filing a complaint would get you nothing. We been trying to clean up this district for years, but some of these locals have friends in high places, if you know what I mean. The boys will rough them up a little, but that's about all they can do. I could maybe pressure that Queenie into coughing up a little dough to help pay for your suit, but it'd—"

"No, you needn't do that," I said hastily. "I think I'll do like you say and skip the whole thing. Next time I'll know better than to go into a place like that."

"Sure, that's the best policy," he said. "Charge it up to experience."

The three cops came out of the joint herding four kicking, squirming youths in front of them. "What you want us to do, Sarge, take 'em in?" one asked.

"Naw, just boot 'em where it'll do some good. Where's the rest of them?"

"They must have beat it out the back. Nobody's in there now but Queenie." The cop shrugged. "The lieutenant told us to layoff Queenie, you know."

"Yeah." The sergeant nodded. "The guy isn't going to file a complaint anyway, so it's okay. Pin a sore tail on 'em so they'll remember they aren't supposed to beat up on strangers."

With considerable enthusiasm, the three did as he directed and two of the youths were propelled violently along the sidewalk and landed on their faces. The other two, a little more agile, were lifted into the air and alighted on their hands and knees. "Beat it!" one of the cops roared after them. The four scrambled hastily to their feet and, limping a little, scurried away.

"Okay, Mister, I guess that settles that," the sergeant said. He got out a pad of paper and a pencil. "Just for the record, I'd better take your name and address. Got some identification?"

I showed him my driver's license and several other cards and told him that I was staying at the Devonshire Hotel. He wrote it all down, then slapped the pad into his pocket. Waving a hand, he got into the squad car. His companions climbed in after him. I stood there watching it until it moved away from the curb and merged with the southbound stream of traffic.

None of it made much sense, but I had the feeling that it was all part of a pattern, a vicious pattern woven by desperate greedy men. Whoever Greco was, he was someone important. He was my starting point. To understand the pattern and get a line on Lila's murderer, I had to get a line on him. According to my watch, it was a few minutes after midnight. I turned and walked slowly north.

I stopped at two other joints and had a drink in each of them before I located the one that the cab driver must have been referring to when he mentioned a second spot similar to Queenie's on the street. It was a long, low, dimly lighted dive called The Hang-Out, containing the inevitable mahogany bar, a few tables and a generous spattering of low-voiced customers, mostly women. The bartender was a skinny flat-chested girl in black sweater and slacks whose dishwater blonde hair was skinned back against her head in a mannish shingle. She came down the bar to me, flicked a wet rag over the wood, and lifted an eyebrow.

"Scotch-on-the-Rocks," I said.

She nodded and popped an ice cube into a glass. I noticed that she slopped the Scotch in carelessly, as though she didn't much care whether she gave full measure or not. She extracted 75¢ from the dollar I gave her and spun the quarter across the bar to me.

A girl with her back to me was saying, "When I turned around, there he was, as bare as the man in the zodiac and when I made it plain that there was nothing doing—"

Her companion interrupted. "How do you like that? The nasty thing! You shouldn't have gone there in the first place though, because—" Noticing me over the other girl's shoulder, she dropped her voice and finished the sentence at a low pitch.

I sipped the Scotch and pretended disinterest. After a while their voices became audible again. The nearer of the two, a brunette with short curly hair, was saying, "...don't know what happened, but no one came around. I'm almost out, too."

The other one replied, "You can always take a walk along Ontario Street. They usually have someone near the Institute of Design. You know how to tell them, don't you?"

"Oh, sure, but I hate having to chase down there. If someone doesn't come pretty soon though, I suppose I'll have to."

Their voices sank lower again. I signaled to the bartender for another drink. When she passed the girls, one of them asked, "What happened to Tony? Didn't he call or anything?"

The blonde shrugged and shook her head. I saw that there were lines under her eyes where youth had flaked away. "Something musta happened," she rasped in a G-major voice. She looked directly at me. "Yessir?"

"Do this again, will you?"

She took my glass and strode away. The brunette looked at me and started to smile, then stopped abruptly. Rather carefully I said, "You aren't the only one who wonders where Tony is."

Her eyes became opaque. "You mean you—?"

I nodded and paid the bartender for the drink she brought. The two girls whispered together for a moment, then one of them left. The brunette inched along the bar until our elbows were almost touching. I could see her better now and, in spite of the pinched look around her eyes, she was rather pretty.

"What do you think could have happened?" she asked.

"I don't know," I said. "I do know that it's damned inconvenient."

"He's always been here by now."

"He didn't hit Queenie's place either," I told her, choosing the words carefully.

"Oh." She nodded several times, as though I'd explained a great many things to her. "It must be something serious then." She stared at her empty glass.

"Would you like another drink?" I asked.

"No...no thanks. Alcohol doesn't give me much of a lift." She gave me a frank look. "I don't do much drinking. I've just been waiting around for—you know."

"Same here."

"Well, we can always—" She hesitated.

"Take a walk?" I suggested.

"Uh-huh. I wondered if you knew."

"Yeah," I said. "Down by the Institute. I was trying to make up my mind whether to go or not."

"I'm afraid I'll have to." She shivered a little. "You know how it is when—well, you know."

"Sure. If you're going, suppose I walk along with you."

"It's all right with me."

I drained my glass and strolled after her to the door. When we were on the sidewalk, I said, "Maybe we ought to take a cab."

"It isn't far." She started briskly south, walking beside me but keeping a discreet distance between us. At the first corner she turned west for a block, then south again at Dearborn and we walked in silence along the deeply shadowed street. She had the lithe stride of a man and seemed to gain momentum with each block. I was beginning to wonder where Ontario Street was and how much farther it was to the mysterious Institute when, abruptly, she slackened her pace and released a sigh of relief.

Ahead of us, a large man was loitering near the edge of a wide strip of concrete, which served as the entrance to a hulking, castle-like building. He stood with his hands pushed into the pockets of a leather jacket, ostensibly watching the sniffing-around antics of a big black Doberman Pinscher that he held on a leash. The dog, sensing our approach, lifted its head and stiffened. The man remained motionless.

"Have your money ready," the girl whispered. She fumbled in her purse and I heard the rustle of paper as she crumpled some bills in her hand.

Having no idea as to what the procedure was or how much money required, I took the $100 bill from my wallet and folded it in the palm of my hand. She walked ahead, pausing a few feet from the dog. "Hello, doggie," she said softly. "Nice doggie." The dog eyed her warily and remained stationary. As though abashed by its unfriendliness, she straightened and smiled at the man. "He looks like a nice dog. How old is he?"

"Five," the man muttered. I could see that he had a weather-beaten round face, the principal feature of which was a pair of shrewd dark eyes. They appeared to be staring blankly out into the street, but I knew that he was watching us intently.

"I didn't think he was more than three," she protested.

"Five," the man repeated.

"Well—"

She moved toward him a little and I saw the slight jerk of their shoulders as their hands sought each other and her money changed ownership. He glanced down at it, put the hand into his pocket, and moved his eyes slightly in my direction. "What about him?" he asked softly.

I stepped around her and slipped the folded bill into his waiting palm. His eyes flicked at it, the hand started toward his pocket then stopped. He licked his lips and looked at the bill again. "All of it?" he asked.

"Yes," I said.

He put the money into his jacket, then made a smacking sound with his lips. The dog bounded toward him, stood on its hind legs, and pawed his chest. He fondled the dog for a moment. The girl, tense with expectancy, watched him with parted lips and anxious eyes. Pushing the dog away, he touched the girl's hand briefly, then extended the hand to me. A small package remained in my palm when he took his hand away. I slipped it into my pocket. Making the smacking sound again, he turned away and strolled slowly toward the corner, coaxing the dog along by gentle tugs on the leash.

"Damn!" she said tersely.

"What's the matter?"

"Matter?" Her dark eyes flashed in the pale oval of her face. "Good lord! Last week it was two and only the day before yesterday it was three—and now it's suddenly five!" She opened her clenched hand, giving me a glimpse of three small capsules. "Fifteen dollars worth! By tomorrow night it'll be gone and I don't get paid until Thursday—" The words stuck in her throat, as though caught in thickening mucous. She looked desperately up and down the deserted street and began to tremble.

"I've got quite a bit," I told her.

She got my meaning. "You feel like throwing a party?"

"Why not?"

"Well—" her shoulders jerked. "I live on Superior."

"I've got it room at the Devonshire."

She shook her head. "No, my place would be better." Something occurred to her. "You won't get anything out of it, you know. I hope you realize that."

"I don't want anything," I said, sliding a hand beneath her arm. "Just company. You don't mind that, do you?"

"No."

We started north again.

CHAPTER TWELVE

SHE WAS almost running by the time we reached the tall building on Superior Street in which her apartment was located. Unlocking the outer door, she hurried into the lobby ahead of me and threw her weight against the call button of the self-service elevator as though she was ringing for St. Peter. As soon as it came down, she flung the door back and held it until I was in the tiny cage with her. Releasing the door, she jabbed at the "9" button, closed her eyes, and sank against me as though she hadn't strength to stand alone. I put my arm around her waist. Through her thin clothing, I could feel the violent trembling of her body. As soon as the cage stopped its upward journey, she straightened like a released spring and clawed at the door. I had to help her pull it back.

She ran stiff-legged down a narrow red-carpeted corridor and stopped beneath a yellow bulb that glowed feebly over a scarred brown door. Her fingers pawed frantically in her purse, searching for a key. She found it at last and tried to insert it in the lock, but her fingers were shaking like blades of grass in a spring wind. The key fell from her fingers and dropped soundlessly onto the faded red carpeting. I picked it up, slid it into the lock, turned it, and pushed the door open. With a grateful sigh, she turned on the lights and flung the purse onto a sofa.

It wasn't much of an apartment. There was a cheap, uninviting sofa, a few chairs and very little else. No pictures, no radio, no drapes, no ornamentation or bits of extravagance or any of the usual little feminine touches. It was like a monk's cell, stripped bare of everything except the necessities.

Without a word, she started for a door, which I figured led to a bathroom. "Hey!" I said. "Where are you going?"

She stopped with her hand on the knob. "I've got to have one right away," she said nervously. "It'll only take a minute."

"This is supposed to be on me," I reminded her. "Can't you wait a second?"

"Well, I need it pretty bad. I thought—"

In the lighted room, she wasn't pretty any more. I decided she was somewhere in her early twenties and, months ago, before dope had started tearing through her veins, she may have been beautiful, but now there was a gaunt, bleak hardness about her dark eyes and the taut lines around her red mouth showed that her lips rarely relaxed long enough to smile. She had a good figure though and nice legs and she looked clean. I knew what I had to do, but I couldn't help feeling a deep pang of pity.

"Hell, I need it, too," I said, "but why use yours when I have all this?" I took the small package out of my pocket, tore it open, and spilled its contents into the palm of my hand. There were a couple of dozen white capsules, each tightly packed with a substance that glistened a little in the incandescent light. Her eyes fastened on them and widened hungrily. "How many do you want?"

She moistened her lips. "I usually only take one. That's all I can afford. But—"

"Would you like a couple?"

"That would be wonderful!" She sighed like a child contemplating a huge pink birthday cake.

"Come here then."

She came toward me, trembling with eagerness, and reached out a hand. I jerked my palm away from her fingers and poured the capsules into my coat pocket. Then, before her startled gasp was complete, I grabbed her arm and pulled her to the sofa. She twisted and fought with a wild animal-like desperation, but I locked her arms behind her, picked her up, and forced her onto her back. Her legs thrashed furiously and she tried to kick me in the face.

"It won't do you any good!" she cried hoarsely. "I told you I'm no good that way! Can't you tell when things are wrong? Please, please, let me have—"

"Shut up!" I said grimly. "What did you do with them?"

"Please, please—!"

I slapped her legs away, pinned her down with one arm, and forced her fingers open, one by one. They weren't in her hands. I felt about her body, searching for pockets in her dress. There were none. I hesitated, inwardly revolted by what I had to do, but I had no alternative. I unbuttoned the front of her dress, pulled the straps of her slip and brassiere away from her shoulders, then forced my hand into the padded cups of the brassiere. Her breasts were cool, hard, and more generous than I expected. I searched the cups carefully but the capsules weren't there.

Her eyes were shut and she was moaning and biting at her lips. "Please, please—!" she whimpered.

"Tell me where they are," I said. "I'm not going to hurt you. I'll give them back to you before I go."

She got one of her arms free and jabbed viciously at my eyes. I held her down with my body, struggled for possession of the arm, captured it at last. Her legs were pumping like a speeding bicycle rider's. I didn't see how she could have secreted them in her stocking without my noticing it, but I pulled up her skirt and searched the tops of her stockings. Where the hell could she have hid them? Some place in her clothes, certainly, but where?

"Give them to me," I told her, "or I'll have to undress you. Can't you see I'm not kidding? I just want to make sure you don't take any for a few minutes. After we've talked awhile, I'll give them back to you."

"No, no, no!" She arched her back and tried to squirm away.

I hooked my fingers into the waist of the dress and ripped it down the front. She screamed hoarsely, but I rolled her over, got the dress out from under her, and dropped it on the floor. The brassiere and slip were next. When I finished, I was breathing heavily from the exertion and she was clad only in a transparent pair of pink panties, a garter belt, and her stockings. Gathering up the rest of her clothes, I released her. She rolled off the sofa, scrambled to her feet, then whirled to face me, eyes wide and rolling, oblivious to her near-nudity.

"Give them to me!" she shrieked. "Please, please, give them to me!"

Ignoring her, I examined every inch of the brassiere with my fingers, felt every seam of the slip, then started in on the dress. They had to be there. I went over the dress twice before I found them, tucked into a tiny hollow of the cuff of one sleeve. I shook them into my palm and let her see them.

"There," I said, throwing the dress to her. "Now, let's talk business."

She flung the dress away and got down on her knees. "Please! I don't know what you want, but give me one of 'em! Just one. I can't—I can't do anything unless—"

"Who's Tony Greco?" I asked.

"I don't know. Please give me—"

"Listen," I said harshly. "Tell me what I want to know and you can have all of them, every one I've got. Understand? You can have all I've got. Who's Tony Greco?"

"I can't tell you! He'd kill me if—"

"Would you rather spend tonight without these?" I shook the capsules in my hand. "And how about tomorrow—and the next day? You've spent all your money. Unless you talk, you'll suffer so much that you'll wish you were dead. It'll be a hell, won't it?"

"Yes, oh yes! But—"

"Then be sensible. You can have everything you want in a few minutes. Tell me about Tony."

"He's a peddler. That's all I know. I've been buying it from him."

"Where does he live?"

"I don't know. I've tried to find out, when—when I had to have some and didn't know where to go, but nobody could tell me."

"What does Tony look like?"

"He's tall and good-looking. I think he has dark hair."

"Keep talking."

"He wears sports clothes a lot and he has a little mustache."

"A mustache?" Danny Horan hadn't mentioned that. "You're sure?"

"Yes, just a little one. Please, can't you give me—"

"Not yet. Do you know a Danny Horan?"

"No."

"Did you know Lila Livingston?"

"I only saw her once. She was at The Hang-Out with someone."

"Try to think. Who was she with?"

"I don't remember. Some man, I think."

"Was it Carlo Ventutti?"

"No. It wasn't Carlo."

"Where does Carlo have his headquarters?"

"I don't know. Not at The Hang-Out."

"Make a guess."

"Some place near Grand Avenue. That's where Tony usually is—and Tony works for him."

"So Tony works for Carlo," I nodded. "Then the dope really comes from Ventutti not from Pete Ponzio?"

"I never heard of Ponzio." She shuddered and clasped one of her bare breasts as though it hurt her. "Please. I can't stand it much longer. Can't you see—"

"In a moment. Tell me this, how long have you been using this stuff?"

"Nearly a year."

"And you have to have three capsules of the stuff every day?"

"Yes—more if I can get it."

"How do you manage to earn enough to pay for it?"

"I don't know. I get it somehow." Her eyes looked blankly about the room. "I've sold everything I own. Sometimes I do extra work. And there are other ways. It's terrible, but I've got to have it."

"How'd you get started?"

"A girl I knew gave me some." Tears brimmed in her eyes. "Please—!"

"Are there many girls like you, many girls taking dope?"

She nodded. "Quite a few. That's why—" She bit her lip.

"That's why Tony has a regular route, why Ventutti has agents posted on the streets at night?"

"I suppose so. Please, Mister, for God's sake, give me just one!" She clasped my knee and looked beseechingly into my face while tears coursed down her cheeks. "I can't stand it any longer. You don't know how it is. I'll go crazy. I'll—"

"Here," I dropped one of the capsules into her hand. With a sob of relief, she ran into the bathroom and returned with a small box. Oblivious to my presence, she took a spoon, some cotton, and a hypodermic needle from the box and spread them on a table. Then, emptying the white powder from the capsule into the spoon, she added a few drops of warm water to it. When it was dissolved, she laid a dab of cotton on the spoon and sucked the dope into the needle through the cotton. When the needle was full she sighed and, holding her lips tightly together, eased the sharp point of it into a vein on her right arm. Slowly, as though experiencing an exquisite pleasure like the first bubble of a seminal spring, she closed her eyes and depressed the plunger.

The effect was startling—and almost instantaneous. The trembling ceased and, as she took a deep breath and removed the needle, the tautness in her face disappeared. Her body seemed to glow and she looked riper and years younger. When she looked at me, it was as though I were meeting her for the first time.

"I'm fine now," she said almost pleasantly. "Do you want to use my needle?"

"No."

"You were lying. You aren't an addict, are you?"

"No. I was lying."

She shrugged and, in doing so, seemed to become conscious of her nakedness for the first time. "Oh my!" she said, looking down at her breasts. "I didn't promise you anything, did I?"

"No, you needn't worry about that."

"That's good." She reached for the rumpled dress and crushed it against her. "When I'm like that, I don't know what I'm doing or saying half the time. I don't—I mean, I'm not much satisfaction to men. I was afraid maybe—"

"There wasn't anything like that."

"Well, fine." She got up and slipped into the dress. One hand rose unconsciously and touched the sleeve where she had hidden the capsules. A look of concern crossed her face and she eyed me uncertainly.

"Here are the rest," I said. I emptied my pocket on the sofa and pushed the capsules into a pile.

She pounced on them eagerly. "Thanks! This is wonderful!"

My mouth tasted as though it had been sucking on an old rubber ball and I could feel my stomach beginning to retch. I got up and walked to the door.

"You're going?" she asked, holding the capsules lovingly in her cupped hands.

"Yes. Goodnight, kid…and good luck."

"Goodnight. Thanks ever so much!"

I thought: *When August comes I'll keep myself cold by thinking of you.* I opened the door and walked out. It was five minutes short of being two in the A.M.

CHAPTER THIRTEEN

I KNEW better than to return to the Devonshire. The police certainly had a description of me by now and would be watching the hotel, waiting for me to try to get to my room. On a hunch, I flagged a passing taxi and told the driver to take me to the Flask Club.

The neon lights on the club's facade were turned off, but the door was still unlocked. Inside, a balding bartender was washing glasses and stacking them on a shelf. He shook his head wearily when he saw me and said. "Sorry. We're closing."

"I'm waiting for Millie Royce," I told him. "She hasn't gone yet, has she?"

"Don't think so. She's probably upstairs changing clothes." He went back to his glasses.

I slid onto a stool and lit a cigarette. Almost all the customers had gone elsewhere to continue their search for pleasure and the joint was virtually deserted. While I waited, tired-footed and homeward bound employees straggled past me, one by one like roaches on their way to a newly leased apartment. I watched them for a while, then noticing a phone booth near the entrance, I went to the booth and looked up Sarah's number in the directory. Depositing a dime, I dialed the number and listened to the monotonous buzz of the ringing signal. I counted the buzzes. When I had counted fifteen and she still hadn't answered, I hung up, checked the number in the directory and dialed it again. Still no answer. Puzzled, I pronged the receiver and retrieved my dime.

Where the hell was Sarah?

The question puzzled me so that I almost missed Millie Royce. She was halfway out the door before I realized that the dark-suited girl in the plain red hat and low-heeled shoes was she. I hurried after her, touched her arm, and said, "Hello, Miss Royce. I hope you don't mind my waiting for you."

She pulled her arm away, then looked up and smiled. "Oh. Hello! I didn't recognize you for a moment."

"I intended to come back earlier but I ran into a little trouble. Feel like having something to eat with me now?"

"I'd like to. What sort of trouble did you have?"

"I'll tell you about it later. Where would you like to go?"

"Any place that's quiet. I'm kind of hungry and I've heard enough noise for about eighteen hours."

"Well, I'm not very familiar with the city—"

"There's a place near my apartment. It's on Diversey Parkway, and it's quiet and has good food. If that sounds all right to you—"

"It sounds swell."

I hailed a cab and helped her in. She told the driver where to go. I watched her, thinking that she looked exactly like a small-town girl in her street clothes and not at all like the singer in a big city hot spot. She had pulled her blonde hair under her hat in some way, making her small pale face look plainer and more sedate. Finished with the directions, she sank back on the seat and said, "Now tell me what you've been doing."

"I visited a couple of joints on North Clark Street. Queenie's Den and The Hang-Out. Maybe you know about them."

"I've heard of Queenie's. Isn't that where...?" She left the question unfinished.

"That's the place," I said, "and that's why I got mussed up. One of the boys thought I was making a pass at his very good friend."

"What were you doing in a place like that?" she asked, laughing. "You didn't go there on purpose, did you?"

"Sort of," I admitted. I grinned across the seat at her. "I was trying to get a lead on a pretty boy called Tony Greco. Ever hear of him?"

"Tony Greco?" She frowned and shook her head. "I don't believe so. What does he do?"

"That's what I'm trying to find out." I decided to change the subject. "How were things at the Flask Club after I left?"

"Hectic." She wrinkled her nose. "I'm always glad to get out of there. Mr. Ponzio was touchier than a mother cat and had nearly everybody in the place on the carpet. The police didn't help either."

"The police..."

"Oh, sure. They came in a little after midnight and went up to his office. That sort of put a damper on things. The girls were fit to be tied."

"What'd they want?"

"It was something about Lila's murder, I think. That's what one of the girls said. They stayed about an hour and he went out right after they left and then things sort of went back to normal. There seemed to be a lot of tension though. Mr. Ponzio was glaring as though he'd been cheated of something when he went out." She glanced out the window. "Here we are—and am I glad! I'm hungry enough to eat almost anything."

As she had said, it was a nice quiet place and the food was good. We each ate an order of barbecued ribs with french fries and drank two cups of coffee. We talked about Ripon and Fond du Lac and how she happened to come to Chicago and my job and a dozen other things. Then over our coffee I brought the conversation back to the Flask Club.

"Did you notice the girl who came down from Ponzio's office just before I did?"

"Not that I can remember. What did she look like?"

"Redhead in a blue suit. Slender. Rather attractive."

"Oh, her. Yes, I saw her. Why?"

"She's Lila's sister."

"Really? Why, I've seen her around the place a lot."

"You mean she came to see Lila?"

"No. I don't recall seeing her with Lila." Millie squinted thoughtfully. "She was with some man usually. I noticed him because he waved his hands a lot and talked so much. Funny how things like that stick in your mind, isn't it?"

This fellow you saw her with, Millie—did you ever hear his name?"

"No. I just noticed them from the bandstand. Between numbers and choruses, you know, I haven't much to do except look at the customers and wonder what I'm doing there. I probably wouldn't have remembered him at all if he hadn't looked like such a character and if they hadn't made such an odd-looking pair."

"What do you mean by that?"

"Well, a looker. Not like Lila, of course. Lila knew how to pour it on and make the most of what she had. This other girl, her sister, was really better looking than Lila, but she didn't fuss with herself or try to be beautiful. Women notice things like that and I thought it was too bad. With the right clothes—"

"I think I know what you mean, Millie. But why were they an odd-looking couple?"

"Well, it's hard to explain, Gordon. She had so much and didn't do anything with it, while he was the one who was all duked up. Girls are supposed to fuss with themselves, but men—"

"Are you talking about his clothes or things in general?"

"Things in general. His clothes were pretty spiffy though. I remember that one night he had on a light grey flannel suit with pleated shoulders, big patch pockets, and large pointed lapels. It must have cost a lot of money and you could tell that he was proud of it. I'd guess—"

"Describe him for me, Millie!"

"You needn't snap at me. Why are you so interested in him?"

"Sorry, Millie. The description so far seems to fit someone I've been looking for. If he is and if she knows him well, maybe I've been barking up the wrong tree. Try to describe him for me."

"Well, as I said, he was always dressed to kill and he talked a lot and he waved his hands when he talked. I'd say he was fairly young, in his late twenties, probably. He had a small mustache—you know, the kind that looks as though it's been drawn on with a pencil—a rather thin face, thick eyebrows, sort of darkish hair—either curly or wavy, I think. I'm not sure—and pretty lips, almost like a girl's. He seemed—"

"I'll be damned," I commented. "It sounds like Tony Greco!"

"It does?"

"It sure as hell does." I rubbed my check. "He didn't have a dog with him, did he?"

"A dog?" Millie's chin dropped. "What would he be doing in the Flask Club with a dog?"

"I don't know," I admitted. "I thought he might have had a Pomeranian or a Pekinese or—"

"Mr. Ponzio has a Peke. That's the only dog that ever—"

"Ponzio has a Pekinese pup?"

"Sure. He likes dogs. He brings it to the club with him fairly frequently." She chuckled. "It always seems funny to see him with such a little pup. Personally, if I were a man, I'd have a big dog—a Great Dane, or a German shepherd, or a Collie. Pekes are all right, I suppose, but they remind me of cats."

She rambled on, talking about the kinds of dogs she liked and the alley curs she'd kept bringing home with her when she was a kid in Ripon. I let it go in one ear and out the other. If what she had said was true, Sarah knew Tony Greco and must have had dealings with him. But she had denied having any knowledge of him. Who was lying? Millie had no reason to lie, as far as I knew—but had Sarah?

"You aren't listening to me!" she accused.

"Sorry, Millie. I was thinking about something."

"I said it was time I was home and in bed. You don't mind if I call it a night do you? I'm really sort of tired."

"Of course not."

I paid the check and walked to the Rienzi Hotel with her, where she had a tiny apartment, she said. When we were in the hotel lobby, she put a small warm hand in mine, thanked me for the ribs, and said she hoped she'd see me again soon. I told her I hoped so, too, and smiling, she got into an elevator and disappeared.

The hotel clock said 3:37. I was beginning to feel as though I'd been pulled through a keyhole, but things were more complicated than ever. From a phone booth in the lobby, I called Sarah's apartment again. I got a lot of buts and no response. Wherever she had gone, she was apparently making a night of it.

I was standing outside the hotel in front of the plate glass windows of an open-all-night beauty salon called The House of Beauty, when a black Cadillac sedan skidded to a sudden stop and a man hurriedly alighted and ran into the hotel. He wasn't anyone I knew, just a man in a blue suit and grey hat who was in a hurry, but the car continued to wait and I still had to make up my mind as to what I was going to do next. I eyed the sedan, not with any great interest and noticed that the driver was a broad-shouldered man and that there was someone huddled in a corner of the rear seat. I couldn't see the driver's face and the person in back was merely a vague outline, but something tickled my curiosity.

I had taken a step forward intending to get a better look at the person in back, when another sedan came hurtling east on Diversey, slowed suddenly and emitted a sound like a kid rattling a ·stick along the metal bars of a fence. Someone screamed. Glass tinkled in the street. The Cadillac, its windows dotted with whitish holes as though someone had pelted it with tiny snowballs, roared to life and leaped away in pursuit of the other car. As the Cadillac disappeared, a man and a girl ran out of the hotel. The man was the guy in the grey hat and blue suit. The girl was Millie Royce.

CHAPTER FOURTEEN

INSTINCTIVELY, I backed into the doorway of the beauty salon and averted my face. Neither of them glanced my way. Grabbing her by the arm, he pulled her across the street and they ran into the deep shadows of an alley just as the eerie wail of a police siren began to rise and fall on the early morning quiet.

Without pausing to think, I ran to the corner, sprinted to the next block, and hid myself in the dark entrance of a cleaner's shop. They came out of the alley a few seconds later, he in the lead and still pulling her forward by the hand. I couldn't see her face, but there was unwillingness in every step she took and I felt, rather than heard, the protests she must have been making.

They headed for a taxi stand on the corner. As soon as I was certain of their intent, I hightailed it into Clark Street and waved frantically at a Yellow that was cruising slowly north. When he stopped, I climbed in and shouted, "Follow that cab!" Leaning over the back of the front seat, I pointed at the taxi that was half a block ahead.

With a grunt, the cabbie spun the wheel and kicked at the gas. "Got it," he growled. "What's up?"

"My wife's in it with some other guy," I told him. "Ten bucks if you keep them in sight without being spotted."

He grunted again, somewhat derisively and settled down in his seat. The car ahead went straight north for three blocks, then turned left and headed west. I sank back on the seat, got out my wallet, and folded a $10 bill between my fingers.

"I don't want no trouble," the cabbie growled a few minutes later, as though the possibility had just occurred to him.

"Ten bucks isn't trouble," I told him.

"What happens when they stop?"

"Go on past and drop me down the block. I just want to find out where they're going."

"You oughta shoot the bastard." His head jerked. "I would if it were my—"

"The hell with him," I said, trying to sound like a broadminded much-cuckolded husband. "He can have her, for all I care. I just want to know where they go when she thinks I'm working."

"Evidence, huh?"

"Yeah."

The red taillight ahead of us glowed like a bobbing railroad signal, then disappeared suddenly. The cabbie braked at the corner, twisted the wheel and the cab squealed into a side street. The bobbing taillight glowed briefly, then disappeared again. When we reached the next street, our quarry was pulling away from the right-hand curb and two shadows were moving rapidly toward the porch of a large frame house.

"Keep on going," I said. "Slow down at the next corner and I'll hop out. Don't stop though. Turn or something so it'll look as though you just happened past." I dropped the folded bill on the seat beside him.

"Right." He braked a little and started to turn. I unlatched the door, waited until we were abreast the crosswalk, then jumped out. Before the door flapped shut, I heard him call, "Good luck!"

I found the entrance to the alley that ran through the block and headed down it, tripping over treacherous cans and pieces of stone as I felt my way through the darkness. Above me, a wisp of a moon sailed tranquilly across a black star-spangled sheet. The house toward which they had gone was the fourth one from the corner. I felt along a wire fence until I found the gate, cursed silently as a sharp piece of metal pierced a finger and fiddled with the invisible latch until it opened. I entered a pitch-black yard.

The entire neighborhood was completely silent. I reached the house, located the back porch, and ascended it cautiously. The door was locked. I eased my ear against it and listened intently for several minutes. There was no sound of movement within. Frowning, I worked my way down the steps and circled the building on tiptoe, staring up at windows as I went. None of them were lighted. No one was in the house—or everyone was asleep.

I stood there in the darkness, wondering if I had made a mistake and then it occurred to me: *They played it safe. This wasn't where they went.* The conviction became stronger and with great care I inched my way back to the alley and studied the houses on either side. The only one in which a light showed was a three-story gabled structure at the far end of the alley. I started toward it.

A fence, a gate, another latch, and several curses later I was in another dark yard, moving stealthily toward the deep shadows of a building. On its top floor, two yellow rectangles showed where light was glowing through shaded windows. I was positive that that was where they had gone. A minute later I was absolutely certain.

The roar of a powerful engine shattered the quiet and bright headlights glared on the street. I dropped flat on the ground, just as the car turned into the driveway and halted.

Rubbing my nose into the dirt, I prayed that they didn't catch me in the beam of their headlights. They didn't. The lights died and a car door slammed. I lifted my head and made out the shape of the big Cadillac. Someone was grunting and cursing, as though trying to get something out of the car. I wriggled toward the car until I could look down the space between it and the building. While I watched, a short stocky man lowered something heavy and bulky to the ground, clicked the rear door shut, bent, picked the bundle up, tottered around the car toward me with it.

He turned, followed the side of the building to a railed porch and grunting frequently, went up the steps. Reaching the top, he banged the door with his elbow. A light came on downstairs and the door opened, dropping a plank of yellow light across the porch. I could make out a pair of legs hanging from his arms and realized that the bundle was the body of a person.

"What the hell happened?" a harsh male voice demanded. "We got chopped. Hold it wide, will ya?"

He maneuvered the dangling legs into the doorway and blocked the light with his stocky body. The door closed. A few minutes later the downstairs light was extinguished. I stayed where I was, trying to add two and two and two and get an answer that seemed reasonable. The legs had looked like a man's; at least they appeared to be encased in dark trousers. Who was he and who was the guy in the blue suit and what did Millie Royce have to do with them? More important, was I making a stupid mistake or did this all have something to do with Lila Livingston's murder? I was still racking my brain with the problem when I heard the dog bark.

At first, it was merely a faraway yipping, then I could hear it quite clearly. The downstairs light came on again and the back door opened a few inches. A small dark shape bounded onto the porch and came leaping down the steps, yipping shrilly. My heart turned over and all the optimism in me drained away. Sure enough, the damned dog started straight for me, stopped stiff-legged when it got my scent, and began barking as though there were fifteen tomcats in the yard.

The door opened and the harsh voice said, "Shut up. Brownie! What the hell's the matter with you?"

The dog barked frenziedly and pawed the ground as though undecided whether to spring at me or not. I could feel the man's eyes probing into the darkness, searching for the dog and I slid my hand down my side until my fingers touched the gun in my pocket. I wished the little bitch would come a couple of feet closer so I could grab her. I'd stop her damn barking once and for all. Fortunately, a moment later there was a clatter in the alley and the shape of a larger dog loomed beyond the fence. It growled challengingly and began barking in deep howling octaves.

"For cryin' out loud!" the harsh voice commented. "Come here. Brownie! Come here! You're waking the whole damn neighborhood! Come here, damn you!"

Reluctantly, the dog retreated toward the porch, barking shrilly every inch of the way. The other dog's howls reverberated through the night. From where I lay, it looked like a large police dog. I wondered if it could leap the fence. If it did, I'd have to shoot it.

"Get in there, damn you!" the harsh voice snapped. The door banged shut. The light went off. The other dog stopped howling and went scratching off down the alley. My lungs started breathing again. I rolled over and looked up at the sky. I didn't know which star had been taking care of me, but I felt grateful as hell.

I got to my feet, made my way to the porch, and crawled slowly up the steps. No sound came from inside. Cautiously, I tried the door. Locked. I shrugged. It would be senseless to try to break in. The dog would hear me or sense me and everyone inside would be warned before I had a chance to accomplish anything. But what was going on? Who had been wounded and what was Millie Royce's role?

For a moment, frustration flooded through me. Descending the steps, I went around to the side of the big house and studied it. The lights were on the third floor and only two windows were lighted. The windows were gabled and a sort of narrow balcony with a wrought iron rail had been built in front of them. A row of flowerpots was on the balcony, nearly filling it, but it might accommodate a man and once there, he might be able to peek beneath the drawn shades. But how the hell to get up there?

I toured the yard and located a two-car garage and a couple of tin garbage cans, but there was no sign of a ladder. I needed something strong and solid, something at least fifteen feet long. Then I noticed the tree. It was quite tall and heavy limbed, but, unfortunately, none of its branches came anywhere near the balcony. I studied it for several minutes. Hell, there simply wasn't any other way. I ran to it, wrapped my legs around its trunk, and started up.

I haven't climbed a tree since I was a kid and, for a while, I didn't think I'd be able to reach the first branch. By using my teeth and nails and sacrificing a trouser leg, however, I managed to catch my heel on a lower limb, and work my ankle into a position of solidity against its rough bark and lever myself up far enough to grasp it. Breathing heavily from the unusual exertion, I paused to rest. The branch was nine or ten feet from the ground and brought me almost on a level with the second floor windows.

Leaves and small branches tore at my hands, arms, and face as I began to work my way upward. When I was on a level with the third floor, I leaned out as far as I could and tried to touch the balcony. I was short three feet and jumping was out of the question. I climbed higher. The branches became thinner and the trunk shrank until it was a mere pole. When I was level with the gabled roof, the tree was swaying dangerously and beginning to lean toward the house. I went up a few more feet, then grasped the thickest branch and swung out into space. My weight brought the top of the tree down against the tip of a gable and I was dangling precariously in the air with a rain gutter a foot away.

With a prayer on my lips, I grabbed for the metal gutter and caught it. Gingerly, I put my weight upon it, little by little. It seemed solid. I abandoned the branch suddenly and clawed my other hand at the gutter. My chest and knees slapped the side of the house and the tree snapped straight, out of reach, leaving me no choice but to inch my way along the gutter until I was above the little balcony and hope that my feet would touch it.

For what seemed like half an hour, but which probably was no longer than four or five minutes, I was suspended between heaven and hell, with hell getting most of the votes. The rough metal slashed and tore my hands, the rough sides of the old house caught at my clothes and rubbed my knees raw; and with every inch I progressed, the rusted cleats that held the gutter threatened to tear loose and send it plunging to earth.

At last I reached a position above the windows. Craning my aching neck around, I peered over my shoulder to ascertain the location of the balcony's railing. It seemed to be directly beneath me. I pawed the air with my feet, trying to establish contact, but my shoes touched nothing. I hung there, gasping for breath and trying to swallow my heart, while I forced my mind to rationalize my predicament. Obviously, there must be several inches of space between my feet and the rail. That meant that there were twelve or eighteen inches between me and the balcony. Not much of a drop, certainly, but enough to make a hell of a noise, especially if I landed on some of the flowerpots.

If I could only touch the rail! I loosened my fingers until I was suspended by their very tips and I stretched my legs until I felt as though the cartilage between my bones was on the verge of tearing loose. My feet still swung freely in thin air. The gutter squeaked ominously. I took a deep breath, let go with one hand, fastened my eyes on the narrow balcony—and dropped.

I landed with a horrendous crash of rattling tin and shattering pots.

CHAPTER FIFTEEN

A WINDOW banged up and powerful hands clutched my legs. They dragged me across the clutter of spilled and broken pots and I fell through space onto the floor of a room. My head cracked against the hard floor and multicolored stars showered behind my eyes. The hands pulled me around and jerked me erect. I blinked, blinded by the bright lights, and threw up a protecting arm over my eyes. A hand knocked my arm down, pawed my clothes, relieved me of my gun. When my eyes managed to become focused, I found myself confronted by the muzzle of a huge automatic. It looked like the open end of a storm sewer.

The man behind the gun was a shriveled grizzled old geezer with tired grey eyes and an unruly shock of brush-like grey hair. He sat in the corner of a rubber-tired wheelchair, attired in loose striped woolen pajamas and he looked as though he might be dead but hadn't seen the papers. But he wasn't dead. In a dangerously quiet voice, he asked, "Who are you?"

Before I could reply, a girl's voice cried, "He's the one I was telling you about! Oh, Gordon, how did you—"

My eyes swung toward the voice. Millie Royce, her blonde hair hanging in a tangled mass about her shoulders, was sitting on the edge of a cot with the end of a bandage trailing from her fingers. The bulky figure of a man, stripped to the waist, was stretched on the cot. The bandage she had been applying was crimson with blood and covered the man's entire right shoulder. I couldn't see his face for—obviously in great pain—he had an arm across his eyes and was rolling his head from side to side.

While I was staring at her, another figure moved into my line of vision. He was short, big-shouldered, powerfully built. I recognized him as the driver of the Cadillac, the man who had carried the wounded man into the house.

"Millie—my lord!" someone said. It was several seconds before I realized that the voice was mine.

"So you're Banner." The old man nodded, then steadied the gun against the arm of his wheelchair. "You dropped in at a most opportune moment. We've been talking about you."

"He doesn't know anything, Carlo," Millie interposed quickly. "I told you he—"

"Shut up," He said the words softly but they had the snap of authority. "You tend to your job, Millie; let me tend to mine." He gestured toward a chair. "Sit down, Banner."

"I'll stand," I said.

The gun described a half-inch arc and the short guy's' foot sent me sprawling toward a chair. Anger flared within me, but there wasn't anything I could do. I sat.

"That's better, Banner. I like to be obeyed. When you're as old as I am, you'll understand that men of my age can't afford to indulge in useless argument about trivial details. Hereafter when I tell you to do something, do it. Things will be much simpler for both of us if you do."

"So you're Carlo Ventutti," I said.

"Yes," A slow smile flickered on his shriveled lips. "I see you have heard of me."

"I've heard that you're a gangster and a dope peddler."

"You've obviously been talking to the wrong people. I'm a businessman, Mr. Banner, simply a businessman."

"You're in a rotten business then."

"Most businesses are rotten. You should know that, Mr. Banner." His eyes sparked faintly. "I suppose you know that I have a right to shoot you for breaking into my home. Why did you come here?"

"I was in front of the Rienzi Hotel when the shooting occurred and I saw Miss Royce leave the hotel with some man. I followed them."

"You came alone, of course?"

"None of your damn business."

"On the contrary. It's very much my business." Without moving his eyes from me, he said, "Jimmy, go down and have a look. I won't need you for a few minutes." The short guy nodded and hurried out the door. "Now, Mr. Banner—" Ventutti moistened his lips a little, "suppose we dispense with the niceties. According to Miss Royce, you're interested in Lila Livingston. Why?"

"Because she was murdered," I said flatly.

"Is that the only reason?"

"It's reason enough, isn't it? The cops think I did it."

"Ah..." He nodded. "You're the owner of the car she was seen entering then. Most likely you're also the man who was seen going into her apartment." His face tightened. "Do you have the money, Mr. Banner?"

"No."

"But you know about it, I see."

"Ponzio gave me a song and dance about it. I'll tell you the same thing that I told him...I haven't got it."

"Perhaps Mr. Ponzio is more easily satisfied than I am. What happened to that money?"

"What business is it of yours? According to Ponzio, it belonged to him."

"Ponzio lied. It was mine. I'm the one who will lose if it isn't properly delivered."

"You mean you gave it to her to take to him and you'll have to dig up another $60,000 if Ponzio doesn't get it?"

His eyes blinked as though I'd fanned a piece of paper in front of him. "Sixty thousand? Who said anything about $60,000? The deal was for a hundred grand."

"Is that how much you gave her?"

"Certainly."

"When she got in my car, she was carrying a package which contained six packets of $100 bills. I was with her sister when the package was opened. The total amount was $60,000."

He squeezed his lips tightly shut and his free hand clenched over the arm of the wheelchair. "There was one hundred grand in that package," he stated. "Millie!"

"Yes. Carlo." She got up from the cot and came over.

"You delivered the package to her as I instructed?"

"Of course."

"Did you open it?"

"No. Why should I? I had no idea what was in it."

"Don't lie, Millie. You know I hate liars."

"I'm not lying." A brittle note crept into her voice. "I wouldn't be foolish enough to take only part of it if I intended to make a break, Carlo. I'd have taken the whole thing."

His eyes flickered between us. "Can you describe the package you saw, Mr. Banner?"

"Sure. It was wrapped with brown paper and tied with string and it was about this big." I indicated its approximate size with my hands.

He looked at Millie. "That right?"

"Yes. Carlo." She dipped her head in a quick nod. "That's what it looked like."

"And you went straight from here to her apartment and gave it to her?"

"I told you. Carlo, that—"

"Tell me again."

"I went straight from here to her apartment. She opened the door and I handed it to her. I didn't go in. I simply put it in her hands and told you you had sent it. As I said, I didn't know it contained money. No one mentioned that."

The man on the cot groaned and rolled from side to side. Millie glanced at him, then bit her lip and remained stiffly where she was. The door opened and the big-shouldered driver came in. Ventutti gestured with the gun. "Tie this man in his chair," he ordered. He pointed at me.

"Carlo—" Millie began.

"Shut up."

She bit her lip again and color fled from her face. I started to fling myself forward, but I was seconds too late. The short guy's fist caught my chin and slammed me back. A rope appeared in his hand and he spun it expertly over my wrists and fastened them to the wooden chair back.

"Legs, too?" he asked.

"No, that'll do." Ventutti jerked his head. "Now string her up. I want to find out if she's lying."

"Carlo!" Millie screamed. Her face went sick with horror. "Don't!"

"I told you to shut up." Without changing his tone, Ventutti added, "Better gag her, Jimmy."

"Right, boss," Grinning, he caught the girl's arm, jerked her off balance, slapped a hand over her mouth, flicked a handkerchief into her mouth and knotted another one over it. Then, still grinning, he dragged her across the room, got a long rope from a closet, and looped it about her wrists. He threaded the end of the rope into a pulley nailed high on the wall and pulled it tight. Stark terror was in the girl's eyes and frantic choking sounds came from her throat. He tightened the rope until her arms were high in the air, then he tied its end to a doorknob. "Okay, boss?" he asked.

"Yes. Suppose you begin by giving her a mild taste of what to expect."

Jimmy went to the closet and got out a lash made from an old fan belt. He swished it through the air experimentally. It whistled cruelly and my stomach cringed.

"She's telling the truth!" I exclaimed. "Can't you tell she's telling the truth?"

"Perhaps she is," Ventutti agreed coolly. "We'll know for certain in a moment." His eyes flickered. "Unless you want to participate, I suggest that you keep your mouth shut during this inquiry, Mr. Banner." He tapped the arm of his chair impatiently. "Go ahead, Jimmy. Get it over with."

"She ain't gonna feel much through that suit, boss."

"Remove it then."

The short guy dropped the lash on the floor and licking his lips, began to undress her. Tears rolled down her cheeks as he tore the jacket and blouse away and when he pushed his fingers into the front of her brassiere, she made a fierce animal-like sound in her throat and kicked desperately at his groin. Chuckling, he caught her leg, pulled her into the air and let her bang back against the wall. He yanked the brassiere away from her young firm breasts and threw it in the corner. Then he bent down and retrieved the lash.

Like a Sunday pitcher playing to a packed grandstand, he brought the lash back and sliced it effortlessly through the air. A long, thin red line appeared across her back. The gag bubbled with her scream and her body rippled with pain.

"Do you care to change your story?" Ventutti asked.

Her eyes pleaded tearfully with him and the gag bulged with the soundless words she tried to force through it.

Ventutti shrugged. "Proceed, Jimmy."

The lash rose and fell and the white flesh of her back began to look like a wall on which someone had scrawled a tick-tack-toe design with red lipstick. Ventutti watched emotionlessly. I had all I could do not to retch into my lap. Jimmy, his eyes filled with hot sadistic pleasure, began to perspire a little.

All our eyes were riveted on the slender swaying nearly naked figure and the angry red slashes left by the lash. The man on the cot was completely forgotten. Ventutti particularly, I think, was taken completely by surprise. I heard him suck in his breath sharply—and then the room roared with the blast of a large caliber gun. Ventutti seemed to rise a little in his chair, then he fell back and began to slide to the floor. The gun roared again. Jimmy, caught in mid-stroke, spun partway around and the lash fell from his fingers. His knees bent and he sank toward the floor like a devout worshipper preparing for a Hail Mary.

Twisting my head around, I saw that the guy who had been on the cot was weaving toward me, glaring about him with pain-crazed eyes. A large gun drooped in his hand. He looked at me, grinned weakly, and took a step toward Millie's swaying body. He dropped the gun suddenly and pressed both hands over the bloody bandage that covered his shoulder and chest. An expression of bewilderment settled on his face. Closing his eyes, he toppled forward and crashed to the floor.

CHAPTER SIXTEEN

THE ONLY SOUND in the room was the hysterical bubbling noise in Millie's throat. Forgetting that my hands were tied to the back of the chair, I lunged forward and fell to the floor with the chair banging on top of me. I twisted around, got to my feet, and dragged the chair along behind me. When I reached a wall, I spun violently around. The chair whirled through the air and crashed against the wall, filling the room with deafening sound. Pain shot through my arms. I got into position again, gritted my teeth, and repeated the maneuver. The chair splintered a little. On the fourth try, a rung loosened and clattered to the floor. With renewed hope, I banged the chair against the wall again and again until, with a wrench that almost tore my wrists off, it fell apart.

With a cry of triumph, I freed my hands and sprang to the doorknob where the rope that suspended Millie was tied. My wrists were bleeding and my fingers felt as though they'd been poking around a whirling buzz saw, but I got the knot loose and released her. She fell into a small limp trembling heap. Stepping over Jimmy, I picked her up gently, trying to avoid touching the welts on her back and cradled her against my chest while I carried her to the cot. When I pulled the gag away from her mouth, she licked at her dry lips and her eyes slid open. They were glazed with fear and pain.

"No, no!" she gasped. "Please, Carlo—not anymore!"

"It's all right, Millie," I said softly. "They won't do it anymore. Do you understand? It's all over."

"Don't hit me!" she moaned, not understanding and trying to avoid my arms. "Please! I'm telling the truth! I don't know—"

"Millie, *Millie!*" I said sharply. "Carlo is dead. So is Jimmy. They can't hit you anymore. Listen to me. Can't you hear?"

The words sank into her consciousness slowly. Understanding came into her eyes. "Thank God..." she whispered.

"Do you think you can sit up?"

I put my arms around her and held her up. Leaning her head on my shoulder, she sobbed quietly for several minutes. I sat there, holding her shaking body against me and staring around at the room. Death had slapped Ventutti in the chest. He lay on the floor beside the wheels of his chair, literally wet with blood. Jimmy had caught the second slug an inch or two above his stomach; and in exiting, the big slug had blasted a hole the size of a man's fist in his back. The floor around him was a slowly oozing pool of crimson, shaped somewhat like Australia. Their killer was stretched in the center of the room with his head propped against an outflung arm. He too had found sleep, the big and final sleep.

She moved against me and I felt her lungs expand as she took a deep breath. "I'm all right now," she said in a tight voice. "What happened?"

"Have a look."

She lifted her head. It took a second for it all to register. Then, "Ralph!" she moaned. She flung herself to the floor and crawled to where the bandaged guy lay. "Oh, Ralph!" She shook him gently as though trying to awaken him. "Say something, Ralph! You can't—"

I went to her and lifted her to her feet. "He's dead," I said. "You can't do anything for him now. Stop torturing yourself."

"Did he kill them?"

"Yes."

"He must have known," she whispered, more to herself than to me. "He did it for me. He heard them." She swallowed and straightened a little, shaking tears born her cheeks. "Thanks, Ralph. I won't forget."

"Here..." I got her brassiere from the corner, picked up her blouse. I handed them to her. "You'd better get dressed."

For the first time, she became conscious of her nakedness. Crimson flooded her face. Turning her back to me, she slipped her arms into the pink loops of the brassiere and fumbled with the catch. I heard her gasp with pain as she tried to reach behind her and taking the clasps from her fingers, I fitted them together.

"Thanks," she murmured gratefully. She put the blouse on and buttoned it. Turning, she looked into my eyes. "What are you going to do?" she asked. "What are you going to do with me?"

"It depends."

"On what?"

"On whether you killed Lila or not."

She was silent for a moment, but her eyes didn't waver. "I didn't kill her," she said. "I took the money to her. You heard me tell Carlo that. She was alive when I left. I didn't know she was dead until you told me." Her lips twisted wryly. "You don't believe me, do you?"

"Should I?"

Her eyes dropped and I knew she was looking at the bodies sprawled on the floor around us. "I don't suppose so," she said slowly. "You think I was one of them. It looks that way, I know, but I wasn't. I had to do things for Carlo. I had to do what he told me to do—because of Ralph." She lifted her chin and sought my eyes again. "You may as well know all of it: Ralph was my husband. He was in Joliet prison until this morning. Carlo got him paroled for me. That's why I came here tonight. They brought him to me, but Ralph didn't want to be seen in my hotel. He insisted on waiting downstairs in the car—and he got shot. Some of Ponzio's men shot him, I think, mistaking him for another of Ventutti's gang. He was unconscious when I got here. And now—" Her lips quivered.

"You couldn't help it," I told her, putting an arm about her. "Listen. You've got to get a grip on yourself. We've got to get out of here. Do you know if there's anyone else in the house?"

"I don't think there is."

"What happened to the guy who brought you here? You know...the one in the blue suit and grey hat."

"He left. He only stayed a minute. Carlo sent him some place."

I got her jacket and held it for her. Remembering my gun, I rolled Jimmy onto his back with my foot and patted his pockets until I felt the gun's outline. I freed it, dropped the gun into my pocket, and walked to the door. "Come on," I said nervously. "It's getting light outside. We don't want to be seen leaving here."

She tore her eyes away from Ralph's body and came toward me. Side by side, we groped our way down the stairs to the first floor. The pup met us on the landing and yapped at us all the way to the front door. I ignored it and so did she. I wonder if she even heard it.

Outside, the pale light of dawn was filtering between the houses and over the street. The air was cool and clear, the street was deserted, not a cop or milkman was in sight. I put a warning hand on her arm and led her down the steps to the street. Walking so close that our hips touched, we strolled casually to the corner, turned, started down a long narrow sleeping street.

"I may as well tell you everything," she said in a hopeless voice after we'd walked several blocks. "I don't expect you to believe me, but I'm going to tell you the truth, as far as I know it and then I'm going to go to the hotel and pack my things and go back to Wisconsin. I'm sick and ashamed of the kind of life I've been leading. I'm going to quit before I forget what he did for me and how he looked on the floor there and—" Her voice choked. She swallowed painfully and squeezed my arm. "I'm going to tell you the truth, Gordon, and let you do what you think best."

"Yes," I said. "Tell me the truth. There's been enough lying and dirty dealing."

"I may as well start at the beginning. I told you I was raised in Ripon. That's true. I lived there with my parents until two years ago. I was a secretary at the knitting factory there. Then I met Ralph one afternoon when I was having coffee in a lunchroom. He wore a diamond ring, nice clothes and had a big car—and he kept looking and smiling at me all the time I was drinking my coffee. When I got up to leave, he followed me out and—well, I'd never met anyone like him and I suppose his big-city ways fascinated me. Anyway, I made a date with him and a week later, I quit my job and came to Chicago. We got married. For three weeks I was the happiest girl in the world. Then the police came. They took Ralph away with them."

I held her arm tightly—and waited.

She took a deep breath. "It was a shock, of course. I thought it was a gag, a trick, something like that. I didn't know much about men and I knew even less about crooks and gangs and rackets and money-hungry cops. My friends were several hundred miles away. Besides, I was too proud to let them know that the police had arrested my husband and that I hadn't a cent in my purse. So, to make a long story short, I got a job as a waitress in a Northside restaurant and hired a lawyer to do what he could for Ralph. He couldn't do a thing. That's what he said anyway. A few months later, Ralph was sentenced to five years in Joliet."

"What had he done?" I asked.

"The charge was felonious assault. They said he tried to kill a man."

"He was working for Ventutti?"

"He wouldn't talk about it, but I'm sure he wasn't. All he'd tell me was that someone had handed him the dirty end of a rag and that he'd get even with them some day."

"Then where does Ventutti figure?"

"I'm getting to that. After they took Ralph to Joliet, I felt as though the whole world had blown up in my face. But I made up my mind to work hard and save money and get a better lawyer for him. It's hard for a girl to save money in a city like Chicago though. I worked long hours and made good tips, but there never seemed to be anything left. Several times I got discouraged and was on the verge of quitting and going home and never coming back, but I loved Ralph and I knew he loved me and I knew that I was the only one who could help him. I had to do something.

"And then one night I got what I thought was a big break. One of my customers asked me if I'd like to make a little extra money. You can guess what I said. The next day he came in with a little package and asked me to give it to a friend of his whom he said would call for it later. I didn't realize it at the time, but he was testing me. I followed his instructions and the next day he gave me $10. I did that for him several times after that and I guess I passed my test, because he came in one night when I was getting ready to go home and he said that his boss wanted to meet me."

"Ventutti?"

"Yes, but I didn't know that at the time. I'd learned a lot working as a waitress and I wasn't a dewy-eyed little girl from the country anymore, but, believe it or not, I didn't know who Ventutti was or how he operated. When I met him, I thought he was just a sick old man who had his fingers in a few political pies. He asked me a lot of questions and, of course, I told him about Ralph. He seemed very interested. Before I left, he asked me if I could sing. I told him I had a fair voice and had sung in some glee clubs and in a church choir, but that I hadn't had any formal training."

"You mean it was Ventutti's idea that you become a singer?"

"It sounds funny, but that's the truth. A couple of days later, he had me brought to him again and he told me that he wanted me to quit my job and do some special work for him. When I asked what it was, he said he wanted me to sing with a small combo that he was going to have booked into the Flask Club. I thought he was kidding, but he assured me that I didn't really have to be a singer and that, if I took the job and followed his orders, he'd get Ralph out of Joliet. As far as I was concerned, that clinched it. I was willing to do anything to help my husband get his freedom. According to Ventutti, he'd spoken to a friend of his who was a state senator and his friend would make a deal with the governor or with someone on the state parole board and Ralph would be released in a month or so."

"Did he mention this senator's name?"

"No. I didn't ask him either. I didn't care how he worked it as long as he did what he promised."

"I don't get it," I said. "Why spot you as a singer?"

"He said that for business reasons he was interested in the Flask Club and wanted someone he could trust to keep an eye on things for him. I know now that that was only part of what he wanted me to do, but at the time, I didn't stop to examine his motives very closely. I was convinced that he could get Ralph out of Joliet and that's all I cared about."

"But why a singer? You could have worked as a waitress or a dice girl or—"

"I know. That occurred to me later, after it was too late. You see, he'd phone me every evening and ask me to do a special number for him. That's what he really wanted. It took me a while to catch on, but I began to notice that at nine o'clock every evening there'd be a lot of the same people in the audience and they'd all be staring at me, waiting to hear what I was going to sing. The rest of the time they didn't pay any attention to me at all, but as soon as it got close to nine o'clock and I was about to sing the number Ventutti told me to, they'd be all ears."

"You mean it was a signal of some sort?"

"Something like that. Last night, for instance, he told me to do *Sweet Georgia Brown.* The night before, it was *Million Dollar Baby.* It has something to do with the dope racket. I think it tells them where they can buy the stuff."

"A code," I agreed, frowning, "but why at the Flask Club?"

"He knew Ponzio was trying to cut in on him, I think, and he got a kick out of using Ponzio's place as a rendezvous for his own men. He had a—a strange sense of humor."

"I'll say." I shook my head. "In other words, Millie, all you did was sing a special song for him every night at nine o'clock and he was to get your husband paroled. But how about the package you delivered to Lila Livingston?"

"You heard me tell him about that, Gordon. It's the only thing he ever asked me to do besides sing that song every evening. He called me at my hotel and asked me to come to his place for a talk. When I got there, he told me that Ralph was due to be released any day and that he'd appreciate it if I'd deliver a package to Lila's apartment for him. That's all he told me. I took a taxi there, gave it to her, and then went back to the hotel for a nap."

"How did Lila act when you handed her the package?"

"Well, she wasn't surprised, if that's what you mean. She opened the door and I said, 'Carlo told me to give this to you, Lila,' and she said, 'Oh, sure. Thanks.' That was all."

"Was she alone in her apartment?"

"No, someone was with her. I don't know who it was, of course, but I got the impression that she had company and didn't want to be interrupted."

"What time was that? Do you remember?"

"A few minutes after eleven, I'd say. Five or ten after."

We reached an intersection and I saw a taxi cruising toward us. I waved at it. I gave the driver a dollar and told him to take her to the Rienzi Hotel. Before the cab pulled away, I smiled encouragingly at her and said, "Send me a card from Wisconsin, Millie."

She nodded. I think she understood.

CHAPTER SEVENTEEN

IT WAS nearly six in the A.M. and in spite of gradually increasing traffic, there were very few vacant cabs available. I pushed my hands in my pockets and strode south. As I walked, a speck of an idea floated in my mind. It was so ridiculous that I brushed it away and tried to think about Ponzio and Ventutti and the $100,000 pay-off they had both mentioned. The speck kept floating back, however, tantalizing my mind and demanding attention. I took a good look at it finally and the more I looked the bigger it became. It ballooned bigger and bigger until it filled my entire mind.

I knew, suddenly, what must have happened.

A cab came crawling along. The driver gave me an oddly appraising look as he stopped and I began to realize that I must be quite a sight. My clothes were torn and dirty, my hands were raw and caked with dried blood, and my face was a mess. I grinned at him, hopped in and told him to take me to the Devonshire.

On the ride toward Ohio Street, I checked and rechecked everything I knew. The picture was there but too many of the pieces were missing. It seemed clear enough to me, but the problem was, would anybody else be able to see it my way? I had to have all the pieces, all the proof, otherwise I'd be no better off than I had been in the beginning.

The cab rattled to a stop in front of my hotel. I paid the driver and got out. There were no squad cars in the street, no cops around the entrance. The key to my room was in my pocket. I strolled through the door and slipped into an elevator. The operator, a young girl with a friendly smile, banged the doors shut and said, "Good morning—what floor, sir?"

I told her fourteen. She leaned on the control and the car shot upward.

I got off at fourteen, ducked down the fire stairs to twelve, and slid the key into the door of my room. It opened noiselessly and, without turning on the light, I stepped in and closed it. I stood still for a few minutes, letting my eyes adjust themselves to the pale shadows and peered about me. Everything seemed to be as I had left it. My suitcase stood beside the dresser, the bedspread was smooth and undisturbed, the soiled shirt I had draped over the back of a chair was still there. The police had undoubtedly searched my room, but they'd been careful to leave things the way they'd found them.

I stripped off my clothes and threw them into the wastebasket. Then, shutting myself into the windowless bathroom, I turned on the light and showered and shaved. As I slipped into a clean shirt, I looked longingly at the bed and wished I could flop on it and sleep for a couple of hours, but I knew that I was pushing my luck and that time was running out. I got my brown gabardine suit from the closet, put it on, knotted a tie around my collar. When I finished, I turned on the room lights for a moment and unlocked my suitcase. The extra $50 I'd tucked into a sock was still there. I stuffed the money into my wallet, turned out the lights, and opened the door. Feeling capable of facing the world a while longer, I walked up to fourteen, rang for the elevator and rode down.

As I stepped onto Ohio Street, a black squad car squealed to a stop in front of the hotel and two cops jumped out. They ran past me into the hotel. I turned and walked hastily away. Thank heavens I hadn't turned on the lights until I was almost ready to leave! They must have had someone keeping an eye on the windows of my room. The hue and cry would be in full swing from now on. Unless I wanted to lose the dice for keeps, I'd have to make every shake a winner.

Grand Avenue was a block south of the hotel. Clark Street was two blocks west. I walked to Grand, had wheat-cakes and coffee in a cafeteria near the corner, then walked slowly down Grand toward Clark. The street was beginning to rumble with early morning delivery trucks and CTA buses, but the sidewalk was deserted. I stood on the corner of Dearborn and Grand and smoked a cigarette, then continued leisurely toward Clark. When I reached Clark, I smoked another cigarette, turned around, began retracing my steps. I had smoked ten cigarettes and covered the two-block route five times before I spotted anyone with a dog. It was a dirty-white chow, unleashed and the man trailing along behind it was a gangly Negro boy in a faded wool shirt and pale blue jeans. The chow went sniffing toward a parking lot off Dearborn, did his business, then ran after its master, who walked slowly north. Within a few minutes, three other pups appeared with their owners, all headed for the parking lot.

It was nearly eight o'clock before anything resembling a Pomeranian or a Pekinese appeared. The pup was a brownish Pomeranian held on a long leash by a girl with thick loose dishwater-blonde hair. She wore a man's leather jacket, a brown wool skirt, red socks, and saddle shoes. The pup darted back and forth in front of her, eagerly sniffing at grass, rocks, and posts. When they reached the parking lot, she bent and released him from the leash and with a shrill yip-yip, the pup scampered off to find out what success his predecessors had had.

I crossed the street and strolled casually toward her.

She was a young kid, fairly pretty and not more than fourteen or fifteen. I stopped a few feet from her and poked a cigarette into my mouth. "Nice pup," I said, holding a match to the tip of the cigarette. "How old is it?"

Her mother hadn't warned her against talking to strange men. "Nearly a year," she replied. She pursed her lips and whistled to the pup, which had just liberally lubricated the wheel of a parked Buick. It cocked its head, gave her a look full of disdain, and went to investigate a nearby Pontiac.

"Pomeranian, isn't it?" I asked.

"Yes."

"Will it get much bigger?"

"I don't think so."

"Cute pup. I don't suppose you'd care to sell it?"

"It isn't mine. I just take it out once in awhile."

"I'd be willing to pay quite a bit for a pup like that. Who owns it?"

"One of our roomers."

"Do you think he'd be interested in selling it?"

She shrugged. "Maybe."

"Is he home now?"

"He's still sleeping."

"Well, I'd like to talk to him about the dog. What time does he usually get up?"

"I don't know." She whistled to the pup again and this time the dog came dashing toward us.

I bent down and rubbed its neck. "You sure are a cute little pup," I said. To the girl, I added, "I've always wanted to own a dog like this. Tell you what, if you'll take me to his owner so I can talk to him about buying it, I'll give you a couple of dollars for a box of candy."

"You don't need to give me anything. It ain't my dog."

"No, but I feel grateful—and giving you the money may bring me luck. Maybe he'll sell it to me."

I pressed a couple of dollar bills into her hand and with the pup capering ahead of us, we walked north to Ohio and then west toward Clark. In the middle of the block, she turned into a huge dilapidated old frame building. I followed her up a dark, narrow stairway to the second floor. Taking a key from her pocket, she unlocked a door. The pup darted into the gloomy interior. I followed her in.

It was a dirty cluttered room, full of grownup's clothes and kid's toys. The air was moist and dank with the stink of diapers and stale whiskey. In one corner of the room, a child's playpen had been erected and a chubby silken-haired baby was busily annihilating a copy of Life magazine.

"Wait here," the girl said. "I'll see if he's still sleeping." She went into another room, leaving me with the kid. It gave me a wide-eyed look, blew spit through its lips, grabbed a fistful of the magazine, and with a delighted coo, tore out a picture of Dagmar. It cooed again, grabbed another fistful, and removed a photo story on the Boulder project. I decided it was a boy, somewhere between twelve and fourteen months old.

The girl came back, looking as though she had been slapped and said, "He says he don't want to sell it."

"That's too bad. I'd be willing to pay quite a bit for a pup like that. Maybe if I talked to him—"

"You better not. He ain't feeling very good. Look, Mister, I gotta hurry up and go to school—"

"What's his name?"

"Tony. But—"

"Say, you don't mean Tony Greco, do you? Is that Tony's dog?"

"You know him?"

"Of course, I know Tony! Where is he anyway?"

"In back."

"I'll bet I can talk him into selling me that dog—" I walked past her into the next room. It was even more cluttered than the first, showing evidence of a wild booze and poker party that must have lasted most of the night. I stepped over a litter of chips and cigarette butts into a kitchen. Greco was in a small bedroom adjacent to the kitchen. When I entered, he was clutching a pillow as though it were a struggling lover and making small blowing noises with his lips.

He wore pretty pajamas. I clapped a hand over a big red rose and shook him. His eyes opened, blinked and he sat up. "Who the hell are you?" he demanded in a soprano voice.

"My name's Banner," I said. I eased myself onto the side of the bed and he cringed away from me as though I might be a carrier of mumps. "I thought you might like to know that Carlo Ventutti is dead."

"You're crazy!"

"Maybe I am. Who killed Lila, Tony?"

"Lila!" His face rippled colors like a child's kaleidoscope. "I didn't even know her! I—" He caught himself abruptly. "Get out of here! I'll call the police. I'll—"

"Go ahead, call them," I said. "They might be interested in your dealings with Ventutti and Ponzio."

The statement affected him like a pail of cold water. He hugged his arms around his gaily-flowered chest and shivered. "I don't know what you mean!" he quavered.

"Look," I said. "You're supposed to be one of Ventutti's boys. Last night you missed your regular rounds and threw in a substitute. I think I know why. I think you were afraid to show your face because you knew that Carlo was getting wise to your dealings with Ponzio or vice versa and it wasn't healthy for you to go out. What happened to the forty grand, Tony? Who got it...you or Sarah?"

He was shivering all over and his teeth sounded like miniature ivory castanets. "Sarah? S-sarah w-who?"

"Sarah Livingston. You know, Lila's sister. You've been meeting her at the Flask Club. Did you know that Carlo had a spotter there and that he knew you were seeing her a couple of times a week?"

"That's a l-lie! Carlo—"

"I'm telling you the truth, Tony. Millie Royce, the girl who sang with the combo, had a tie-in with Carlo. He knew you were meeting Sarah there and, of course, he knew you were using her and her sister as go-betweens for a deal with Ponzio. But someone killed Lila—and now Ventutti is dead. Where does that leave you?"

He looked as though he was going to faint.

"This may amuse you," I went on, watching the thin line of hair on his upper lip quiver with apprehension. "Yesterday evening Danny Horan paid a visit to Sarah's office. Sarah wasn't there at the time, but I was. Danny wanted the Livingston Agency to locate you for him. Silly, wasn't it? You and Danny knew each other pretty well, didn't you? After all, you were both peddling dope, both working for Ventutti. But Danny paid a retainer of $100, described you pretty accurately, and hired her to find you. What does that sound like to you?"

"I d-don't believe you! Danny wouldn't—"

"You're right, Tony. Ordinarily, Danny wouldn't do a silly thing like that. If he'd really wanted to find you, he'd have known where to look. Or he'd have had some of the boys go through the neighborhood asking questions. He certainly wouldn't have hired a female private eye to do the job for him. You know what I think?"

"W-what?"

"I think it was supposed to be a sort of warning. I think Carlo sent him to Sarah as a subtle hint that he knew that you and she were playing patsy. I think he knew who killed Lila—and I think he had a pretty good idea as to what happened to the $40,000 she took from the pay-off. Who got it, Tony? That's all I want to know. Who got the $40,000?"

A wild look came into his eyes. Turning suddenly, he snaked a hand beneath the pillow. I caught the glint of a revolver and swung a fist into his belly, then another at his face. He coughed a high note and collapsed with the gun dangling in his fingers. I caught it up, threw it into a corner, and reached for him. He had a small-boned body, as delicate as a girl's and he didn't weigh more than a hundred. I picked him up and shook him like a woman cleaning a dust mop.

"Who got it?" I asked. "Who got the $40,000?"

"I d-don't—"

I gave him the treatment until his face was as white as paper and his eyes were beginning to rattle in his head. Then I flung him against the wall and began searching the room. I went through his clothes, his dresser, his trunk, his closet. I examined the radio, the pictures on the wall, the bottoms of the dresser drawers, the insides of all his shoes. For a while, he lay limp and motionless as though unconscious, then he pulled himself into a trembling huddle in a corner of the bed and watched me with wide fearful eyes. I found nothing.

I picked up his gun and put it in my pocket. "Get off the bed," I said.

"Y-you w-won't find—"

"The hell I won't." I reached for him and with a weak shriek of terror, he scuttled off the bed and stood shivering beside it. I tore the sheets away and flung them onto the floor. The mattress was next. I rolled it back so I could see the springs beneath it. Then I pounded it with my fist in a search for concealed objects. There were none. The pillow remained. I picked it up, squeezed it between my hands—and felt the hard flat bulge. Grinning, I plunged my arm into the pillowcase and brought out a packet of money.

He screamed and flung himself on me.

I rammed an elbow into his gut, then turned and laid a solid right against his mouth. He fell back, spitting blood, while I examined the packet. The bills were crisp new unsullied by use in trade. The packet had originally held a hundred bills, each $100 in denomination, but it looked as though a few of the bills had been removed.

I was counting them when a crisp voice behind me said, "Don't move, Gordon. If you do, I'll shoot."

CHAPTER EIGHTEEN

I TURNED my head slowly. Sarah stood in the doorway with a small nickel-plated automatic in her hand. She looked as though she were almost ready to collapse, but there was a hard, determined glitter in her green eyes.

"Sarah!" I said. "For God's sake—so it was you all the time!"

"Not me," she said clearly. "You're the one. You killed her."

"Have you lost your mind? You know I didn't kill her! I didn't—"

"Keep quiet, Gordon," She motioned with the pistol. "I know you've got my gun. Throw it and the money on the bed."

I tossed the packet of money onto the mattress and started to reach into my coat pocket.

"No," she said, narrowing her eyes. "Don't try to reach for it like that. I don't want to have to kill you. Leave the gun in your pocket and take off your coat. Don't try any tricks. I'm a good shot."

I unbuttoned my coat and pulled it off. With a sigh, I dropped it onto the bed. Behind me, Tony was making happy sounds and getting to his feet.

"Oh, Sarah!" he said in a high nervous voice. "You came just in time! I can't tell you how scared I was! He came in and—"

"Shut up, Tony," she interrupted coldly. "If you weren't such a fool, this wouldn't have happened. I told you to get rid of the money and to act completely normal, but you wouldn't take my advice."

"But Sarah—!" he protested, looking as though he were getting ready to cry. "It wasn't my fault. Really, it wasn't! I had to keep the money. Where would I have put it? If I hadn't—"

"I told you to shut up!" She squeezed her lips tight and included him in the arc of the gun. "We're in enough trouble as it is. There isn't time for a lot of argument. Carlo's dead and we have to move fast before Ponzio finds out what has happened."

"The Livingston Agency!" I said bitterly. "What a laugh. I'll bet your father's spinning like a pinwheel."

"Leave my father out of this!" she snapped. Her red hair seemed to crackle like a hungry flame. "He was a good man but he died and left us without a cent. Thank heavens, he taught me to be a good tail. You didn't know it, but I was right behind you all night."

"So that's why you didn't answer your phone."

"Of course. I knew you'd go charging around like a horse in a burning stable and I had to make sure you didn't stumble over something that wasn't any of your business. Every time I let you get out of my sight you did some damn fool thing. Like mailing that package. You not only took it out of my apartment and mailed it to yourself like a soap opera sleuth, but you had to rush into the Flask Club and 'save' me by telling Ponzio what had happened and what you did with it! I could have killed you with my bare hands when you started babbling in front of him like an idiot!"

"It looked to me like he was getting ready to kill you!" I retorted. "You'd still be chewing on that gag and straining at those ropes if it hadn't been for me!"

"That's how little you know. He'd have had to let me go."

"Like hell," I said. "I don't know what you're trying to prove, Sarah, but Ponzio wasn't fooling. You were damned grateful when you walked out of there. It was a question of give him the dough—or else."

"That's the way it looked, Gordon. But I had an ace up my sleeve. I could have made a deal with him if I had wanted to, a deal which would have made him glad to forget a little thing like $60,000."

"Look who's talking," I said mockingly. "A little thing like $60,000! You didn't even have sixty thousand cents yesterday. Now you're talking as though you owned a piece of the U. S. Treasury."

"Maybe I do." Her red lips curved into a frigid smile. "At least I won't have to worry about insulting landlords and two-bit clients for a while. I'm going to wear good clothes and travel and have fun. You're the only thing in my way now, Gordon—and you're not much of a problem anymore. I'm going to see that you get the chair for killing Lila."

"Why me?" I asked. "You know I didn't kill her."

"You're in my way. I can't have you interfering in things any longer. With Ventutti dead, we'll be able to make millions."

I shook my head. "You don't make sense, Sarah. No jury will ever believe that I killed Lila. I'll tell them about you and Ponzio and Ventutti and Tony and how you've all been——"

I was interrupted by a loud chorus of barking from the rear of the house. It sounded like a pack of hounds closing in on a rabbit, with each dog proclaiming its right to the first bite. Sarah and Tony Greco stiffened.

"What's that?" Sarah asked sharply.

"The dogs," Tony said. "There must be someone in the alley."

"Go and see who it is!"

I saw my chance. Holding Sarah's eyes with mine, I flung an arm out, caught him around the waist, and pushed him toward her. The gun in her hand made a sharp cracking sound, like a lead pencil being broken by strong fingers and Tony's frightened yelp climbed toward high-C. I dove at her legs, knocking him ahead of me, as the gun cracked a second time. I felt a dull pain stab at my shoulder, but then my arms were around her kicking legs and she was twisting on the floor like a cat, trying to free an arm so she could aim the gun at my head. I swarmed onto her, caught her arm, yanked it behind her. She screamed furiously and clawed at my eyes with her other hand. Her nails cut down my cheek like the tines of a sharp fork, leaving parallel paths of bleeding pain. Then she sank her teeth into my shoulder. Cursing, I buried my head between her breasts, found soft flesh, clamped my teeth on it, and yanked harder on her arm. I heard the gun hit the floor and felt her go suddenly limp.

Then someone picked up the room and dropped it and everything went black.

An agile orange dancer was licking at my wrist. I moved my arm and stared dully at it. It was a tiny flame. It leaped and wriggled and rapidly became larger, spreading toward me like a living yellow liquid. A stench assaulted my nostrils and I became conscious of running feet above me. Voices were shouting hoarsely and the air was filled with a dry brittle crackling sound. The flame was licking at my arm again. Fire!

The word washed through my mind, dissolving some of the dullness. I rolled over and bumped into a soft object from which a low moaning sound was issuing. My hands pulled at it and the shape began to have meaning. A name rose in my throat.

"Sarah!"

Dense clouds of smoke were billowing around us and one wall was a solid mass of flames. The hot acrid air tore at my throat and lungs and choking, I got to my feet and lifted her in my arms. I found the door and stumbled into the kitchen, reeling under her weight and the suffocating fumes. Glass was breaking. The shouting above us was louder. The pounding feet were heavier and closer. Suddenly, like a spectre, a black shrouded figure appeared amid the flames. He saw me, shouted something, and plunged toward us.

I was gasping for breath. Somewhere beyond everything a siren was wailing plaintively. The fireman, flailing his arms to ward off flame and smoke, reached me and extended his arms to take Sarah.

"The baby!" I shouted. "Did you get the baby?"

"Where?"

"In front!"

Shielding his face with an arm, he turned and plunged back the way he had come. Holding Sarah tightly against my chest, I followed, driven by fear and desperation. Somewhere along the way I must have blacked out again, because all I remember is reeling against fire-speckled walls and falling forward foot by foot toward where I hoped safety and life was waiting. I kept thinking: *I've got to get out!* And we did.

A calm emotionless voice was saying, "Dynamite probably. A flash fire is the easiest thing in the world to start in an old building like that and they're damn near impossible to put out. They were lucky to get out alive. Another three or four minutes and—"

"Sarah—"

"Hey, he's coming out of it. Better call the doctor."

"Gordon! Can you hear me? Gordon?"

A girl's voice, an anxious voice, a voice I ought to remember. Before I could fit it to a chord in my memory, a strong cool hand clasped my wrist and a man's voice asked, "Are you conscious, Mr. Banner?"

I heard a tired voice say, "Yes. All right."

"How do you feel?"

"Hurt all over. Can't see."

"You were badly burned, Mr. Banner. The reason you can't see is because most of your face is bandaged. You'll be all right in a week or so, however. How does your left shoulder feel?"

"Sore."

"Yes. We found a shallow bullet wound there. If the bandages feel too tight, tell the nurse and she'll relax them a little. How are your legs and arms?"

"Can't feel them."

"Mmm. There should be some sensation in them. I'll have another look at them in a few minutes. You were very lucky, Mr. Banner. The worst you can look forward to is a little skin grafting later on."

"Sarah?"

"Miss Livingston is doing nicely and so is the baby."

"Tony?"

The voice hesitated. "He didn't get out. The police think he was dead before the bomb landed. There's a police officer here now, waiting to talk to you about it. Do you feel strong enough to talk to him for a few minutes?"

The girl's voice said, "The police can wait. Doctor, I was here first."

"All right, I'll tell Lieutenant Fielding that Mr. Banner is very weak and has to rest a little longer."

"Thank you. Doctor."

"Not at all, Miss Royce. I'm inclined to think that you might be good medicine for him."

He moved away and a small warm hand grasped my fingers. "Gordon, it's Millie. Remember me?"

"Sure, pretty girl. Bet your back is sore."

"That isn't all that's sore. I'm wearing a few bandages myself. I hope you'll forgive me, Gordon. I had to lie to you an awful lot, not because I didn't trust you but because there were other people involved and I didn't dare take any chances. I'm really from

Wisconsin, like I said, and part of what I told you about Ralph was true—but it wasn't all true. That sounds complicated—and I guess it is complicated—but, you see, Ralph wasn't my husband."

"No?"

"No. Ralph was an agent for the Federal Narcotics Bureau. I've been working with them, Gordon, trying to find out who was behind the dope ring in Chicago. I got a job in a place where we knew some of the peddlers used to meet, and I told them a story about Ralph being my husband and being in prison so they'd become interested in me. Ralph really did spend a few weeks in prison, so there'd be a record on file and so Ventutti's boys could check without jeopardizing me. It looked like a nice setup, but we weren't getting any place. We knew they were using dogs in some way, but we couldn't figure out how the dope reached the peddlers and where the dogs went when they ran away."

"Ran away?"

"Yes. The dogs were trained to run away as soon as the leash was released, taking the dope with them. We were never able to catch any of the peddlers with dope in their possession and not having a lot of manpower, we were stuck when it came to trying to trail the dogs. Now we know that Greco was their trainer. We found a garage full of dogs out in back of that building. It'll be a long time before any of them go around again with packages of heroin fastened to their collars. I'm going to see that you get credit for that, Gordon. If you hadn't led us to Tony Greco and if we hadn't happened to hear the dogs barking out in back, we might have let them get away."

"Heroin?" I asked dazedly. "That's what it was?"

"Yes. They've been smuggling it in from Europe and Cuba and cutting it with milk sugar. They've had dozens of peddlers working regular routes in the city and they've been making millions. At first they sold it cheap—at their own cost, nearly—but lately they've been charging the addicts outrageous prices. As much as $5 a capsule, I understand. It's the cruelest business in the world—and the most heartless. I was thinking of the misery they brought to thousands of addicts, Gordon, when I lied to you. If it hadn't been for them, I'd have told you the truth. But I couldn't take a chance, not with all their suffering in front of my mind."

"Who killed Lila?" I asked slowly.

"Tony Greco probably. We don't know for sure. We do know that Ventutti and Ponzio were involved in a pay-off and that part of it disappeared. We think Lila held out $40,000 and that Tony waylaid her in her apartment and killed her for it."

I stared into the darkness of the bandages over my eyes and tried to shake my head. "No," I said positively. "Not Tony."

CHAPTER NINETEEN

IT WAS Sarah then? You mean Sarah killed her own—?" There was a note of incredulity in Millie's voice.

For a moment, pain flooded me and I had to bite my lips to keep back the cry that rattled in my throat. When it subsided, I said, "The doctor said Fielding is waiting to talk to me. Who else is out there?"

"Frank Vance. He's my boss."

"Narcotics Bureau?"

"Yes. He's chief inspector in this district."

"Fine. How badly is Sarah hurt?"

"She has a lot of minor burns. Nothing serious, according to the doctor."

"Do you think they could bring her in here?"

"I think so. I'll ask, if you want me to."

"Do that, Millie. Tell Fielding and Vance that I'm ready to talk and that I'd like to have Sarah here."

"All right. I'll tell them." Something soft and warm touched my mouth fleetingly. I thought it was her lips—and suddenly I felt strong and good and whole.

A door opened and whispers rustled on the still air. The door closed and I was alone for a while. I took a deep breath and, blinking at the darkness that surrounded me, strove to organize my thoughts. The door opened again and footsteps approached the bed. Millie's hand slipped into mine.

"They're here," she said. "Lieutenant Fielding is at the foot of the bed. You know him, of course. Mr. Vance is at your right. He's short and fat and hasn't much hair." She squeezed my fingers. "And this is me again. A nurse has gone to get Sarah.

The doctor said it would be all right to bring her in, in a wheelchair."

"Sorry to find you like this, Banner," Fielding's voice said. "It's too bad we didn't catch you at the hotel this morning. You made a lot of trouble for yourself by ducking out."

"I'd have been in more trouble than this if you'd caught me," I said slowly. "You intended to arrest me, didn't you?"

I tried to visualize the scene. Fielding probably had his hands on the bed's rail and his lean face would be staring at my bandaged head, watching my lips. Sarah, when they brought her, would be pale and bandaged and swathed in a hospital gown. Vance was short, fat, bald. I was a stiff, still, gauze cocoon.

The door opened again and I heard the muted swish of rubber tires on tile flooring and the faint click of a nurse's heels. Then the heels retreated and the door closed with a hiss that seemed to proclaim finality.

"Sarah's here now," Millie said.

"Good. This is a different sort of ending than we planned, Sarah," I said. "But this is the way it has to be. Lila had all the beauty and fun, you told me once—and you had all the brains. You forgot to say that you were both greedy, that you both loved money, and that you were jealous of Lila because she seemed to live an easier life than you did. In a way, you were both true sisters under the skin because you were both unscrupulous when it came to getting what you wanted. Most of the time you and Lila wanted different things, except when it came to money. That's something you both wanted. And you were the brains, so you were the one who thought of a way for both of you to get your hands on a lot of it, once and for all."

"What are you getting at, Banner?" Fielding asked. "Are you accusing Miss Livingston of—"

"Let me say it in my way, Lieutenant," I interrupted. "Sarah knows what I'm getting at, I think. Don't you, Sarah?"

"No," I heard her say in a choked tired voice.

"All right," I said, "play it that way if you like. But it all has to come out. It wasn't Lila's fault that she was beautiful and that she attracted men. And it was pure chance I suppose that your father died and left you the agency. You started out to make a female private eye of yourself and you had tough sledding. Bills piled up. You got deeper and deeper in debt. And then, quite by accident I think, you discovered that Lila had had a baby, a child born on the wrong side of the sheets, whose birth had been kept secret from you and her friends. That may have shocked you at first, but then you saw a chance to ridicule and embarrass her and like a sure-enough detective on a real case, you started gathering all the facts. That's when you found the big gimmick; that's when you saw a chance to jump into the big time and get your hands on some really big money. But you needed Lila to help you because Lila was close to Pete Ponzio. By working through Tony Greco and Lila, you built yourself a pipeline to both Ponzio and Ventutti, the two who had most to say about distribution of dope in the city."

"You sound like an idiot—" Sarah began.

"Maybe I am an idiot," I said. "I certainly haven't exhibited much sense in the last couple of days; if I had, I wouldn't be where I am now. But that's beside the point. Ponzio and Ventutti, they were the big boys—and you knew that their problem was distribution. I don't pretend to know much about the rackets, but I do know that peddling dope with the okay of a crooked big-shot cop is a lot easier than peddling it under the eyes of an honest cop. I think you pointed out that fact to Ventutti and you made sure that Lila made the picture clear to Ponzio."

"Say, what's this about crooked cops?" Fielding growled.

"Let's hear him out," a quiet voice to my right said. It was the first time Vance had spoken. His voice had the ring of authority.

"The deal was this," I went on, tightening my fingers on Millie's. "Ponzio and Ventutti were to kick in with $100,000 apiece. In return, they were to be guaranteed a foolproof method of distribution. It sounded like a good deal to Ponzio and Ventutti, especially after they found out how the distributing would be handled and were given a chance to see it in operation. The price sounds like a lot of money to us, but to them it was peanuts, because all they had to do was jack up the price a little and it'd be squeezed out of the addicts in a hurry. Anyway, they liked the deal and they got the money together on the date agreed upon."

"My lord!" Sarah exclaimed in an aggrieved tone. "Is this what you brought me in here for, to listen to a crazy story he probably heard on a cheap TV show or—"

"There was nothing cheap about this show," I retorted. "It was put on to the tune of $200,000—and the only reason it blew up in your face is because you and Lila got piggish and decided to grab all the take instead of splitting it three ways, as you'd originally agreed to do!"

There was silence for a moment.

"Why don't you be smart, Sarah?" I asked softly. "Why don't you admit your part in the scheme? You'll never get any of the money now anyway. Tell them the whole story. Tell them who killed Lila—and why."

"Why should I?" she snapped. "You're the smart one. You're the one who knows it all. Why don't you tell them?"

"I will." I filled my lungs slowly, then said, "Fielding killed her. He's the crooked cop who agreed to—"

"Why, you—!" The bed trembled and an avalanche of pain flashed over me as hands clawed at my throat. I heard Millie scream and Vance shout something. Then the blackness inside my bandages became intense.

CHAPTER TWENTY

"WHAT in the world made you think of Fielding?" Millie asked an hour or so later. "It never occurred to Vance or me to suspect him!"

"I think I would have missed him, too," I admitted, "except for one small slip he made. Remember what I told you about being in Lila's apartment and persuading Sarah to let me call the police? Well, when I put in the call, I gave the police operator the address and told him someone had been murdered. I didn't mention Lila's name and I didn't tell him her apartment number. I intended to watch the street from the window and let them in when they came. But then Sarah discovered Lila's body was gone and we had to think up a story fast. At the time, I was too excited to notice, but later I remembered that Fielding came right upstairs to Lila's apartment without being told where to go."

"That's right. He knew the building and he knew that she had been killed!"

"Of course. Fielding had fallen for Lila like a lot of other guys, but he made the mistake of fathering a child for her. He's married and the scandal would have wrecked his career if she'd made a fuss about it. But she didn't. I think Lila was a good loser. Sarah had the bright idea of using the kid to put pressure on him—and he fell for it—but she made the mistake of thinking that she and Lila could grab all the money and still force him to do the distributing. But Fielding liked money as much as they did. He was waiting in her apartment when she went back to change her dress. He killed her and grabbed the bulk of the dough. The $60,000 in the package was Sarah's share and Lila was taking it to her. That's why Sarah turned up at Lila's apartment. She came to find out why Lila hadn't come to her office with the money."

"Gosh, yes," Millie said thoughtfully. "I should have thought of that! If Ventutti had been sending the money to Ponzio, he'd have told me to take it to Ponzio instead of to Lila. They both sent their money to her and she was going to make the split."

"It adds," I agreed. "I wish I could have seen Vance slug it out with Fielding. Did he get a confession?"

"He will. Vance is a pretty tough guy. He had Fielding's squad car taken apart and he found several hundred capsules of heroin under the seat and over $5,000 in brand new $100 bills in the dash compartment."

"It's too damn bad," I said. "If Lila hadn't gotten her hooks into him, he might have turned out to be a pretty good cop. What happened to Sarah?"

"She did a fainting act. Vance says she's sure to get a few years for conspiracy to violate the federal narcotics law."

"Tough."

"You keep worrying about Sarah and Fielding," Millie said. She sounded as though she were pouting. "What about us?"

"I'm afraid to think about it," I admitted. "If what the doctor says about these burns is true, I'm not going to be carrying samples of Tacoma flour around for quite awhile. I may have to go back to Fond du Lac and hibernate for five or six months."

"I'm going to drive to Ripon in a week or so. Want me to give you a lift?"

"Millie," I said fervently, "don't ever make any pick-ups! I made one yesterday—and look what happened to me."

"I'm not picking you up, Gordon," she said sweetly. "I'm picking you out. There's a difference, you know."

The soft warmth touched my mouth again and this time I knew what it was. I was being picked out. I decided I liked it.

THE END

PRICELESS ART, BEAUTIFUL DAMES...AND MURDER!

Tony Pearson was a pro-golfer wannabe. He couldn't cut it on the PGA tour. He couldn't even cut it as an assistant club pro at a local country club. Then Max Baird came into his life. Max Baird, a known gangster with a reputation for dope smuggling and prostitution. But Baird was trying to clean up his act, and when he hired Pearson to be his club pro at his lavish golf course, it was just another small step in trying to make his operation look "legitimate." But an unfaithful floozy of a wife, an unscrupulous business manager, and a fake Rembrandt all led Tony Pearson into a convoluted web of conspiracy and eventually...first degree murder, a crime for which Pearson had been neatly framed. Only a passionate ex-lover, an aging confidence man, and a sympathetic cop stood between Tony Pearson and the gas chamber in one of the hottest murder mysteries you'll ever read...

POLICE LINEUP:

TONY PEARSON
His life was full of failure. First as a pro-golfer, then as a lover. But the one thing he was good at was staying alive—but for how long?

FERN DAVIS
This dark-haired beauty was a talented artist and a helluva golfer. Her one weakness? Falling in love with the wrong guys.

MAX BAIRD
He wasn't afraid to get tough and nasty, perhaps even pump a bullet into somebody—and he had the reputation to prove it.

STEPHEN LOCKE
Handsome, intelligent, and incredibly vicious when he needed to be, this slick hustler was always one step ahead of the game.

VALERIE BAIRD
This sultry blonde got her hooks into an aging mobster loaded with cash; but there was one thing she loved more than money—sex.

JOE STILCH
Behind this badge was a no-nonsense policeman who sometimes had a weakness for pitiful suspects with tall stories.

CHAD LUPO
He was the muscle end of Max Baird's operation—incredibly loyal and not about to pull his punches.

MIDGE
His talents at picking locks helped save a couple of lives, even if he did get a bash in the head for it!

KILLER TAKE ALL!

By
JAMES O. CAUSEY

ARMCHAIR FICTION
PO Box 4369, Medford, Oregon 97504

*The original text of this edition was first
published by Graphic Books*

Armchair Edition, Copyright 2015 by Greg J. Luce
All Rights Reserved

*For more information about Armchair Books and products, visit our
website at...*

www.armchairfiction.com

Or email us at...

armchairfiction@yahoo.com

PART ONE
Stymied

CHAPTER ONE

THE first thing I noticed about the girl was her swing. She stood at the far end of the driving range, methodically drilling brassie shots into the raw April wind. She was tall, dark-haired, with good hips that pivoted beautifully into her downswing. You see far too few women who can belt a golf ball like that. There was a haunting familiarity about her, but she was not quite near enough for me to make out her features.

I started to amble over when a voice squealed from the clubhouse, "Yoo-hoo, Tony! Sorry I'm late."

I turned with a stiff smile. It was Mrs. Metzger. She is plump, blonde, and invariably late for her weekly golf lesson. She came panting up with her caddy-cart and I almost told her how she looked in those tight red slacks. But Shattuck, Briarview's head pro, had given me strict instructions about being nice to her. The lady's husband was a club wheel. Shattuck would have ordered me to sleep with her had she offered to underwrite his next pro-amateur tournament.

Mrs. Metzger is a teaching pro's typical nightmare. *Now watch, honey.* Every time you lift your head you see a bad shot. *Don't be a woodchopper.* And she kept saying I was just the handsomest man. And such a better teacher than that gruff old bear, Shattuck.

It went on like that for the next twenty minutes, with the Metzger asking me to show her an overlapping grip far too often. She liked me to touch her. She was getting to that kittenish stage they sometimes reach after the third lesson, when they ask you what you can teach them besides golf. I had the answer for that one, but Mrs. Metzger wasn't going to like it.

I kept stealing glances at the dark-haired girl down the range. She was all business. Crisp iron shots, a man's stance. Once she paused thoughtfully to light a cigarette and I got a clear look at her profile.

Recognition came with a searing jolt. Her name was Fern Davis.

Eight months ago, Fern and I had been engaged. Engaged, and terribly, head-over-heels in love.

Six months ago I had been on the tournament trail trying to earn honeymoon money, when Fern had married someone else. A stranger. I had found out about it when I'd come back from the winter tour, flat broke and jobless.

I stood staring numbly at Fern, and the Metzger squealed, "Look, Tony!" Her spoon shot had popped all of sixty yards in the air.

"Wonderful," I grunted. "You should break five hundred today."

"That's not funny." She dropped the honey child accent. "You're paid to teach me, not watch other people."

"Keep your head down and you won't notice those little things."

The Metzger didn't like it. She was paying five dollars a lesson for the exclusive attention of a golf pro, Tony Pearson. She was being cheated. She glared, then abruptly turned and flounced back toward the clubhouse. Shattuck would chew me about it but at the moment I didn't care.

Fern and I stared at each other across a gulf in time. She walked toward me with that remembered mannish stride, carrying her golf bag. When she spoke it was friendly, unashamed.

"Hello, Tony."

"How's married life?" I meant to sound casual, but it came out as a snarl.

Fern studied me somberly. "You've changed, Tony."

"You get old," I said. "And you get disillusioned. No explanations?"

"Would they matter?"

"No," I said. "I guess they wouldn't."

Six months of marriage hadn't hurt Fern's looks. Her soft mouth still hinted of vulnerability, those dark eyes still were as stormy as on the night she had given me back my ring. The wind came up and a few drops of rain spattered Fern's golf bag. I was trembling. I blurted something about only a fool playing in the rain.

"I like to play in the rain, remember?" Soft cool voice, a little husky. "It's a good chance to be alone, to think." She walked toward the starter house, a lonely figure in gray slacks carrying a heavy golf bag. I wondered why she wasn't playing with her husband. Maybe he didn't play.

To hell with her. Someday I'd be able to remember her without it being an open wound. I struck out for the pro shop, bracing myself for Shattuck's chewing.

Shattuck is a Briarview fixture. A great tawny man with sincere gray eyes, he is most especially sincere when selling a club member a new set of custom woods, eighty dollars a matched set. He frowned when I came in and motioned me back toward the deserted locker room.

"Tony, I'm worried about you." He made it sincere, paternal.

"Look, your Mrs. Metzger—"

"She's not important. What's important is that since you've come back from the circuit you've had a chip on each shoulder. It's not my fault you're a failure, Tony." I felt my mouth tighten but he continued. "Failure. Live with it, mister. Think it every time you look in the mirror. You're not Snead or Middlecoff. You're just a sour assistant pro who's been letting the shop go to hell. You think a club pro only teaches and plays in weekend pro-ams? He also sells clubs. He encourages new memberships. He's a personality kid and public relations man and assistant greens keeper. Understand?"

I said I understood.

"Then smile at the customers, Tony. Be glad you're working at Briarview. So you shot a sixty-four once and tied the course record." His voice softened. "So did I. Fifteen years ago. Thought it was the beginning of something. I hit the tournament trail like you did—and failed. Took me a long time to grow out of that phase, son. Just like you're going to do. Or I'll have to fire you, Tony."

He left me alone in the locker room.

The first reaction was fury. A blazing rage, shot with nausea. I started out into the pro shop to tell Shattuck he could shove this job sideways, and just before I reached the door caught a reflection of myself in the mirror and stopped dead.

A stranger glowered at me. A tanned bleak stranger with blond hair bleached to cotton by the sun. A brooding stranger who could drive a ball three hundred yards and three-putt from five feet. A failure, with tattered dreams of glory.

But I couldn't really blame Fern.

We had first met at a Briarview pro-am. She played a man's game of golf and her paintings had been displayed at the Laguna Art Festival. There was a wildness in her. Some of her friends were homosexual art critics. Some were smooth gangsters who had made their pile in Eastern rackets and retired to the expensive Laguna sunshine.

Fern was intense as a dark flame, insecure as quicksand. Her parents had separated when she was a child, leaving her to be raised by her uncle, a Laguna art ceramist. All things considered, he had done a good job. Fern and I clicked, right from the start. Those first three months we shared a crazy splendid kind of magic all our own. We fought, yet the fights only sweetened our reconciliations. Fern wanted a quick marriage. She wanted me to land a rich country club berth and settle down.

But I had visions of hitting that tournament trail and bringing home a million dollars to marry Fern in style. Fern insisted on following the sun with me. I told her it was no life for a woman, living on hot dogs and beans, sleeping in flea-trap motels. We argued. It became an issue all out of proportion. Our last session had been a furious one. *"I won't wait for you, Tony. It's now or not at all, darling."*

Stubborn female pride, I had thought. She would wait. But she didn't.

And Tony Pearson had broken his heart on the tournament trail.

That time at Pinehurst, remember? You qualified with a sixty-six. Then withdrew after a disastrous eighty-three on the second round.

Then Oakmont, a month later. It was the second day and you were right up there with Burke and Littler, tied for first place. You had to come in the money. It was your last chance. It takes dough to follow the circuit and you had exactly twelve dollars left in the world. Came the fourteenth, a wicked par five dogleg. You put the first drive out of bounds and the gallery murmured. You teed the second ball carefully and hooked deep into the rough. You gave the gallery a sick smile. Your nerves were shrieking piano wire, you wanted to vomit.

The rest of the round was a bad dream. Tony Pearson, another flash in the pan from Hickville. Cracked under pressure. Out of the money.

Those who can, do. Those who can't, teach.

Live with it, Pearson. Someday you'll be a big club pro like Shattuck. You'll own a percentage of the club bar and a piece of the pro shop. A distinguished graying citizen making fifteen thousand a year, beaming sincerely at well-heeled club members. And Fern will be just a painful memory.

My anger at Shattuck faded. I went out to the pro shop and helped unpack a new display of irons. Tomorrow I would interest some club member in trading in his old irons. Shattuck would like that.

At seven o'clock I dutifully swept out the shop and locked up. Outside it was dusk and the rain had died to a fine drizzle. I went over to the driving range and switched on the spotlights. For the next three hours I savagely belted out drives. It was no good; I still had that unpredictable hook that had ruined me at Oakmont. About ten o'clock the rain came down hard. I drove home to my Belmont Shore bachelor apartment and went to bed.

Next day was a humid Saturday. All morning I rang up greens fees at the pro shop and practiced being cheerful. I even sold one club member a new set of woods. In the afternoon I relieved the starter and it was four o'clock when I saw Fern. She came up to the first tee with that heavy golf bag slung over her shoulder. As always, she disdained a caddy-cart. Looking at her, I had trouble breathing.

She wore green shorts and white halter. Long, honey-tanned legs, and the halter tight over fine deep breasts. When she saw me at the starter window she paused. I got the impression of a startled uncertainty.

"Hi!" I tried to make it sound relaxed. "How'd you do yesterday?"

"Seventy-nine." There was a breathless catch in her voice as she gave me her greens ticket. I tore the ticket slowly and handed back the stub, hating myself for the way my hand shook.

"I've got a twosome at four-ten if you'd like to wait." My voice, tight, thick.

"No, thanks. I want to go around alone."

She walked nervously up to the first tee. She took three practice swings and made a point of not looking back at me. Her drive was straight and true, landing somewhere, beyond the two-hundred-yard marker.

There was no affectation in her. She really wanted to be out there in her own quiet green world. It reminded me of the times we used to quarrel, how she would invariably head for the golf links. Alone. I used to kid her about potential catatonia, hurt withdrawal from the world.

I was still thinking about her when I closed the starter shack at five and went into the clubhouse. Shattuck was in foul humor.

"You sold a set of woods to a guy named Peterson this morning?" His voice was too bland.

"Sure. Proud of me?"

"You overall owed him twenty dollars on his old woods, Tony. Why?"

He was actually angry. I mumbled something about reconditioning the old woods and Shattuck snapped, "We inventory trade-ins at two dollars a club. It's all they're worth. Will you please consult me next time you decide to give away club equipment?"

It stung. But I forced a smile and he grunted, "Stick around. I'll be back by seven."

It was five, it was five-thirty, and nobody came into the pro shop. I chain-smoked, trying to put Fern out of my mind. Trying to hate her, and failing. After a time I went back to the locker room and found Tommy. Tommy Blake is a tow-headed fourteen, very eager. He scoops practice balls off our driving range and runs odd errands and dreams of being a top pro.

"I got the locker room all swept out," Tommy said respectfully, "just like Mr. Shattuck said."

The locker linoleum sparkled.

"Good job, Tommy. I'm going out for a few holes. Watch the shop, will you?"

He nodded uncertainly. Shattuck would never let Tommy run the pro shop by himself. But what the hell, I thought; I'll be back before seven. I only wanted to talk to her, to get some kind of explanation. I didn't know what the hell I wanted.

I got my clubs and headed across the first fairway, walking fast. She would be on the seventh hole by now, a long par five.

The eighth tee was deserted. I stood panting. I had run the last hundred yards. Then came the lurching fear that she wouldn't show at all, that she'd played the back nine instead.

Then I saw her through the oaks surrounding the seventh green. When she saw me she got a white trapped look.

"Fern?" I made it cheerful, the most natural thing in the world that I should suddenly appear on the eighth tee. "Mind if we finish the front nine together?"

Fern minded. She came up to the tee, lips tightly compressed. "Why, Tony?"

"Don't you think I'm entitled to some sort of explanation?" I swallowed. "Hell, I didn't even get a Dear John. I had to hitchhike back to California, ragged and broke. Shad was decent enough to put me back on the Briarview payroll, but it was a week before I scraped up nerve to go around to your uncle's. That's when he told you you had just married some guy named Steve Locke."

"You think it was rebound, is that it?"

"I want to know if you love him," I said stubbornly.

She looked at me with a queer remoteness.

"I'll tell you what you don't want to hear, Tony." Fern spoke with carefully controlled effort. "With you it wasn't real. We fought too much over trifles. It was unstable, an adolescent love. With Stephen it was different—"

"He was there and I wasn't, huh?"

It was the wrong thing to say. She teed up her ball without another word. We drove off together and walked down the fairway.

Fern's second shot was a spoon. The ball faded into a trap just short of the green.

"Your right hand's riding a little high," I said inanely.

No answer. My hands were sweating as I came up to my ball. I took out a five iron. It was a poor shot. Sand sprayed from the same trap. Fern's smile was impersonal.

"Too much right hand," she said in a fruity voice. "Head down and follow through."

I laughed. We studied our trap lies. My ball was completely buried in the sand. I took out my wedge and exploded. The ball dropped two feet past the pin and rolled to the far apron.

Fern didn't congratulate me. She took out a seven iron, squinting man fashion into the sun. It had become a silent deadly duel, to win this hole.

Her chip shot was clean, but strong. We both needed twenty-footers for our par. I started to line up my putt and she said, "I'm away, if you don't mind."

"Go ahead." I held the pin.

She putted, playing the break high. At the last possible second the ball curved sharply downward, hesitated on the lip, and plopped in.

I studied my putt. It was slightly uphill. I putted too strongly and my ball rimmed the cup and slithered past. Just like at Pinehurst.

"You're one up," I said tightly.

"Look," she said in a choked voice, "it's no good, Tony. It was over eight months ago. Why don't you go to the clubhouse?"

"Sorry I bothered you, Mrs. Locke." I felt suddenly tired as I picked up my bag. "It sure as hell won't happen again."

I turned away and she said, "Damn you," in a fierce whisper.

That left just one thing to do. I dropped my bag and started for her. Her eyes got large and dark. Her lips kept saying "No," soundlessly as I grabbed her and then she came alive, fighting, twisting her head away, and all at once her long body spasmed against mine and she was clinging to me like a drowning woman. She was kissing me and crying.

It seemed a very long time before I let her go. Fern was wiping away tears, trying to smile. "I can't see you again. This is wrong.

The only reason it happened is that three days ago I found my husband doing the same thing with another woman. And I still love him, Tony."

It left absolutely nothing to say.

We walked off the eighth green in silence.

At the ninth tee, a stranger waited for us. A tall tanned man leaning on his caddy-cart.

When Fern saw him she made the smallest possible sound and I was suddenly no longer holding her hand. She said in a flat dull voice, "Hello, Stephen."

Stephen's smile was brilliant against his dusky tan. "You're a hard wife to find." His voice was deep and resonant. He turned a piercing blue gaze on me and I felt the impact of his personality like a sledge.

He had that indefinable charm possessed by certain movie stars, by titans of industry and top-flight salesmen. Drive. Personality plus. Every country club boasts at least one such. They are usually scratch players and throw money around like confetti and have their pick of the club wives. Invariably they own a Jag and belong to a prominent yacht club.

"Hello, Steve," I said numbly.

He nodded and didn't bother to shake hands. "Would you like to play into the clubhouse, darling?"

"You and Tony play." Fern was bleak, withdrawn. "I'll gallery."

Stephen gleamed at me and teed up his ball. There was a smooth thrust of power in his swing. The ball took off in a flat soaring arc. About two-eighty, straight and true.

I drove listlessly and walked down the fairway, looking straight ahead. Stephen was talking urgently to Fern. Something about taking three days to find her, but it had to be a golf course. How what happened had been a mistake, a stupid misunderstanding.

I came up to my ball and selected a brassie. The green looked more than two hundred yards away, but the late afternoon sun can play strange tricks with distance.

Stephen had out-driven me by a good fifteen yards. He was holding a two iron and smiling patronizingly at my brassie. It rankled. I slammed the brassie back into my bag and took out a two iron. It was a poor choice. My shot landed thirty yards short of the green.

Stephen was laughing as he substituted a spoon for his two iron. The old Hogan trick. I wanted to hit him.

His ball split the pin all the way. I saw it bound on the distant green and stop dead.

As we walked down the fairway I caught sight of Shattuck standing in the doorway of the pro shop. He would be unhappy about my leaving Tommy in charge, but at the moment I didn't care. I only wanted to finish this hole and get the hell away from Mr. and Mrs. Stephen Locke.

I came up to my ball and hit a solid wedge that held the pin. When we reached the green Stephen putted almost carelessly. A ten-footer that rolled straight into the cup for an eagle three. Fern's face was pale and set as I picked up my ball, conceding.

Stephen came forward smiling, blue eyes friendly. "Thanks for the game," he said pleasantly. "Incidentally, you forgot to wipe off her lipstick."

He hit me with a short right that traveled no more than ten inches.

It was the hardest punch I've ever received in my life. When the rockets stopped flaring in my brain I was sitting helplessly on the green.

I tried to get up. My arms and legs were paralyzed. A jealous husband with a Marciano punch. I finally got to my feet and stood swaying. My entire face was numb.

They were walking side by side across the roadway to the parking lot. Once Fern looked back. Stephen helped her into a red Thunderbird and they drove away.

When I went into the pro shop Shattuck fired me.

CHAPTER TWO

"I DON'T care whose fault it was." Shattuck's smile was paternal, but there was a hot angry light in his eyes. We were all alone in the pro shop. "You're no good to me, Tony. Look, why don't you hit the spring circuit and starve a while? Live on hamburgers and failure until you decide a club pro's life is the best there is. Then come back to Briarview. Two weeks' severance pay okay?"

I said it was fine.

Shattuck punched the cash register and counted it out. "Luck, Tony. I mean it, boy."

"Thanks." There was no point in shaking hands. I walked outside to my ancient Ford convertible.

Driving past the stone pillars that framed the driveway I took a long last look at Briarview. My jaw throbbed. Stephen knew how to throw a punch. I drove slowly toward Seal Beach and turned right on the coast highway. It was one of those warm California nights with the air full of salt freshness and the Pacific dreaming under a fat orange moon. A good night to be with your girl, making plans or making love. Somewhere else in the night Stephen and Fern were reconciling. I thought about them as I drove past Naples—the new flagstone-and-glass motels on the bay front—into the soft glitter of downtown Belmont Shore.

My apartment was three blocks from the beach, a converted rear duplex with double bed and hot plate in lieu of kitchen. Mrs. Finch charged me sixty a month with a straight face and took pains to remind me that come July she could rent it for ninety. I carefully stowed my golf clubs in the closet and opened the bureau drawer. There was a virgin fifth of Haig there but I decided not to touch it. I had to focus on the plight of Tony Pearson, unemployed.

On the nightstand was my pocket board of chessmen, arrayed in a titanic end game. I scowled at them, wondering how white could possibly mate in four. Someday I was going to look up the solution.

I sat on the studio couch and rationalized. The smart thing was to find a job immediately, some swing shift aircraft deal so I could use every waking second to perfect my game. Maybe in six months, a year, practice would pay off.

I got out my putter and some balls. For two hours I practiced putting on the threadbare rug. When I went to bed I dreamed about Fern.

Next morning I was shaving in my two-by-four bathroom when the sharp rap sounded on the door. Mrs. Finch? My rent wasn't due for two days.

"Come in," I called, and the door opened. It was Stephen.

For a moment I just stared, lather drying on my face. He stood tall and sleekly handsome, almost filling the doorway. He wore softly tailored beige slacks and a white linen sport shirt that must have set him back forty dollars.

"Shattuck said I might find you here." He said it humbly, as if it explained everything. "May I come in?"

I nodded mutely, wiping lather from my face. His gaze darted about the room, encompassing everything in one quick sweep, me, the shabby bureau, the chessmen on the nightstand.

"You play chess I see." A warm smile. We were chess pals. He peered at the board. "Alekhine and Marshall, isn't it? Baden-Baden, 1925? Queen to bishop's six and mate in four?"

"Yeah," I said sourly, studying the board and wondering why I hadn't thought of that rook move before. "All right, what do you want?"

"To apologize, Tony."

His smile would have made an angel weep. His blue eyes were a little ashamed. Somehow his richness made this room a little shabbier, more down at the heels. He was of the elite, the white-flannel yacht club boys, the Austin-Healy crowd. Rich tan and cultured baritone. Today he was slumming.

"So you've apologized," I growled. "So I kissed your wife, so you got me fired. Beat it."

A dreamy look came into his eyes. I tensed. He had me by twenty pounds, none of it fat, but I hoped he'd swing. Instead he chuckled and sat on the bed. His grin was rueful and charming as all hell.

"I don't blame you for being sore, Tony. Look, would you like to be head pro at Point Rafael?"

"Huh?"

"Starts at eight thousand a year, plus a pro shop rake-off. It's no charity; we really need a home pro." He grimaced. "Fact of the matter is, I'm in a spot. I promised my boss I'd produce a pro within twenty-four hours."

This was too wild. I sat weakly on the bed. Point Rafael was an exclusive new course not too far from Laguna. Veddy upper crust and loaded with money. It simply didn't make sense.

"Your boss?" I said.

"The owner, Max Baird." He said it like announcing Caesar. "I'm his business manager, attorney, and nursemaid. You've heard of Baird?"

"Something to do with tuna canneries, isn't he?" Then memory came and I blinked. "Didn't he get a big play in the papers two years back? F. H. A. contracting scandals, smuggling dope on his tuna boats? He's the Frank Costello of the coast, something like that?"

"The grand jury refused to indict him," Stephen said quietly. "Sure, he had greased a few officials to get loan priority, what contractor hasn't? But that dope angle was pure vomit. The tabloids smeared him because one of his friends was a high-rolling gambler who knows the Sunset Strip boys. Guilt by association."

His smile was etched with strain. It was terribly important that I believe him. But Max Baird was a name with blood on it, one of the twilight names like Frank Costello and Joe Adonis. And Fern was married to this man who worked for him.

I said, "Trying to sell me on Max Baird?"

"He's—eccentric. One of those self-made men that worships strength. Last week he fired the club pro, Loomis, because he was a short knocker. Couldn't drive a ball over two-fifty."

Tommy Loomis was a former PGA champ, and one of the finest golfers on the coast. I said slowly, "I don't get it. I'm just an assistant pro. What makes me so special?"

"You hit a long ball." Stephen was patient. "Baird likes that sort of thing. Besides, he's an avid duffer with a roundhouse hook and the disposition of an army mule. He just can't take instruction. Fern said—" He flushed. "She said you were a good teacher."

I almost grinned at him.

"You probably won't last over a month," Stephen said stiffly. "But I've got a hunch you just might work out. Well?"

It was the undertone of challenge in his voice, the arrogance. Cheap psychology—and it worked. I stood up, said, "I'll drive out to Point Rafael this afternoon. Okay?"

He looked delighted as we shook hands. He had the personality of a chameleon. One moment you got the impression of a brilliant sophistry, now it was all boyish awkwardness. "Mind filling me in on your background, Tony? Max might ask."

I didn't mind. I told him about Tony Pearson. High school and city college golf champ. How my parents were killed in an auto smashup while I was in Korea. My caddy days at Briarview, then the assistant pro job. The tournament trail and failure. I told him nothing about Fern. And, as I talked, I kept studying Stephen's elegant profile. This was the man who had taken Fern. He must have been violent and ruthless in courtship, like an attacking army. A brilliantly sincere errand-boy for a retired mobster. He had a chemotropic charm and could chill you with one sneak punch.

After he left I sat on the bed, smoking moodily, trying to plumb the fascination of Stephen Locke. Many days later I realized that evil has its own deadly *glamyr*. In the zoo, you may stare at the shimmering little piranha for a long time. At the oiled sleekness of a coral snake. Later I developed a theory. The stalking carnivore excretes an aura that dulls the perception of its prey. Carnivores may be two-legged. You may meet them at business luncheons, cocktail parties, anywhere, brilliantly adapted to their jungles of steel and stone—or their country clubs.

After a time I went into the bathroom and finished shaving. I kept telling myself it was some sort of mad joke. Then I tried to tell myself it was the money, a chance to save a few bucks before hitting the tournaments again.

But I kept thinking of a cool determined girl with hair stroked by midnight and a haunted look in her eyes. I had to see Fern again.

If Stephen had considered that angle, possibly he wouldn't have been so quick to offer me the job.

Only one thing bothered me. Maybe he *had* considered it.

CHAPTER THREE

THAT afternoon I drove out Highway 101, past Newport. It was a good clear day, with the wind creaming the Pacific off Laguna as I hit the long coast stretch into Point Rafael.

Small, even for a beach town, the place consists of a new pink motel, three filling stations, and two drive-ins. A rotting pier with a *Condemned* sign on it juts two hundred yards out into the surf.

And there is the Lee Shore Hotel.

By daylight the hotel is merely stunning. The swimming pools glisten aquamarine through a forest of palms. Three stories rise into flying buttresses of stone lace. By moonlight it is a palace of champagne witchery, a maharajah's dream. Two years before the scandal sheets had blasted it as a Babylon temple of sin, catering to jaded movie stars and degenerate millionaires, a place where anything could be bought in those plush suites for the right price. Anything.

I turned left at the inland cut-off and drove back through rolling green hills a half mile before I hit the winding road to the golf course. The clubhouse was a fieldstone miniature of the Lee Shore, surrounded by palms and tropicals. I parked the Ford between a black Eldorado and a Lincoln Continental, and walked into the pro shop.

A short wizened man was leaning over the glass showcase. He had the bright feral gaze of a lizard. "Are you a member, sir?"

"I'm looking for Steve Locke." Now he would turn on that aloof smirk reserved for visiting non-members. He would tell me he didn't know any Stephen Locke. And this would all turn out to be an elaborate nasty joke.

But he beamed as if I owned the place. "Yes, *sir!* You must be Mr. Pearson. I'm Chad Lupo. Care to look around?"

I said thanks and went outside past the frosted-glass starter house. The first hole was a rolling emerald dogleg, lined with live oaks and cottonwoods. A blue lake bisected the fairway, curving back toward the huge putting green by the clubhouse. I saw Fern, all alone on the green, concentrating on a putt.

I walked over and said, "Hi."

She missed the putt by a foot and stared as if I were a man in a dream. Again I got the impression of shock, of controlled fear.

"Relax." I made it a sneer. "I only attack wives on Thursdays."

"Why did you come here, Tony?"

"Your hubby offered me a job. Monarch of Point Rafael."

It rocked her.

"Beggars can't be choosers," I said. "This job might give me a stake, if it lasts long enough."

"You won't like Baird, Tony. He's—he's vicious. You'll be his third pro this year." She touched my hand with swift urgency. "Listen, how much more of a stake do you need?"

"A grand or so. Why?"

"I'll lend you a grand, Tony." Her gaze was intense, unflinching. "It's not charity. Call it an investment in your future. You can give me your personal note and pay me back out of your first big win. Fair enough?"

I looked at her. She flushed, but kept those dark eyes steady. I said savagely, "Husband offers a job; wife offers a thousand to turn it down." She tried to turn away and I grabbed her arms. "Why are you so afraid of Stephen? And why so damned anxious to get me away from here?"

"All right." Her voice was tired. "Forget it. It's just that Stephen has—whims. Sometimes they hurt people."

"Question," I said awkwardly. "Do you really love him?"

Nothing changed in Fern's voice, or her eyes. "Yes, I love him very much, Tony. See you around."

She walked like a queen toward the clubhouse. I wondered why she was lying.

The whole thing was too pat, too wonderful. Rich husband gets itinerant pro fired. Offers him dream job on a whim. It just didn't jell. Suddenly the lush expensive links, the sunlight glitter on the blue lake, seemed ominous, unreal as a Hollywood set. I started for the first tee, wondering where the gimmick was.

A dark heavy man occupied the tee, practicing drives. He looked keenly at me. "You're Pearson?"

Everybody knew me. It was all part of the act. "I'm Pearson," I said. "You must be Mr. Baird."

"Max to you." He had a bear's handclasp. His eyes were green ice under grizzled brows. "So you're Steve's latest find. He told me you were a good teacher."

Gruffness in his voice, bordering on challenge. He looked about fifty, thick and hard. His hair was silver wire over mahogany features. Greek, possibly Sicilian. My answer sounded flip.

"Depends on my material, Mr. Baird."

His grin was humorless. "Belt one, Pearson." He handed me the driver.

"Go on, belt one."

I hefted the club, fighting a slow red anger. He had more money than manners. In just one minute I was going to tell Mr. Baird where he could stick his driver and his job.

I teed up a ball and swung. It was one of the longest drives of my life. The ball hissed in a flat white trajectory, just above the lake, gradually soaring, finally dropping with a good overspin bounce on the fairway. Three-thirty, at least.

"Not bad," Baird grunted. "Now watch."

He took the driver and teed up another ball. He took his time addressing it. He had a baseball grip, a spraddle-legged stance. With that vicious swing, he looked oddly out of place at plush expensive Point Rafael. I had a vision of him on a tuna boat in the blue water past Clemente. A dark angry Greek with fish scales shining on his denims, roaring at his crew to grab those albacore jigs. Max Baird, formerly Max Bardos, who had clawed his way up from bait boy to become owner of three canneries and a fleet of tuna boats. Owner of the Lee Shore and Point Rafael country club. A ruthless amoral gangster with the wistfulness of a child.

He hit the ball cleanly and it hissed away in a white streak. A hundred yards out it hooked sharply into the lake.

"I hook," Baird said bleakly. "Irons and woods. You're going to fix it, understand? *Without* changing my swing. As of now, you're hired. Seven hundred a month and what you can steal from the pro shop. If you try to change my stance or grip like Loomis did, you're fired."

I almost told him to go to hell. What checked me was the gruff overtone of pleading in his voice. I caught a glimpse of naked vulnerability, the fierce dumbness of a man too proud to beg. It went far deeper than a golf swing. He needed something money couldn't buy.

"You're asking a miracle," I said.

"So I'm willing to pay for it. Can you deliver?"

"Try that swing again."

I watched him for five minutes. His feet were planted wrong; he had far too much right hand. If he could possibly slow down his wrist action he'd have an even chance of hitting a straight ball. But Max Baird wasn't a man who changed his style.

"Well, Pearson?"

Suddenly, I wanted this job. I wanted just once in my life to have my own pro shop. I wanted the chance to be near Fern, to tear her thoughtful mask away and find out what had happened between us. But I shook head and said, "Sorry, Mr. Baird. I can't help you unless you're willing to swing properly."

I left him on the tee, staring after me. Dark proud man built like a barrel, too stubborn to change his stance or grip.

But there was one way to cure his hook. An unorthodox way, a joker's way. I kept thinking about it as I walked under the palms toward the parking lot. Finally I shrugged and turned into the pro shop. Baird might fire me later, but later wasn't important.

Lupo gave me a bland smile. "Tough, isn't he?"

"Not so tough." I selected a driver at random from a display rack and went behind the counter. "Where's the screwdriver and lead?"

The little man found them and watched expressionlessly while I took the backing plate off the club head.

"Weighting it, huh?"

"Got a better idea to slow down his swing?"

He gnawed at his lip. It had never occurred to him.

I really weighted that club head. When it was finished I checked it on the scales. It came to E-9, which is about the same as putting a half-pound weight on the end of a tennis racket.

"Good luck, baby," said Lupo as I left the clubhouse.

Baird was still on the first tee. The eagerness in his voice belied the scowl. "Forget something, Pearson?"

"Try this on for size, Max." I handed him the weighted driver. He hefted it uncertainly.

"Feels clumsy. What's the idea?"

"Hit the ball with it. Just once."

He grunted and teed up a ball. His swing was exactly the same, an inside-out roundhouse. There was only one difference. The ball creamed far out over the lake, rising, hitting the fairway two hundred and forty yards away.

Baird said something softly in Greek. He stared at the driver, then teed another ball. The result was almost the same, except that this time the ball faded slightly to the right.

"You son of a bitch," he said with emotion.

"Am I hired, Mr. Baird?"

"Tony, you clever bastard, and don't forget it. Tell Max what you done."

The bastard business prickled, but I let it lie. I told him about the factors of swing versus club head speed and made it sound simple. "Pretty soon, Max, you'll start compensating for that weight and pushing the ball to the right. Then you'll fire me the way you did Loomis."

He chuckled and clapped my shoulder. His fingers were tool steel, digging in, hurting. I kept my grin in place.

"You're coming out to the house." It was an imperial command. "You can have the guest house next to Lupo. You'll be a resident pro. Tomorrow you hire a greens keeper and two assistants. Next week we throw a pro-am, get some of the La Jolla snobs out here. You're going to give me class, Tony."

He kept talking about it as we walked into the parking lot, all of his plans for Point Rafael. He waved happily at a twosome coming off the eighteenth tee and they came over.

Even for Point Rafael they were something special. The man was bronzed and handsome, a red-gold crew cut and vital smile. The woman was a pale exquisite madonna. Her hair was soft platinum and her features had the classic purity of a medallion. She kissed Max on the cheek. "I broke ninety, darling. George was gallant in defeat."

"No spot next time," said George warmly. "She beat me four and three. Does it rate a drink?"

"Champagne at my place." Max was expansive. "Meet my new pro, Tony Pearson. He just cured my hook. Tony, this is Val, my wife. George Fair's a Newport real estate thief."

It brought me a friendly nod from George and a long look of appraisal from Valerie. Val's eyes were gentian blue, and she had that trick of looking at you as if you were the only man in the world. George didn't offer to shake hands. As far as he was concerned Max had bought himself another new toy for seven hundred dollars a month.

"We'll take my wagon," Max said. "George, you and Val can follow us out in your heap. I got to orient my new pro."

Max's wagon turned out to be the Eldorado. I mumbled something about not wanting to leave my battered Ford and Max paid absolutely no attention. "You got brains," he said, slapping my knee with those iron fingers. "We'll get along fine. Within a month you'll have me shooting par golf, Tony."

He almost made you believe it. He was much man. I began to understand the drive and enthusiasm that made him a coast legend. We drove up the steep grade, past a flagstone ranch house, then a copper-and-glass modern, screened by live oaks and poplar. Once I glanced in the rear-view mirror. George and Val were a hundred yards behind us, and George was driving a black Porsche with the top down. He had one arm around Val's shoulders and she seemed to like it. Laughing, platinum hair streaming in the wind. Max kept on talking about the club and never once glanced into the mirror. Maybe he was part Eskimo, I thought.

The house turned out to be white Colonial set in a rolling green vista of elms, with a sprinkling of guesthouses between the pool and flagged tennis courts. From the shoulder of the house you could see down a long bluff path that sloped to a private cove and landing. Max pulled into the half-moon driveway behind two Jags and an Austin-Healy. "Val's friends." He sniffed at the little cars. "Newport yacht-club stinkers. She and Steve are hogs for class." His grin turned wistful. "Like I am. Did you know Steve started out as a bait boy?"

"Really?"

"Hell. He ran away from his hometown when he was fourteen. First time I saw him he was a snot-nose kid starving on the San Pedro wharfs. He had a kind of eagle look about him, even then. Sharp. Hungry. I gave him a job and he worked his can off for Max. Nights he read books. Law books, Shakespeare, the works. It gave me an idea. I owned my first cannery by then and was beginning to stick my fingers in other pies. I needed brains, the kind of shyster brains you can trust. Lupo was all I had, and he was only muscle. So on Steve's seventeenth birthday I sent him off to Stanford to be a lawyer. He cried. You know he graduated *cum laude?* Smartest investment I ever made in my life. Now Steve gets twenty grand a year to run things for me. He worries about taxes and the monthly take at the Lee Shore while all I worry about is curing a hook so Val will play golf with me."

I slowly revised my opinion of one Stephen Locke, playboy. Max glanced back toward the graveled hill road. Val and George were taking their time about getting here.

"I want you to move into one of the guest houses," Max said. "You might as well live here like Chad and Steve."

"Baird and family," I said slowly.

"Exactly." Max missed the irony. "Listen, Tony. Two years ago I'm a big name in the headlines. They make me out to be a wheel in the syndicate. They call me doper, pimp, mobster. It makes Max wonder what he's getting out of life. So Max retires and becomes a country gentleman. He buys himself a beautiful wife and country club. Real fine. Steve says I'm spread out too thin. He says the Shore is a white elephant that's costing me a grand a day. He begs me to sell—"

He broke off, glanced back at the white graveled roadway. No black Porsche. No Val and George. It was making me nervous. "Why don't you sell, Max?"

"I've got other assets," he said bitterly. "They get sold first. If I sell the Shore, Point Rafael becomes a different kind of town. I like it the way it is. Clean. Nice people. They respect me."

I was trying to figure out what selling the Shore had to do with Max's self-respect when the Porsche whipped onto the gravel in back of us. I heard Val's throaty laughter mingling with George's. She looked flushed and bright. Max got out of the Cad and walked into the house. I followed him.

I wanted to see what was happening in the Porsche, but I did not look back. Neither did Max.

CHAPTER FOUR

THE PARTY was going full blast. In one corner of the great vaulted living room at an ivory grand piano, sat Stephen, improvising. Next to him sat a willowy redhead singing a Cole

Porter parody in unexpurgated French. There was a portable bar by the terrace, and couples playing darts and arguing over score. Everybody had drinks. The men showed that careless assurance that comes of enough money and enough time to spend it. The women were leggy and tanned. Even in denim shorts they looked sleekly expensive. Fern was nowhere in the room.

Stephen stopped playing when we came in. The dart game came to a gradual halt. Max said with a soft restrained violence, "Thought I told you to stay at the airport."

"His plane's late." Stephen got up quickly and handed Max a telegram. "He'll land at the Los Angeles airport sometime tonight. I left a call for him on arrival."

Max relaxed. Some of the stillness went out of the room. He grinned at the guests. "Hi, everybody. Potluck on the terrace okay?"

It seemed to be fine. Everybody nodded politely and smiled. Then they went back to their dart game. Max might have been part of the fireplace for all the attention they paid him. That redhead was eyeing Stephen with a possessive speculation.

Val and George came in. Val squeezed Max's hand perfunctorily and hurried over to the dart players. One of the men murmured something and Val threw back her head and laughed. Max watched her with a dumb hurt look.

"Tell Chad to bring me a sandwich in the den," he told Stephen. "Call me when Ramos gets here."

He walked slowly past the french windows and up the lucite staircase. I felt puzzled and a little sorry for him.

"He's got a mile-wide inferiority complex," Stephen said softly. "He thinks Val's friends laugh at him behind his back. It's one of the reasons he wants so terribly to be a sharp golfer, to belong."

I couldn't resist the thrust. "Too bad nobody ever sent him through Stanford."

Stephen winced. Then he grinned. "He likes to throw it into me about owing him my existence. Which, of course, I do. How about some food?"

Dinner turned out to be smoked turkey buffet on the outside terrace, with a white-coated Filipino mixing gibsons, and George and Val very gay over the scotch foursome tourney they were planning for next month. I smiled with my mouth and made polite noises and sat on the stone parapet munching a drumstick, and I watched the willowy redhead.

Her name turned out to be Lorraine, and she had hot black eyes that focused entirely too much on Stephen, and not enough on Paul, her stocky unsmiling husband. I saw Stephen bring her a fourth gibson, and bend over her whispering something, and take entirely too long to tell her what he was undoubtedly telling her, and I noticed how Paul began talking loudly about his new cabin cruiser and the Acapulco cruise he and Lorraine planned for June. Lorraine ignored him completely.

These were the hollow people, the Metzgers and Shattucks of Point Rafael. Their world consisted of Sunday foursomes and Catalina regattas and casual infidelity at the weekend club dance while their mates were too potted to care. Val and George Fair were entirely too much of a twosome. But she laughed loudly at Paul's banalities and kept stabbing glances at Stephen and Lorraine. She looked actually jealous.

Fern appeared on the terrace, cool and distant in a green linen dress. Stephen got up solicitously and helped her to buffet. "How's the headache, darling?"

"Fine, Stephen." She made a point of not looking at me. Finally her eyes flicked mine and to me it was a glance alive, electric. But she had put up an intangible barrier that I intended to tear down before the evening was over.

Maybe Stephen sensed it. "How about chess, Tony? Spot you a rook."

He was calm, matter-of-fact, rather than patronizing. He was obviously a superior player. I wanted to hit him.

"Fine," I said, following Fern with my eyes as she went back through the french windows into the living room. Dusk was falling, with a damp evening breeze that promised rain. Johnny, the houseboy, brought us a stand and chessmen.

"You can have white," I said. "We'll play even."

Once, when I was seventeen, and the wizard Steiner was giving a simultaneous exhibition in Los Angeles, I held him to a draw. I was a competent player.

But I had never played anyone like Stephen Locke.

His gambit was a formless attack, without apparent purpose or shape, exploding into a brilliant middle-game.

It hinted of a mind incredibly complex and patient. He smashed me with almost contemptuous ease.

"Again?" Stephen asked.

We played again. From inside came the soft throb of Cuban drums and I saw that Val had turned on the hi-fi and was dancing very close with George. The dart couples were drinking too much and arguing. Fern was playing dominos with the wizened man I had met at the clubhouse.

"Chad Lupo," said Stephen, following my glance. "Lupo did big time in Folsom and came out a very fine domino player. He's Max's bodyguard, valet, and watchdog. He'd die for Max. He's hurt and puzzled that Max prefers the simple life to the rackets."

"So those headlines were right," I said. Stephen's smile was twisted.

"Past tense, Tony. Two years ago Max withdrew from certain— enterprises. He got a respectability obsession. He married a well-bred tramp named Valerie, but in his own eyes he's still a boorish Greek fisherman who embarrasses her friends. He kicked his hundred-dollar-a-night call girls out of the Lee Shore, and smashed the roulette tables. Now the Shore is costing him, but he won't give it up. It's a symbol, like the country club. He's selling the Rembrandt instead."

"The what?"

"He bought it right after the war, from a private collector. One of the big Nazi looters who needed quick cash for a trip to Argentina and the obscurity that a hundred grand could buy. Technically, the picture still belongs to the Dutch Government and Max is in illegal possession. It's a self-portrait in miniature, and priceless I've managed to contact a South American collector who has offered three hundred thousand for it. Very hush-hush deal. His representative flew in from Venezuela today to see if it's a genuine Rembrandt. Checkmate in three, I believe."

I studied the board. He had cracked my fianchetto like a walnut. My king was doomed. I shrugged and stood up.

"Let's go inside," Stephen said. "Smells like rain."

Inside, the sob of violins filled the living room and Val was dancing with her eyes closed. George looked smug as he held her. I looked around for Fern and felt a hollow ache when I saw she was no longer in the room. I wanted to ask her many questions, to kiss her violently until her composure was shattered in tears and reconciliation. But after all, I was of the hired help. I went over to the bar and had a double rye. It helped.

Johnny, the little Filipino, must have had supersonic eardrums. It was impossible to hear the front door chimes, but he did. He flitted past me to the hall, came back with a tall man, dark, with a pencil mustache and beautiful, liquid black eyes. Stephen said, "Mr. Ramos?"

"The same." A crisp bow. Ramos handed him a card.

"You are Mr. Baird?" He spoke flawless English, with only the faintest trace of accent. His face was thin, saturnine, wary. He had come to decide whether a piece of ancient canvas was worth three hundred thousand dollars.

"Baird's upstairs," Stephen said. "This way, please." He winked at me. "How would you like to see a real live Rembrandt, Tony?"

Damn him. I had to find Fern. But I shrugged and followed them upstairs. Once I glanced back.

George and Val were no longer in the room. The french windows were open and I could see them on the terrace, a merged shadow, moving with the music. Lupo sat toying with his dominos, staring at them with an unwinking basilisk fixity.

We turned right at the top of the stairs, and went down a hundred yards of jade pile broadloom to a small oak door. Stephen knocked twice. Then twice again. The door opened and Max stood dark and squat in blue denims. He shook hands with Ramos listlessly.

"Tony's never seen an old master," Stephen said lightly. "Is it all right?"

Max gave me a quick look and shrugged. "Why not?"

It was a strange room. The first impression was one of cheap surrealism. The tattered fishing net on the knotty pine wall was out of decor with the walnut hi-fi, the comfortable Morris chair. In the middle of the room was a curiously shabby poker table. The green baize was torn. A mounted blue fin stared glassily at us from beside the barred windows. Next to it was the metallic glint of brass, which on closer inspection turned out to be a knuckle-knife. I saw a dollar bill, framed.

And I saw the Rembrandt.

Indirect lighting from the ceiling bathed it in rich umber. It was Van Ryn himself, staring at us from a gold frame. The king of shadows had limned himself in a cynical mood. The eyes, heavy-lidded, half-humorous, half-bitter. The tired mouth, curved richly at the corners, with his secret smile at the world.

Max closed the door. Ramos crossed the room and stared intently at the portrait. "My den," Max told me somberly. "Over there is my first buck. That net I started with, thirty-five years ago. That blue fin cost my brother his life. I'll tell you about it sometime. The knuckle-knife I'll tell you nothing about. Sixteen years ago, playing stud with another Greek named Dandolos, I won sixty grand at this table. It gave me my start. Everything in this room has got a story."

The story of Max, I thought. Bait boy to owner of a Rembrandt. The American dream. Ramos said reverently, *"Senor* would it be permissible to remove canvas from its frame?"

Max nodded bleakly, and took the portrait down, placed it carefully on the table, and Ramos bent over it like an eager Doberman.

"Three hundred grand," Max said in a harsh voice. "I hope you know your paintings, mister."

Ramos straightened up to his full height. *"Senor* Baird," he said with dignity, "for three years I had the honor to represent the South American Academy of Art. After the war I was retained by the French Government as consultant to authenticate certain old masters that Goering had looted from Paris. I acknowledge one equal in my field, an Englishman named Joseph Revere."

Baird chuckled humorlessly. "Once I paid Revere five grand to tell me this was the real McCoy. If you're his equal, you're pretty good."

The Latin looked at him with a faint smile. "Six months ago, in Rio, I authenticated *The Madonna of Brugas,* by Michelangelo. A Brazilian collector was paying a half million for it. Since the war, I have had occasion to verify Renoir's *Two Sisters,* and Gauguin's *Night.* Both priceless. And presumed to have been lost during the war. Certain old masters are lost forever to the museums of the world. But collectors like yourself still gloat over them in private rooms—if they had the right price shortly after the war, and contacted the right individuals."

Ramos peered at the portrait. Slowly, and with infinite delicacy, he removed the frame backing plate. "A very valuable commodity, to be kept in one's den."

"It's a very special den," Stephen said quietly. "It's bugged like the First National Bank. Takes Max ten minutes to turn off the alarms before he can even go in."

"Right." Max grinned at Ramos. "Steve, here is another precaution. His bedroom's next door. Only Steve and I know the door combinations. Not even my wife knows. See those bars on the windows? They look flimsy, but touch them and you get a thousand volts. Try to bust down the door and—"

The scream came ripping up out of the night. A woman's shriek, full-throated, and iced with terror. It choked off in crescendo, and for one suspended fraction of time Max and Ramos and Stephen stared at me.

The scream belonged to Valerie Baird.

CHAPTER FIVE

STEPHEN was out of the door and halfway down the hall before anyone else moved. Baird came abruptly to life and pounded after him. Ramos and I bringing up the rear.

Halfway down the hall, Baird and Stephen stopped dead, staring over the balustrade at the frozen table below.

The dart players were huddled in a silent group by the bar. Valerie stood just inside the french windows, very pale. Only George Fair was missing. Chad Lupo stood at the foot of the staircase looking sorrowful.

"Little accident, Max," he said cheerfully. "I'm throwing darts and miss the target. George's cheek got a little scratched. Isn't that right, Val?"

Val nodded woodenly. Max stared down at her, at Lupo, and suddenly he looked tired and shrunken. Out on the terrace I caught a stir of white. Johnny, the houseboy. He was bending over a huddled figure that held its face in both hands: George. Evidently Lupo had a variety of functions in the Baird household.

We went back to the den in strained silence. Ramos put on an urbane smile but his fingers shook slightly as he took out a magnifying glass and pored over the portrait. He was obviously unused to this sort of thing. Stephen stared at me. We were both wondering what Lupo had done to George's face with that dart. I made a mental note never to make a pass at Valerie.

Ramos made a small sound and put away his magnifying glass. He said, enunciating deliberately, *"Senor,* your joke is in execrable taste. Where is the Rembrandt?"

Max seemed to hunch a trifle. "I don't get you, friend."

"The Rembrandt, *senor,"* Ramos said with a sour smile. "It is not likely you would expect a man to fly five thousand miles for the express purpose of telling you the obvious—that this canvas is not even a good imitation."

For the space of three seconds, nobody breathed.

Stephen said coldly, "That painting was authenticated by Joseph Revere six years ago. What are you trying to pull?"

"Please do not take my word for it," Ramos said wearily. "Ask any local art dealer. For this, you do not need an expert."

Max's eyes were terrible. "You telling me I paid a hundred grand for a fake?"

"I'm sorry. My principal will be disappointed—"

"Damn your principal to hell," Max said, and shivered. "That Dutchman, Neider. Smart Nazi bastard. A hundred grand sacrifice! I wonder how much he paid Revere."

"You can still sell the Lee Shore," Stephen said.

Almost casually, Max slapped him. "Get out," he said. "All of you. Out of here!"

We went downstairs in thick silence. Stephen told Ramos how sorry he was to have wasted his time. Ramos was frigidly polite.

"It happens more often than you might believe. Shortly after the war the market was deluged with old masters that had been ostensibly looted from Europe. Frankly, I would have been surprised had the portrait been genuine—although I did expect a better imitation."

Lupo was sitting alone at the portable bar. "The party's over," he said solemnly. "Val went to bed and Fern took a walk. Everybody else went home. Who's for dominos?"

Stephen ignored him. He was apologizing to Ramos for Max's bad manners as I walked through the french windows to the terrace.

There was a raw dampness in the air, and you could taste rain. I thought about Max, in his den, staring at a fake Rembrandt for which he had paid a hundred thousand dollars. And I thought about Fern as I walked down the flagged terrace steps.

She was out there in the windy darkness, restlessly avoiding me, yet knowing it was inevitable that I would ask her questions about the tension that filled the house of Max Baird. I found her by the swimming pool, near the guesthouse. She was sitting in a deck chair. Her cigarette defined a long red spiral that died with a hiss in the pool.

"You're late, Tony." Her profile was still, reflective. "I've been expecting you for an hour."

I found another deck chair and sat next to her. "I've been studying a fake Rembrandt."

"Fake?" Her sharp intake of breath.

She listened tautly as I told her about it. "Poor Max," she said, standing. "I've got to go inside, Tony."

"We have things to talk about," I said.

The night wind came up and we felt the first raindrops. Spring lightning flickered on the south horizon.

Fern took a long deep breath. "All right, Tony. We may as well get it over with. Let's take the Thunderbird."

We walked across the graveled drive and got into the little sports car. Rain spattered the windshield as Fern drove silently past the cottonwoods. She turned off the private road suddenly and cut the lights. I lighted cigarettes, making a ritual of it. She inhaled deeply and blew smoke at me in a long shuddering stream. When she spoke the words were stiff and badly rehearsed.

"I'm a fickle bitch, Tony. I only married Stephen to spite you. He had a good job, looks, money. You had nothing. That's what you wanted to hear. Wasn't it?"

"Thanks," I whispered. I was shaking with a dry chill anger.

I reached for her shoulders, turning her, my hands gripping her shoulders hard, and she did not cry out. She came easily into my arms and her mouth was slack against mine, her whole body yielding—and cold. She had prepared herself for this, and she was limp, uncaring. I could take her, now, and she would accept it in flaccid silence as punishment deserved. I let her go. "I'm supposed to hate you now," I said with a tearing bitterness, "and go away. Is that the idea?"

"Damn you," Fern said wearily. "All right. I met Stephen three days after you hit the tournament trail. I tried to fight him, Tony. Honestly, I tried. You've absolutely no conception of his strength. It's the way he plays chess or fights—or makes love. He's utterly invincible when he wants something." Her voice broke. She looked up, her face a pale lovely oval in the darkness. "I'm not sure, even now, what Stephen feels for me."

"What do you feel?"

"Attraction," she said softly. "And fear. He can still look at me across the room and turn me into water."

"Even when you found out Max dominated him like a puppet?"

"Steve kept telling me it was only temporary. How very soon we were going away—" She bit her lip.

"Big killing?" I wanted to hurt her. "Rome and Antibes and Paris? Was making love to Val part of his job, or did he throw that in for a bonus?"

It was a blind brutal stab, based on what she had told me at Briarview, but Fern's head went back as if I had slapped her. Her knuckles were white against the steering wheel.

"It was a week ago," she said tonelessly. "Steve thought I was playing golf. I decided to go shopping instead and came back to the house to change my clothes. I opened the door to our bedroom and—"

"I don't want to hear about it."

"It didn't make sense at the time," she mused. Val isn't Steve's type. But something happened tonight that makes sense. Horrible, frightful sense. I'm leaving Steve tomorrow. He doesn't know yet. But it doesn't mean I love you, Tony. I've got to have time to be free, to think clearly. It's a question of evaluating what Fern Davis is, where she's going. She's not going to make the same mistake twice. Maybe in six months or a year, I can look at you objectively. Not now. Can you understand?"

Lightning crackled in a white silent blow against the night. We sat motionless in the drumfire of rain, waiting for the snap of thunder. It reminded me of another night a year before, when Fern and I had driven down to Newport for charcoaled filets at Hugo's, and had drunk too much wine and kissed shamelessly at our table, very young and very much in love. And had driven home in the rain, very gay, until our tire had blown. Fern had insisted on helping me, and we both had laughed like fools, changing that tire in the rain. I sat hating Stephen. I thought about his apparently formless chess attack, but with a hidden meaning behind every pawn move. With Valerie it had not been just a casual roll in the hay. I said tiredly, "Explanation completed. Let's go back."

She started to turn on the ignition, then hesitated. "You only came down here because of me. Isn't that right, Tony? You're not going to stay?"

"Why not? Head pro at seven bills a month. It's what you wanted for me a year ago, isn't it?"

"Tony, you'll hate it!" A quiet desperation in her Voice; "It's like a prison."

"With bars of gold. We'll both have what we want, baby. You'll be alone and free and I'll have a cushy job and bored club wives to solace me for a lost love. Maybe I'll try Val. That is, if Stephen gives her a good recommendation."

Fern's breath was a dry sob. She moved in the darkness, and one hard little fist stung me high on the cheek. I tried to grab her wrists as she twisted behind the wheel, roweling me in the ribs with an elbow, panting with angry effort as I caught her in a bear hug. She was a feline fury, impossible to hold. Golf and tennis had given her good muscles and a man's coordination. She fought with elbows, fists and butting head.

I was wedged back in the corner of the seat, trying to keep her arms imprisoned, and I remember how the blue-white lightning glare showed me her face, all wet and contorted, and how I shouted at her to stop before she got hurt. Then my voice was lost in the thunder as her long body spasmed against mine and her hands came around hard to lock behind my neck and pull my face down to hers.

And it was a fierceness, a consuming violence of passion, with all the bittersweet hunger of lost months coupling us into an aching crescendo of need. Afterward she lay crying softly, her fingertips like moth wings on my cheek. I held her very close and murmured meaningless endearments as to a frightened child.

"I love you, Tony." Tired rusty voice, vulnerable softness of her, and the faint sweet pressure of fingertips.

"I love you, Fern."

"Sparkling conversation," she said gently, raising up and turning on the dash light. "Don't look at me for a minute, please, darling. I'm such a mess."

Her torn dress and tangled dark hair made her even more poignantly desirable. But I dutifully watched the rain and lit twin cigarettes while she repaired the ravages with lipstick and comb. Then she snuggled against me with a contented sigh and for a time we smoked in silence. The rain had stopped.

"You're leaving Stephen tomorrow." It sounded too masterful, but she replied in a still small voice, "Yes, Tony."

We made plans. A quick Reno divorce, then a justice marriage. We'd follow the tournament trail as man and wife. I wanted to wait until next year's spring circuit, but Fern murmured, "No, Tony. It's something that will always be between us, something we both have to get out of our system before we start keeping house."

She was right. Tomorrow we would tell Stephen. He was very civilized, he'd understand.

Yet as we drove back to Max's I felt a gnawing worm of doubt. Fern was holding something back. Something about Stephen. I would ask her, but not then. Later, I thought. Tomorrow.

A hundred yards from the house I got out of the car and kissed Fern good night. I was walking toward the front veranda when the front door opened and Stephen came out. He stood very tall in the doorway, looking at me.

"Thought you'd gotten lost, Tony." His smile was boyish, eager. "We've worked up a fishing spree at dawn. Ever catch albacore?"

I hesitated. "What about the course?"

"Lupo can watch the clubhouse until we get back. Max has a fast boat. We'd be at San Clemente by dawn, back for breakfast before noon. What say?"

"Sounds good," I said cautiously. At least it would give me a chance to talk to him about Fern. "Tough break for Max on that painting."

"Very tough. He can't stand being suckered. I'm going down to the boat now to check on the trolling gear. See you at five, sharp."

I watched him stride along the path toward the boat landing. He was whistling softly. I turned and went into the living room. Johnny, the houseboy, was emptying ashtrays and cleaning the portable bar. Lupo sat by the fireplace, absorbed in dominos and a half-empty decanter of his favorite bourbon. He looked oddly meditative. An hour ago he had maimed a man who had kissed his boss's wife.

His wizened face studied me briefly, then went back to the dominos. "Where you been?"

"Walking in the rain. Where do I sleep tonight?"

"Second house east of the pool. You make his bed up, Johnny?"

"Yes, sar," Johnny grinned. "Fresh linen, clean guesthouse, you bet. Just like home."

He wheeled the bar back toward the kitchen and I told Lupo good night. "Just one minute, Tony."

I looked at him. His face was a study in stone.

"You seen Steve this last hour?"

"Just passed him as I came in. Why?"

His gaze was sleepy, toad-like. Finally he shrugged. "It's your business, chum. Steve's been outside for the past hour. When he came back inside he was white. Said you were out in the car with his wife. He sat right there and inhaled a pint of scotch in fifteen minutes. Said he was going to kill you."

"You're kidding," I said slowly.

"I never kid," Lupo said. "Good night."

CHAPTER SIX

THE GUESTHOUSE was nice. Birch walls, a fireplace, maple provincial furniture. Nothing but the best for Max's serfs. I set the Capehart for four-thirty, and went to bed. Sleep came slowly.

Stephen wasn't the type to bare his cuckolded frenzy in public. It didn't quite make sense. Yet Lupo had no reason for lying. Come morning I'd tell Stephen, everything open and above board...

Five o'clock found me shivering on the boat landing below the house. It was that gray hour between night and dawn, and the cabin cruiser was a white bird poised in the morning swell. I clambered aboard, and was fumbling in the rack for a pole when Stephen came on board. He wore denims, yacht cap; and he looked white and drawn.

"Max has a hangover, Tony. The party's off. Unless you don't mind making it a twosome."

That suited me fine. I was on the point of telling him we'd catch damned few long fins in April when he brightened and said, "Look, we'll just go out of the cave. Snag a bonita apiece and come back for breakfast on the terrace. What say?"

I hesitated. His grin was rueful. "Frankly, I got potted last night. I said some pretty rough things about you and Fern. We've got to talk it out, Tony."

All this time he was fiddling with the ignition, and abruptly the engine kicked over, racketing the dawn stillness. I shrugged. At least it would give us a chance to get things out in the open. I hoped he wouldn't get nasty.

The cruiser moved leisurely out of the cove and headed east, toward Clemente. It was a calm morning, with the water greenly translucent in the dawn, and once I saw a seven-foot sand shark, cruising lean and lethal just below the surface, and two terrified flying fish that broke water and sailed for thirty yards above the whitecaps.

"Is there anything Max can do about the painting?" I asked.

"Nothing," Stephen said bleakly. "Six years ago I pleaded with him not to buy the damned thing. But owning a Rembrandt fitted his dream of class. Naturally he couldn't insure it without answering some embarrassing questions. Now he has to sell the Lee Shore."

"Doesn't he want to?"

"The only man that will give him a decent price is a smooth gangster from Beverly Hills named Castle. Castle's smart enough to realize the one way to make the Shore payoff is to import hundred-dollar call girls, private rooms with roulette tables, the works. Only Max doesn't want his fair Point Rafael soiled with bad gangsters. He wants to keep this part of his life shining and uncorrupt." Stephen reached into his jacket pocket and brought out a pint of bonded bourbon. "Open it, Tony? We could both stand some anti-freeze."

I took a deep slug. It was good whiskey. Stephen kept his eyes on the compass as he reached for the pint and downed almost half of it.

"Hey, you're driving, remember?"

He took another slug and grinned, showing even white teeth. "Breakfast, man. Say, why don't you set the jigs? We might pick up a few strays on our way out."

I went back to the stern and fumbled with the trolling gear. We were a half-mile out, and Point Rafael glittered like a great emerald in the dawn. Stephen began to sing *High Barbaree* in a rollicking baritone. His mood had certainly improved. I was feeling sorry for him when the engine died with a cough and he came out to the stern.

"Let's try the green feather this time," he said happily. Except for a faint flush around the cheekbones, the bourbon hadn't touched him. "Longfins are fickle as hell. Last time they wouldn't touch a spoon."

He helped me string the jigs, whistling. "Strange thing, Tony. Ten years ago I hated this. Poor little bait boy, hungry for the rich things of life. Now I'm a gentleman fisherman and love it. All because of Max."

"He treats you like a son."

Stephen's smile flickered and died. "Max is a lot like my old man, Tony. Tough and arrogant and stubborn. I grew up in a filthy little coal town in Pennsylvania. I'm half Croat and half Hunky, and you couldn't pronounce my real name. My old man and my brothers worked in the mines. They hated me. So did my mother. The blue-eyed little brother in a family of black Croats. Living proof of my mother's infidelity. My old man used to get drunk on payday night and come home and kick the hell out of me. Sometimes he'd kick the hell out of my mother. I used to hide under the bed with my hands over my ears, crying, while my mother got it. Then he'd come after me. He'd laugh as he dragged me out from under the bed. I remember he had big hands, a miner's hands."

He stared at me blindly. This was the real Stephen behind the brilliant mask. A terrified child, reared on pain and hate.

"In between paydays it wasn't so bad. I had school. The other kids hated my guts, but teacher loved me. Mrs. Larkin said I was a 'prodigy'. She talked to the school superintendent about giving me special instruction after hours, so that I could skip two grades. I had it all figured. I was going to leave home in two years and work my way through Penn State and become a lawyer."

His face was mottled now, and he breathed heavily as he stared at the whitecaps. But he spoke with a painful intensity.

"Just two more months and I was going to skip the ninth grade. I was so proud that day I took my report card home to the old man. All A's. And a nice letter from Mrs. Larkin saying I could skip the ninth grade if I went to summer school. I had forgotten it was payday night. My old man came home drunk and ugly. I showed him the report card and the letter. He laughed. He tore the letter up. He told me next week I was starting in the mines. Said it was time I started paying him back for my keep. I started to cry. He slapped me. He backed me against the draining board and kept slapping me with those gnarled hands. We were in the kitchen. He kept laughing and telling me I had too much education already. I kept trying to scream at him and tell him how

I had to go to Penn State. He kept laughing. There was a bread knife on the drain board. I grabbed it and stuck it in his belly. I twisted it. He looked surprised. Then he thrashed like a chicken. Blood all over the linoleum. Nobody else was home. There was sixty dollars in his pocket. I hopped a fast rattler to Pittsburgh that night. I was out on the road a year before I hit California… Panhandling, shining shoes, living as a dirty bait boy.

"Then I met Max. One look at him and I knew he was soft inside. Soft, because he'd always wanted a son."

I stared at him, my throat dry. Stephen's blue eyes were ineffable, his smile nailed on.

"Did you know I can read people, Tony? I can look at them and extrapolate behavior curves, like a sibyl. It's a gift, like wiggling your ears, or second sight. Five minutes after I met Max I knew he was ultimately going to put me through college. Ten minutes after I met you I knew you were going to make love to Fern. And eventually wind up in the gas chamber at San Quentin. For murdering me."

His fist was a white blur in the sunlight. I tried to dodge, and a sledgehammer hit me behind the ear. I went down hard and slammed into the railing. Stephen stood over me, hands hanging at his sides. His smile was the essence of mockery. The blue of his eyes was hot and intense. "Get up, lover. It's mate in two."

I came up fast, throwing punches blindly, conscious only of wanting to blot out that sneering handsome face. It was like fighting a ghost. He moved like a ballet dancer around the live bait tank, shooting long straight ones that hurt, that pulped my lips and closed one of my eyes, that made raw meat out of the thing that had once been my face.

He could have put me away easily. He didn't try. I missed a roundhouse hook and spun off balance, across the railing. As I careened wildly, trying to find the deck with my feet, Stephen moved in, his eyes sparkling, and hit me with three short lefts that turned the Pacific into a floating redness as the sun pin-wheeled crazily and I fell sideways to the deck.

I got up, lurching against the cabin hatch. My fingers closed around something hard. A tuna gaff. As Stephen came in I set myself and swung. I missed.

"That makes it even," Stephen said dreamily. He was very calm, a surgeon operating on a favorite patient. "Try again, lover."

He was crouched, his grin anticipant as I stumbled toward him with the gaff. Then somehow the gaff was ripped from my fingers and clattered on the deck. Stephen feinted me into throwing a futile right. Too late I saw his shoulder hunch. Something clicked. The sun gushed crimson. I was on my knees, shaking my head, watching the blood drip down to make small red spots on the deck. Stephen was laughing.

"There has to be enough blood for both of us," he said. "You understand?"

Somehow, I got to my feet. My hands weighed fifty pounds. I could not get my guard up. Stephen surveyed me clinically as I reeled toward him. Just one punch. I had to hit him once before I passed out. Only he wouldn't stand still. He kept hazing into two people, two grinning Stephens. Now he was frowning. He moved in and said, "Plead manslaughter. You might get off with ten years."

A bomb exploded in my solar plexus. I was down by the side of the bait tank, huddled into a retching ball of pain. Something struck the deck next to my face—Stephen's yacht cap. All during the fight it had stayed on his head. Stephen stood poised on the railing looking down at me.

"Don't forget," he called. "Manslaughter, Tony. So long."

He dived gracefully off the stern. There was a splash. The sunlight was blinding. Then the sun went out.

The sun was high on the horizon when I came to. The cruiser was drifting free in the offshore swell. I grabbed dizzily for the stern railing and clung there until the sky and sea stopped revolving and my eyes focused.

The ocean crawled like warm green oil and there was no sign of Stephen anywhere. I stumbled past the bait tank to the wheel, and fumbled with the ignition. The engine sputtered, caught with a roar.

I brought the cruiser into the cove almost an hour later. Fern stood on the landing, waiting.

Her face was pale but there was no sign of surprise as she stared at my battered face, at the blood on the deck. It was more of a bitter resignation.

"What happened, Tony?"

I told her painfully about it. "He's crazy," I mumbled through puffed lips. It was all I could do to stand erect. "It's his way of getting even for last night. Where is he?"

"Tony, listen." Her voice was low, quick, urgent. Her grip on my shoulders was surprisingly strong. "Listen carefully, darling. Take the diagonal path up to the driveway. I'll be waiting—"

"Here comes Lupo," I said.

Her whole body went rigid. Without a word she turned and started up the diagonal path to the guesthouses. Lupo came down the main steps to the landing. He looked at me, his olive face unreadable. "Where's Steve?"

"That's what I want to know. He clobbered me, then swam ashore. Seen him?"

Lupo looked sardonically at the blood on the deck, at me. "No, I haven't seen him. You stuff him in the bait tank?"

I told him about it. He nodded calmly. Come on," he said. "Let's tell Max."

We went up the steps to the main house. Twice I stumbled and almost fell.

Max was sitting by the fireplace, talking with two men I had never seen before. One of them was a pale man with white creamy hair and mustache. The other was short, balding, nervous.

"You're sure," Max said. "No possible mistake?"

The bald man's accent was crisp clear British. "No mistake. I don't even need to fluoroscope the paint samples. It's a wretched copy, not over twenty years old." He straightened erect, frowning. "Frankly, Baird, you puzzle me. Had the Rembrandt been genuine, I would have had no choice but to report it to our West Coast office. You realize that?"

Max nodded wearily. "I had to know. Thanks, Favian. I'll send you a check."

"Fine," Favian nodded. He glanced curiously at my face as he went out. Max sat staring into the fireplace.

"Beat it, Castle," he said without looking up. "We've got no business. I'll close the Shore down before I let you get your tentacles into it."

"You can't afford to," the white-haired man said in a voice of soft music. "It's draining you, Maxie. Hang on to it and you go under. You want to be a country baron, you got to pay. And Castle's got the price."

Max cursed him listlessly. "I suppose it's just coincidence that you stopped by this morning?"

"I get hunches," Castle murmured. "It won't be so bad, Maxie. I'll keep the Shore respectable." He laughed without sound. "Think about it. Think about losing a grand a day until you finally lose your little country club. You always were a percentage player." He stood up and saw us. His pale features were finely cut. His eyes were passionless, the color of half-frozen water. "Hello, Lupo," he said.

Max didn't even glance at the man as he went out. Max was staring at me, and his face was all animal, querulous with suspicion.

"Where's Stephen?"

I told him about it. It didn't seem to register. He stared at Lupo, who said quickly, "Blood all over the boat. No scales. No fish. Somebody used a gaff." Lupo had sharp eyes. "Incidentally," he added as an afterthought, "Steve gets loaded last night. It seems Fern and Tony are having a ball out in the rain. Steve talked bad action before he went to bed."

Max sat very still, gathering himself. When he spoke, the words seemed squeezed out of him by a relentless external pressure.

"Early this morning I put through a transatlantic phone call. To a limey named Revere, an art critic who six years ago told me that my Rembrandt was genuine. Revere died six months ago. Cancer. But his partner tells me this Revere had integrity. That he was the greatest when it came to old masters. That if Revere said it was a Rembrandt, that's what it was. And that bald guy who just left," Max breathed. "He's an art expert from Lloyd's. Very reputable. He came out to the coast to appraise some movie colony art collections for insurance. He just verified the painting as pure phony."

Max got to his feet in one fluid motion.

"You come out of nowhere," he said with deadly softness. "Recommended by Steve. By coincidence that same night I discover my Rembrandt is a fake. I remember how we all get excited when Val screams. How maybe you're the last one to leave the den."

He was adding it up, and it made sense. Fatal sense, like Stephen's queen gambit.

"Know what I think?" Max said. "I think you pulled a gypsy switch last night. I think Steve suspected you, that you had a fight about it this morning on the boat. I think you killed him. I think you know right now where the real Rembrandt is. Tell it over again, mister. Tell it different."

"Hell! You heard the story. Stephen planned…"

Lupo chopped a judo punch into my spine. A thoughtful punch. I tried to get up. Lupo kicked me carefully in the kidneys.

Max looked down at me. His dark face was patient, almost kind.

"Let me tell you something about Lupo. Sometimes he is very useful."

Lupo bent over me.

"We've got lots of time," Max said.

CHAPTER SEVEN

WATER thundered over me in an icy cascade. I gasped, tried to rise. "Easy," Max said, setting down the water carafe. "We'll try it again, Pearson."

"He's pretty good," Lupo said. "Three times he tells it the same way. He must have rehearsed."

Max stood biting his lip, not liking it. His stoic face was heavy with indecision. "So make it four times," he said. "Start over again, Tony. From where Steve first offered you the job."

At first I had cursed them and tried to fight. But Lupo had convinced me of the futility of that. He had convinced me with his clever sadistic hands and his knowledge of nerve centers. One of my wild kicks had found his face, bringing blood. Yet he exhibited no anger. I was merely a job to be done, a pleasant job. And Lupo was a craftsman.

I told it again, omitting only the part about Val's infidelity. There was no point in shielding Val, but I had no wish to involve Fern. Once my voice faltered. Lupo prompted me. I passed out again.

When I came to, there were voices in the room. A harsh deep voice that counterpointed Max's rumble of protest.

"You can take him in later, Stilch. In a minute he'll confess—"

"I'll take him in now, Mr. Baird."

"Like hell," Max said. "I happen to be a personal friend of Jed Wells, the county sheriff. Call him. He'll tell you—"

"Jed's on vacation in Oregon." The voice held respect, a curious bleakness. "Sorry, Mr. Baird."

I stirred, got to my knees. Strong hands jerked me erect. The room whirled. I was staring into a young-old face with a flat mouth and high Indian cheekbones. Blond hair, crew cut. He was big, about six-four. He had tremendous hands. At first glance he looked sleepy. Then you saw the eyes.

"Can you stand all right?" Dispassionate voice, a little tired.

I nodded and he let go of me. Lupo was standing to one side and a little behind Max. He looked wistful. The big deputy turned to him. "You mark him up?"

Lupo shook his head. Max said quickly, "I'll show you the boat."

"We'll bring him along," Stilch said.

"Sure," Lupo said.

They took me outside, and down the steps to the cove. Max took Stilch on board the cabin cruiser. The big deputy asked Max a great many questions. He picked up the gaff with a handkerchief, staring at me. I sat on the edge of the landing, fighting to keep from passing out. The sun burned down from an acetylene sky, and wavelets lapped gently against the pilings. A small army of fiddler crabs played hide and seek in the rocks. Lupo squatted next to me like a conspirator.

"Last chance, Tony. We can write Steve off as an accident. I can testify I saw the whole thing from the landing, that it was self-defense. All Max wants is his pitcher. Where'd you stash it?"

I said nothing. The deputy came back to the landing with Max.

"Let's go, Pearson."

I stood up. He put handcuffs on my wrists. Max was frowning. "Incidentally, Stilch, who called you?"

"Mrs. Locke. We may need a statement from her later." Stilch was deferential, now. Max Baird was a power in Point Rafael. He was money, to be treated with respect.

"When Wells gets back, tell him to call me," Max said.

"Yes, sir." Stilch took my arm, led me up the bluff steps. Max and Lupo stood motionless on the landing. We reached the highway patrol car parked in the shell drive, and Stilch opened the door.

"They work you over?" he asked conversationally.

"What do you think?"

Oddly enough, I felt no pain. I was in a suspended state of shock. Later, the pain would come.

We arrived at the county seat twenty minutes later. Stilch took me up stone stairs through a glass door, and we turned down a long asphalt tile corridor. We passed frosted glass doors, and turned into a large office bisected by a wooden railing. It had all the functional beauty of an operating room. Fluorescents overhead, gray steel filing cabinets, impersonal metal furniture. A rawboned man with flaming red hair sat at a desk in front of the railing.

"Hi, Barney," Stilch said. "Bring in the recorder, will you?"

We went back of the railing into a smaller room that said *Sheriff's Office* on the frosted panel. There were a desk, bookcase, four chairs.

First, Stilch removed my handcuffs. He sat behind the steel desk. "Turn your pockets inside out, please."

I emptied my pockets. Wallet, pocket comb, car keys, cigarettes, and matches. While Stilch was studying my driver's license, the redheaded deputy came into the office wheeling a tape recorder stand. Stilch said, "Baird told me most of it. I want your version." He flipped a switch, said to the recorder, "Interrogation of Anthony J. Pearson, twelve-forty p.m., April twelfth, by Joseph Stilch. Witnessed by Bernard Krafve."

It took almost an hour. Stilch interrupted me several times. His questions were brief and pointed. I started with Briarview, Stephen's job offer, Max's violent discovery that his Rembrandt was a fake, the beating Stephen had given me some hours ago. Finally Stilch turned off the recorder and sat looking at me out of those sleepy brown eyes.

"Point of order," he said. "I'm not interested in Baird's painting, or your hypothesis as to what might have happened to it. I'm only concerned with what happened to Steve Locke. You were a quarter-mile offshore, right?"

The trap was obvious. "Closer to a mile," I said.

Stilch made a steeple of his fingertips, brooded at it. "It's too wild, Pearson. Why not plead husband-and-wife triangle? Locke invites you for a boat ride. Kicks hell out of you and you defend yourself. At the worst, manslaughter. A sharp lawyer might get you off with five to ten. In three years you'll be eligible for parole."

My face was throbbing. "Don't you see?" I whispered. "Stephen planned the whole damned thing! He made some kind of deal with Ramos. Ramos was the last one to leave the den when Val screamed. He pulled a gypsy switch—"

"Sure," Stilch said affably. "And Mrs. Baird, downstairs, screamed deliberately to bring everybody out of the den long enough for Ramos to swap paintings. Now, since Lupo prompted Val's scream, it corresponds that he's in on it too. And we mustn't leave out the chap who got hit with the dart. Ergo, Steve Locke and Mrs. Baird and Lupo and George Fair all conspired to frame you for a murder that never happened—"

The redheaded deputy snickered. Stilch lighted a cigarette and smiled at me through the blue haze of smoke. "You still don't want to change your story?"

"Turn me over to Baird," I said nastily. "He'll have a confession out of me inside an hour."

His Indian face was unreadable. "Supposing we find only your fingerprints on that gaff?"

"You'll find Stephen's too."

"Will we?"

I felt the noose tightening. "I told you how it happened!" My voice was raw, almost a whisper. "He's setting me up so Baird will think he's dead, so Baird won't try to find him!"

"Look at it our way, Pearson. You make a pass at Locke's wife. He creams you. Later, you shake hands and he offers you a job.

We've got Lupo's statement that Steve threatened to kill you for taking a moonlight drive with his wife. Next morning you take him for a boat ride. You come back alone, with a yarn which no jury could possibly swallow." He leaned across the desk, big shoulders hunched. "And your gypsy switch angle is out. Know why?"

I shook my head, unable to speak.

"Because a three-hundred-year-old Rembrandt is a brittle thing. You don't roll it up your sleeve or do disappearance tricks with it. If you do, it cracks. Do I make sense?"

I thought about it. He was right. I said tightly, "Can I call a lawyer?"

Stilch said slowly, "I'm going to hold you on suspicion, pending discovery of the body. Right now it's too circumstantial to actually book you. If Locke's body turns up, a homicide charge is automatic. If it doesn't—then it's strictly up to the sheriff. He gets back Monday."

He was playing it safe, this soft-spoken giant. He didn't care whether I was guilty or not. I leaned over the desk. "Can I ask one question?"

"Go ahead."

"In spite of everything, you think I'm telling the truth. Don't you?"

A dusky flush mottled his cheekbones. He looked at the redheaded deputy. "Take him to the infirmary, Barney. Give him a private cell."

In the infirmary the white-smocked nurse burned my cuts with iodine and informed me that my nose was not broken. Barney took me to my cell. It was quiet and cool. I lay on the bottom bunk looking at the mattress overhead, thinking.

Fern had been waiting for me on the landing. She had seen my battered face, the blood on the boat. She had not seemed surprised. She had hurried off to call the county sheriff's office.

Fern painted well. Could she have faked the Rembrandt? Right now, Stephen and Ramos were disposing of the painting through underground channels. Within a few days Fern would take a long trip abroad, the grieving widow. I had a searing vision of her with Stephen on some sun-drenched beach in Rio. I could see them laughing in the expensive playgrounds of the world, in Antibes,

Lisbon, Paris, safe, unhunted, secure. My right fist ached. I realized I had been pounding the steel railing of my cot. Slowly the hate drained, leaving me weak and empty.

I thought about Stephen's white smile over a chessboard. He had planned a long-range death mate. Stephen, the superior being, enduring Max's thousand petty tyrannies, lusting after the treasure that hung on the wall of Max's den. Once in possession of the Rembrandt, Stephen had to disappear, permanently. For Max would be implacable in pursuit. Inevitably, he would find Stephen, though the search might lead halfway around the world.

From the first moment Stephen had met me on the golf course, I had not had a chance. He had catalogued me like some common variety of bug. My reactions were predictable, easily foreseen. He had known I would accept the job, that I would make love to Fern. He had used it as a motivation for his death.

I finally slept.

On the fourth morning I asked to see Joe Stilch. The turnkey gave me a queer look and shuffled away. Several hours later Stilch came to my cell.

"So far you're lucky. We've checked the cove and surrounding beaches. No body—so far."

"What body? He's probably in Brazil by now."

Stilch leaned against the bars. "I'm going to give you break, Pearson." He made it confidential, man-to-man. "I'm going to take you back to the office, and we'll erase your statement. You can admit the way it really happened. Locke started it, didn't he? We found both of your fingerprints on that gaff. You wrestled for it, and—"

"Oh, go to hell."

"You're a fool." But he said it without conviction.

"Listen," I whispered, "I'm telling the truth and you know it! Give me a lie-detector test..."

"Inadmissible as legal evidence. Sorry."

"Then how about a lawyer?"

"You can talk to Jed, Monday."

"Meanwhile you just hold me on suspicion? I thought I was allowed one phone call—"

"Who told you?" Stilch said, and walked away.

PART TWO

In the Rough

CHAPTER EIGHT

THEY released me on the fifth morning. It was Friday. They opened my cell door and took me past the tiered cells to the corridor that led to the sheriff's office. Stilch sat sullenly at his desk. The lawyer was a frail waspish man with a great shock of white hair. He glanced at me without interest, turned back to Stilch.

"Book him or release him," he said. "I don't care which."

Stilch looked angry and indecisive. "Can't you wait until Monday?"

"You want me to call Judge Carver?"

Stilch shrugged and handed me a brown manila envelope containing my personal effects. "Word of advice," he snapped. "Try to leave town, Pearson, and we'll re-arrest you."

The little man sniffed. "Come on, Pearson."

It was like a dream. I followed him down the asphalt tile corridor and out into the bright sunlight of the parking lot. He opened the door of a gray Buick hardtop and I got in. He went around and got behind the wheel.

"My name's Martin Fitzpatrick." He didn't bother to shake hands. "Don't bother asking who retained me, because I won't tell you. Here…"

He counted five hundred dollars into my lap. I looked at the money. "What's this for?"

"A plane ticket. Personally, I can recommend Waikiki. It's nice this time of year."

"I see." Understanding came slowly. "I'm supposed to run?"

"Fast and far. Where can I drop you?"

It was all happening much too fast. "My car," I said. "It's still at the Point Rafael country club."

He nodded and drove. He found the coast highway, and he hit ninety on the stretches. Within twenty minutes we were turning up the drive of the Point Rafael clubhouse. I saw my Ford sitting forlornly in the parking lot where I'd left it.

"Get out, Pearson. That does it."

"Just a minute!" I blazed. "You think I'm crazy? If I run, it means I'm automatically guilty—"

"Or if you stay." He was cold, incisive. "Frankly, no jury in the world will believe your story. But Stilch believed it. It's the only reason I was able to bluff him with a habeas writ. Had he actually booked you I couldn't have done a thing. You've got two days before the sheriff gets back. He'll arraign you. Max Baird happens to own him."

"Your client," I said. "He wouldn't, by any chance, be Stephen Locke?"

The little lawyer sighed. "If you wish, Pearson, I can drive you back to the county seat. Is that what you want?"

I got out of the Buick and slammed the door so hard I almost broke the window. Fitzpatrick drove off without looking at me. I walked over to my Ford. It started on the first try.

Before I drove out of the lot, I made a wide turn next to the clubhouse. A freshly painted sign out front proclaimed the new course pro was named Dan Brewer. Max hadn't wasted any time.

For five miles I drove automatically, in an access of fury. I drove east, along Highway 101. Rage slowly gave way to a cold appraisal of my chances. Someone wanted me out of jail. Max? Stephen? An impatient horn blasted me out of my reverie. I veered sharply to the right side of the highway, making room for the black Pontiac behind. As he shot by, I caught a flashing glimpse of the green Mercury trying to pass on my right.

Those three seconds were an eternity. I remember yanking the wheel hard to my left, and the squeal of the Mercury's brakes and how my Ford fishtailed, swerving to the left lane next to the highway railing with the Pacific shimmering two hundred yards below, and the sound of metal ripping as the Ford rocked on two wheels, then abruptly righted, slewing back across the highway.

I was back on the far shoulder, pulling to a slow stop. I sat sweating. Then I got out and surveyed the left side of my car. A scraped fender. Streak of white paint from the railing. Near miss, no cigar.

I got back behind the wheel, staring at the bright swirl of traffic. I was trembling. It is so easy for a man to die. A sudden horn blast on a sharp curve. A shove at a busy intersection. A push from a high window.

I started the car and drove slowly, hugging the far right lane. It would be convenient for Stephen were I to have a sudden accident.

Abruptly I made my decision. When a break came in traffic, I made a sharp U-turn and drove back toward Point Rafael. I had to see Fern, alone. I had to look into her face while she answered some questions.

I drove up the private road that led to Max's house and parked in the half-moon drive. I walked around to the front door, and stopped dead. Val and Fern were on the front patio. They sat in white wrought-iron chairs eating brunch.

Val saw me first. She stared at me, then stood up. Fern was wearing a plain black dress without ornament of any kind. She looked pale and drawn.

"You've got nerve," Val said whitely, "coming here. How come you're out of jail?"

I forced a grin. "Coming, Fern?"

Fern didn't move. She said clearly, "Coming where, Tony?"

What rocked me was the freezing hatred in her voice.

Fine, dark eyes biting into me with contempt.

"Fern, for God's sake," I blurted. "I've got to talk to you—"

"I don't want to talk to you, Tony." She was a bleak lovely stranger. "Please go before I call Max."

"I'll call him." Val turned and strode into the house. I stared at Fern. Five nights ago we had made love. We had made marriage plans.

"You'd better go, Tony." Fern's eyes were brimming. "Please, before Max comes."

It was the same feeling as when Stephen had hit me in the plexus. She gave me no opening, no chord of remembered contact. I turned away with a sick realization of defeat. As I got into my Ford I saw Val come out on the porch. With her was Max.

I love you, Tony. Husky voice, vulnerable quick passion. Lies, all lies. I drove in quiet madness, all the way back to Belmont Shore.

*   *   *

In my apartment I shaved and showered. Then I put on a clean suit. Somewhere in the web there was one weak strand.

Ramos.

I brewed coffee, scalding and black, and smoked two cigarettes. I picked up the phone and dialed the Long Beach Art Center. They were very helpful, very informative.

His name was Juan Ramos. He was reputable and respected. He had once written a textbook on how to differentiate old masters from fraudulent copies. He was currently affiliated with an art dealer in Los Angeles.

When I found Ramos I was going to interrogate him. Chad Lupo had taught me a few things about interrogation.

I went out and got into the Ford. I drove carefully through the noonday traffic.

The building was a venerable six-story brownstone located far out on Wilshire. The lobby was dark and cool, with electric-eye elevators that opened with automation politeness. I got off on the fourth floor and walked down a hundred yards of green-carpeted corridor to a chartreuse cork door. The pastel letters said simply, *T. Wallquist.*

It was like walking into the Louvre.

Across a fantastic expanse of jade Persian carpeting a blonde receptionist sat at a Jacobean refectory desk. Indirect lighting brought out amber highlights in the mahogany paneling. Near the desk was a group of marble statuary, life-size. The walls were a riot of paintings. I recognized a lordly Reubens in a gilt frame. Van Gogh was a brilliant splash of color next to a somber Goya. I cleared my throat, disturbing the cathedral hush. The blonde gleamed up at me.

"Good afternoon. May I help you?"

"Is Juan in?" I had done an hour's research in the library and rehearsed this twice, but it still sounded awkward and forced.

"Juan?" Her smile faltered, then came back with renewed candlepower. "Oh, you mean Mr. Ramos?"

"I've been out of town all week," I said apologetically. "The other night he called about the Vermeer."

"A Vermeer," she said, brightening. She got up and went past the snow-white statuary to the west wall. She looked at least forty, but her body was a sculptor's dream. She indicated a small canvas reverently.

"Burgher's Wife," she said, watching my reaction. "Of course you can't get the *life* in a reproduction, but this should give you some idea—"

"They're all reproductions," I said, staring around the room. "Representing originals for sale?"

"Of course. This particular canvas is owned by a client in Belgium. Mr. Wallquist listed it last month."

"I've got my heart set on *Delft Study.* Ramos has a line on it. He left word the owners might sacrifice it for sixty thousand. Where can I get in touch with him?"

She went back to the desk, nibbling her lip. She picked up a catalogue, leafed through it. "He hasn't listed it yet, I'm sure. Do we have your name on file?"

I gave her the name of Donald Carter, and an address in Pacific Palisades. She said thoughtfully, "Juan came back from Venezuela three weeks ago. He usually stays at the Beverly-Wilshire, but I haven't seen him all week. Until last Friday he stayed in his office, working on reproductions." She touched a stud on the desk. "Perhaps he left word with Mr. Wallquist."

Ramos had flown up *three weeks ago.* Yet Stephen had told Max that he had flown in from Venezuela that same night.

"May I help you?"

He had come soundlessly through the velvet arras in back of the desk. He had gray, quick-sliding eyes, a porcelain smile. The Ascot and the silver goatee were the last fortissimo touch.

"Oh, hello, Mr. Wallquist," the blonde said. "This is Mr. Carter. He's interested in *Delft Study.* Mr. Ramos—"

"Right this way, please," Wallquist said.

I followed him through the arras into an office that was a mauve miniature of the reception room. As he preceded me through the doorway I saw a birch door across the hall with *J. R. Ramos* in raised, knife-edged script.

"Juan's a junior partner," the art dealer said, following my glance. "He spends most of his time abroad, inducing wealthy old families to part with their treasures. Some of the families, of course, are more old than wealthy." He smiled. "Your particular Vermeer is held by an English earl who I hardly think would let it go for sixty thousand."

I looked hurt. "Then why did he call me?"

"Possibly to interest you in something else. When was it you saw him last?"

"October," I said. It was a poor guess. Wallquist's smile congealed. Last October Juan Ramos had apparently been on some other continent.

Wallquist's gaze traveled over my fifty-dollar charcoal flannel suit, the twelve-dollar brogues. His smile became a smirk. Quite obviously I could not afford a Vermeer reproduction, let alone an original.

"Juan called me last night from San Francisco," the art dealer said blandly. "He's attending an exhibition there this weekend. He may be back in town by Tuesday. Can he call you?"

I said that would be fine. "On second thought, why don't I call him? What's his hotel?"

"The—Mark, I believe." His gray eyes were utterly opaque. "I'm not really sure. Now if you'll excuse me—"

"I understand Juan is very good at reproductions." I stood up, wanting to smash him like a fat grub worm.

"Juan's a very talented man."

At the doorway I paused. "Come to think of it, you could interest me in another painting. I might go considerably higher than sixty thousand."

"Really?"

"A Van Ryn self-portrait. Small, almost a miniature."

He moistened his lips. I was finally getting to him. "No such portrait exists. I don't recall—"

"Before the war it hung in the Prague. Currently it's owned by a private party. You'll have Ramos call me?"

He looked at me with cold hate. I grinned at him and walked out. As I passed the blonde she gave me the number-three smile, reserved for sixty-thousand-dollar customers. I wondered what she would have done had I wanted a Michelangelo.

Driving down Wilshire, I tried to classify Wallquist. A reputable apple-cheeked art dealer, with a Latin partner very good at reproductions. If you had a spare hundred grand and lusted after a certain old master, they'd be delighted to contact the owner. If his price seemed too high, maybe they'd steal it for you.

Ten minutes later I walked into the lobby of the Beverly-Wilshire. The desk clerk was a polite sallow man who called registration, and then informed me that Juan Ramos had checked out last Monday afternoon. His forwarding address was Caracas, Venezuela.

I thanked him, and walked slowly over to the phone booths. I called the Mark Hopkins Hotel in San Francisco. They had a Gonzales registered, but no Ramos. Naturally. I smashed the receiver back on the cradle and started outside.

She was waiting for me near the potted palm by the lobby entrance. A dark, full-breasted woman in a white sharkskin dress.

"My name is Consuela Ramos." Her voice was a muted bell. "You are looking for my husband?"

CHAPTER NINE

HER face was finely chiseled copper. She had attractive, black eyes. I gave her my Sunday smile. "That's right, Mrs. Ramos. Any idea where I can find him?"

She turned to the green leather couch by the palm. "Juanito," she said.

"*Sí*, mama?" The boy looked up from his book. He was about seven, the male image of his mother.

"Please take a walk by the pool, Juanito. Come back in ten minutes."

The boy nodded with adult gravity. He walked through the lobby without looking back. Consuela and I sat on the couch. She said simply, "I have asked the clerk to tell me of any messages or inquiries." She hesitated, took the plunge. "You are of the policia?"

"No," I said, and she relaxed, visibly. "But I've got to find your husband, Mrs. Ramos. Didn't he fly back to Caracas on Monday?"

"No, *senor*. I feel he is here, in Los Angeles. Where did you see him last?"

If it was an act, it was a good one. Suddenly I liked her. And felt a touch of pity for what I had to do.

"Your husband," I told her bluntly, "may be in trouble. He could be a thief."

Consuela sat motionless. Her shining dark eyes searched mine. "What has Juan done?"

I told her briefly about Max's Rembrandt. She listened impassively. "I can tell you very little, *Senor* Pearson."

"What does Juan do for a living?"

"He paints," she said simply. "He makes contacts for *Senor* Wallquist. I met Juan twelve years ago. He was very poor, very proud." Her eyes were luminous with recollection. "He had a great talent and was ashamed of it. He had the gift of mimicry. He copied the great religious masterpieces of the church, the Goyas and the Rafaels. He was a pious man, yet embittered because he could only reproduce, not create. He met *Senor* Wallquist four years ago, at an art exhibition in Buenos Aires. It was a great opportunity for Juan. That first year he made twenty thousand dollars. Only he would be abroad for months at a time. Things went bad between us. Juan had a passion for the rich things of life, the gaming tables. Once, in Rio, there was a woman—"

She stared across the hotel lobby. I sensed strength in her, and a bitter pride.

"Always, Juan has come back to me. Two months ago he came home with a great desolation in his face. He paces our house like a tiger. There is a secret weight upon his soul and I am afraid. Then—a letter from *Senor* Wallquist. Juan is drunk with joy. He kisses me many times, and speaks of much money, a second honeymoon abroad. We fly to Rosarita Beach. Juan leaves me at the hotel. He has business here on the coast for a few days. Then, last week, Juan phones me. He will be delayed a few more days."

"When did he phone you?"

"Last Sunday. There is a coldness in his voice that frightens me. But I—I wait for him. Each day is a year. I say many prayers to the Virgin that he is not involved in some dishonest thing." Her fingers touched the tiny gold cross at her throat. "Yesterday, I call his hotel. They tell me he has checked out three days ago. I come at once." She looked up at me and said fiercely. "He is not a bad man, only weak. What has he done?"

Suddenly, I hated Ramos. I reached over and touched her hand. It was cold as stone. "Did you ask Wallquist about him?"

"He said Juan is in San Francisco." Her eyes held a primitive flame. "Could it be another woman?"

I thought about Val. Fern. "No," I said.

"I shall be at this hotel, *senor.*" She stood up. "When you find Juan, will you call me?"

"I'll call you, Consuela."

She walked across the lobby like some proud splendid animal. I never saw her again...

Driving back to Belmont Shore, Fitzpatrick's five hundred dollars felt uncomfortably warm in my wallet.

Flight money. I was supposed to run. Until Max Baird caught me. Or Lupo. Max was a big man, and he had the connections, the power. He would never believe that Stephen was still alive, that he had set up a Venezuelan art agent to fence the Rembrandt through underground channels.

If I stayed in town, I was dead. The county sheriff would be back Monday. Max would make a quiet phone call. And within an hour, Tony Pearson, a nobody, would be picked up on suspicion of murder.

Circumstantial, but men had died in the gas chamber for less. *Jealous lover kills husband.* The usual headlines, the quick trial. Plead manslaughter, Stephen had said. Damned considerate of him. A good lawyer might get me off with five to ten.

It was after four when I got back to my apartment. I was brewing fresh coffee and thinking about the weak, elusive Ramos, when the door opened. It was Joe Stilch. He came in soundlessly, closing the door behind him.

"You might at least bother to knock."

"And give you a chance to lock the door? After all, I haven't a warrant."

181

He no longer looked sleepy. He looked big and angry, a little tired.

"Why? You need a warrant?"

He didn't answer at first. I got out an extra cup for him and poured coffee. "Black," he said. "No sugar." He moved to the bed, sat warily. I handed him the cup, wondering what in hell he was after. He looked at the coffee and sighed. "Driving out here, I wanted to break your neck. No cop likes to be played for a fool. Then it came to me that I couldn't really blame you. You were gambling they wouldn't find the body. You had nothing to lose."

It was like a cold wind blowing through the room. My throat felt dry. "Are you trying to tell me—"

"Funny thing," he mused. "I believed you. There was a kind of pitiful integrity about your story that got me. The wilder the yarn the bigger the sucker." He sipped his coffee. The cup looked like a demitasse in his huge fist.

"Drink up, Pearson. Let's go."

"Where?" I whispered. But I already knew.

"Mrs. Baird found him three hours ago," Stilch said bleakly. "In the cove. The crabs have been at him for five days, but it's definitely Steve Locke. Both Mrs. Baird and Mrs. Locke made positive identification. The M.E. fixes the time of death some time Monday morning. The time you took him for a boat ride, give or take a few hours."

"Listen," I husked. "I didn't—"

"On your feet, Pearson." He stood up, big hands hanging loose at his sides. "Technically, I'm out of my own territory. But we'll call this one a citizen's arrest. And please resist me." He gave me an iron smile. "Just a little."

Certain decisions are made without conscious thought. Panic flames in a soundless spasm of time. *Do this and you die. Do this and you may live.*

It all happened too abruptly. Stilch standing over me like an executioner, looking eight feet tall. My right wrist moved without volition. It flicked the cup of scalding coffee squarely in Stilch's face.

He made a soft sound and clawed at his eyes. I was down, rolling, as he hit the chair where I had been. The crash shook the whole room. He came up fast for a big man, face contorted, eyes closed.

For perhaps three seconds he stood motionless in the center of the room. Then his hands came up, shoulders hunching. The hands were open, fingers stiff. He squinted and came at me.

I grabbed the coffeepot off the hot plate. It was hammered aluminum, with a nice heft. As Stilch came in I brought the coffeepot down on the right side of his head.

Hot coffee scalded us and I went momentarily blind. Stilch's right hand was a snake striking and there was a soundless explosion in my left shoulder. The entire arm went dead. I flailed wildly, and the coffeepot slashed across his temple. Stilch caved to his knees, clawing blindly at my groin. His breath made a curious whistling sound.

I brought my knee up squarely into his forehead. He toppled sideways, hands plucking at the carpet.

I stepped gingerly over him and opened the door. I was panting like a spent miler. A few minutes later I was on the coast highway, driving toward Laguna. My insides felt like whey. My left arm ached as I tried to flex my fingers. Stilch had tried for my carotid artery, where a slicing palm chop kills.

I was scared. Never in my life had I felt so alone. Within a half hour the roadblocks would tighten, the descriptions would clack out over a dozen teletypes. The net would close, inexorably. Another triangle killing. Jealous lover slays husband. They had the motive, the witnesses, and my fingerprints on the gaff. And they had the corpse.

Ramos, I figured. It had to be Ramos.

Stephen had contacted him, had arranged the switch in paintings. Stephen had planned to disappear permanently, framing me for his murder.

I could see Stephen, laughing inside as he swam to shore. Swimming to a secluded spot outside the cove where Ramos was waiting with dry clothes and a fast car. Ramos killing him instead. Planting his body in the cove. Checking out of the Beverly-Wilshire a few hours later.

Exit Ramos with three hundred thousand dollars' worth of painting which he would not now have to share with Stephen.

Stephen had finally met his chess master…

It was around five when I drove into Laguna Beach. A prowl car wailed past, and I froze behind the wheel. But they were only after a speeding Chevy. As I passed them I stared stonily ahead.

I had to ditch the Ford, and quickly. For a few days I could only hole up in some beach hotel. With luck I might even reach an airport.

My left arm ached in dull surges of pain. In a fair fight Stilch would have broken me, no hands. No cop likes to be played for a fool and I had made a fool of Joe Stilch. When they finally found me and brought me in, I could see Stilch's sleepy smile as he walked into my cell. An hour alone with him and I would be very glad to sign a confession.

I drove aimlessly through the heart of Laguna. Ceramic shops and shining new motels. Oceanfront homes in redwood and glass. The shimmer of blue neon in the dusk, *Hidaway Bar.*

A year ago I had taken Fern to the Hidaway often. We had made lovers' plans and laughed together over gimlets.

Under stress, man can be a weak, regretful animal. I retrospected bitterly, going back to the exact point in time when I had first met Fern. And I saw myself suddenly as an adolescent. Life had always given me a second chance. Life was a scotch foursome with changing partners where a shanked iron shot did not matter, because your partner would always sink that fifty-foot putt to tie the hole.

A year ago, I had closed my eyes to Fern's insecurity, had gone to the golf wars full of fatuous confidence that she would be waiting when I returned. I had underestimated her need.

The thought hit me like a sledge. I slammed on the brakes so hard that there was an indignant horn squall from the car behind. I whipped into the Hidaway parking lot and fumbled for a cigarette.

I had gone to Max Baird's house at noon. Val had been surprised to see me. An hour later she had found Stephen's body. She had found it in the cove, where the county deputies had failed to find it for the past five days.

I thought about Fern. Tired voice, dark eyes dull with contempt. Could it have been an act for Val's benefit?

Fern had sent me away hating her. Women in love can do cruel, unpredictable things to save their men. Could Fern...?

I went into the bar and found a phone booth. Information gave me Baird's number. I dialed, my fingers slippery with sweat. If Baird answered I could hang up.

"Meester Baird's residence." It was Johnny, the houseboy.

"Is Mrs. Locke there?"

A pause. He had recognized my voice.

"Mrs. Locke not home. Sorry."

"Johnny, this is Tony. I've got to talk with Fern—"

"Sorry, she not home." He sounded unhappy, "—now."

Someone else could be near him. Baird or Lupo or Val. Somebody else could be tracing the call on an extension.

"Tell her I'm in Laguna," I said. "Fern knows the place. We used to drink gimlets there. If she's not here by six, I'm coming after her. Tell her that, Johnny."

"I hang up now," Johnny said.

I held the phone a moment, listening. I thought I heard another soft click of an extension. I couldn't be sure.

I took a long deep breath and went back to the men's room. I washed my face and combed my hair. Stilch had torn my coat sleeve and my shirt was minus two buttons. I adjusted my tie carefully, hiding the missing buttons. It seemed terribly important that nobody noticed them. I went out to the bar and ordered a vodka gimlet.

It was ten after five. One gimlet later it was five-thirty. Once, this bar had held a special magic for me. The green baroque mirror over the bar, the driftwood and fishing nets on the walls, the vivid murals depicting leering pirates and their women.

But now the murals were faded, and it was just another bar where the laughter was too loud and the juke too discordant.

I had made a desperation gamble. At any moment two big state troopers would walk through the door. They would take me in, not gently. I had roughed up a cop, possibly fractured his skull.

Time to run, still time.

I ordered another gimlet.

It was five after six when Fern came into the bar. She came in quietly, walking like a queen. She was alone.

CHAPTER TEN

WE SAT in a dark corner booth, not talking. Fern finished her gimlet and looked levelly at me.

"Hungry, Tony?"

I nodded. She beckoned for the waitress. We ordered steak sandwiches, fries, and coffee. Fern was studying my face with cool detachment.

"You've matured," she said. "The Tony Pearson of twelve months ago would have hated me for what I said this morning. It would have taken him a week of sulking before he came back. It took you only five hours."

It stung, but I deserved it.

Fern added quietly, "You understand, of course, that I was afraid of Val. She's been studying me minutely all week to make sure I'm a shattered widow. I had to reject you in front of her. Otherwise you'd have stayed until Max came out. He would have killed you."

Understanding came, and shame. "Then you hired Fitzpatrick," I said. "But that morning, when I came back alone on the boat, why did you call the sheriff's office?"

"You'd rather have Max let Lupo continue to work on you?"

"Sorry." I looked down at the table. Fern's hand found mine. The juke was playing *Lisbon Antigua,* the way it had twelve long months ago. For just a moment we recaptured a very special mood. Then the steak sandwiches came.

We ate, hungrily. I told Fern about Wallquist's art emporium, about Ramos checking out of the Beverly Wilshire three hours after killing Stephen.

"There's one missing factor," Fern mused. "I'm sure Val was in on it. She's leaving Max."

"He'd let her?"

"He doesn't know. This afternoon I went into Val's room to return a sweater I borrowed from her last week. I was hanging it in her closet when I saw her two bags, packed. When I went downstairs she was telling Max she had a headache and couldn't go to the Shore with him tonight."

The waitress brought coffee, hot and black and delicious. I lighted cigarettes. "Fern, where do you think she's going?"

"To join Ramos, possibly. Wait here a minute, Tony."

She got up and walked back toward the phone booth at the end of the bar. I sat, extrapolating. The sands in our hourglass were running out. We could sit here for hours making futile plans, and in the end the police would find us. In trying to help me, Fern was making herself accessory after the fact. I felt anger and self-contempt. I tossed a five on the table and started outside.

"Tony!"

Fern caught me at the door. She grabbed my arm, dark eyes snapping. "Idiot! They've got roadblocks out by now. You can't drive three blocks in your Ford without being picked up—"

"All right," I growled, as we went outside. "It was stupid to call you in the first place. Who did you phone?"

"A friend." She was smiling a secret. "First, we're going to prove your innocence to Max. He's the only one powerful enough to help us."

I made a polite noise of disbelief. Fern's Thunderbird glistened blood red in the lights of the parking lot. She opened the door, slid behind the wheel. "Get in," she said dangerously. "Tony—"

"Oh, hell." But I got in.

She drove fast and smoothly through the south end of town. She was driving toward Point Rafael.

"First," I said caustically, "we tell Max the whole story. Then he apologizes while Lupo disembowels us—"

"Don't you *see*? If I can convince Max that Ramos forged the painting, he'll help us. He's a hard man, but he's fair. And he respects me. I think we'll find that proof in Ramos' office."

She had it all figured out. I leaned back in the seat and gave up. It was a warm night, and the moon washed the Pacific with platinum. A fine night to be off to Mexico for a six-week honeymoon.

I saw two black-and-white prowl cars parked at the corner intersection, and stopped breathing. Fern hit the green light at fifty miles an hour. Then we were on the long coast stretch, doing eighty.

"Relax," she said confidently, "they're looking for a blue Ford." She turned on the radio and there was the soft tinkle of a piano. I tried to relax, but my thoughts kept flashing back to Stephen. Patricide at fourteen. Bait boy at fifteen, Stanford graduate at twenty-one. Master chess player, lover, thief. Graduated from life at twenty-eight, *cum laude*.

A random thought struck me. I glanced sideways at my girl. Her face was pale and set, eyes fixed on the highway.

"Stephen never really loved you," I said.

"No," she said softly. "Although I did not fully realize it until a few days ago. A month after we were married he asked me to paint a replica of the Van Ryn. It was to be some kind of joke on Max. I refused. He insisted. I pointed out that Max would hardly appreciate that type of joke. He backed off. A cool smile. But from then on it was different between us." She shivered. "He was like ice. He'd hurt me in bed. Around people he was terribly polite. Very correct, with all the cruelty and hatred behind the mask. I couldn't understand. I kept loving him. I'm sorry, Tony."

"He fascinated you. The way a snake might."

"I wouldn't give him a divorce. In a way he was trapped. Max had taken a liking to me, and Stephen would never risk Max's disapproval. So it became a silent angry stalemate, my hanging on, Stephen trying to break me." There was a broken catch in her voice. "Two Sundays ago I answered the phone. A man's voice, with a faint Spanish accent. He wanted Stephen. After Stephen hung up he had that white calmness that meant he was excited inside. We had a scotch foursome at the club that day. He told me to go without him, that he had to go into town on business. I felt unaccountably furious with him. After he left the house, I stayed. I was outside by the pool when he came home an hour later. When he got out of the car he was carrying a small flat package. He looked at me and went into the house quickly."

"The fake Rembrandt," I said slowly. "He met Ramos in town and picked it up."

"Two days later I saw him making love to Val. I went away. But when he found me at Briarview, I was—glad. Can you understand, Tony?"

I said nothing. The Thunderbird rounded a high curve, and you could see the waves foaming over the rocks below, white lace and jade in the moonlight. I stared at them, full of hate and bitterness for a dead man.

"When I first saw you at Point Rafael," Fern said, "I was afraid. That night when you told me Max's Rembrandt was a forgery, I knew Stephen planned to frame you. Yet a tiny part of me still loved him. This afternoon when Val and I went down to identify the body, I cried. He looked like a tattered side of beef. Please be patient, Tony. I don't want his ghost to come between us..."

I reached out and switched off the ignition. The Thunderbird coasted on a dead motor.

"Pull over," I said harshly. We floated to a stop on the bluff shoulder. I took her in my arms. She was trembling. She tried to speak and I stopped her mouth with mine. I held her very close. After a time she sighed and burrowed her head into my chest.

"No ghosts?"

"No ghosts, Tony."

I turned on the ignition. Fern touched the starter. Her smile was tremulous and bright.

"I love you, Tony."

We drove through the night. There was no need for words. Ten minutes later we rounded the long bluff curve and came into Point Rafael.

The Lee Shore was a festival of light and color. Cads and Buicks shone in the festooned lights of the parking lot. I saw people in evening dress walking through the doorway arch. The pink marble facade was ablaze with colored spotlights, and you could hear the faint sob of violins from the swimming pools.

Fern slowed to a stop a hundred yards later. A dim figure waited in the palms.

"Hello, Midge," she said. "Get in."

He was a wizened Negro no more than five feet tall, wearing horn-rimmed glasses. I opened the door for him and Fern introduced us. "Midge Combs, Tony Pearson."

We shook hands. Midge had a seamed intelligent face, a tired smile.

"You work at the Shore?" I asked.

"I quit ten minutes ago," Midge said. His voice was husky velvet. He glanced at me quickly, at Fern. "This the boy they looking for?"

"He's the boy," Fern said. "Why did you quit, Midge?"

"Castle wanted me to play deckhand on his yacht," Midge said with soft dignity. "He lent it to some friends last week for a La Paz cruise. I refused. Next, he wanted me to wear a big turban and tight gold pants. To usher at the private shows. He said I was too small to tend bar. He prefers strapping Nubian types."

"What kind of shows?" I asked, knowing the answer.

"The penultimate, man. Fifty skins admission, and they pack those back rooms." He made a sick grimace.

Fern made a reckless U-turn beyond the parking lot, almost colliding with an oncoming Jaguar. The Jag's horn blared, then it turned into the parking lot. Two blondes got out; tall sleek showgirl types. One of them wore a pink evening dress; the other, black satin slacks. They walked across the lot, holding hands.

Castle was drawing a crowd tonight. The whisper had gone out to the well-heeled sensualists and the jaded millionaires. *The Shore's wide open again.*

If you liked your kicks frantic, if you craved sin at any price, the Shore was the place to go. Here was madness for sale, sweet and terrible.

"So Max sold the Shore to Castle," I said.

"He had to," Fern said. "Without the Rembrandt, he was strapped. The last two nights he's gone down to the Shore and come back brooding drunk. Let's change the subject. Midge, tell Tony about yourself."

Midge sighed. "A few years back I had fame. The cat burglar of Westwood. I'm quite good at opening locks. In Quentin I took up painting. I met Fern last year at the Laguna Art Festival. Poor child thinks I have talent."

"He's a genius," Fern said with that breathlessness peculiar to artists discussing each other's work. "Very advanced color sense. I keep hounding him to have a showing—"

"I'm modest," Midge said, deadpan. "Fifty years from now I'll be another Matisse. Fern got me a job tending bar at the Shore. If it hadn't been for her I'd doubtless be back in Quentin." He hesitated. "I hope you aren't carrying heat."

I said no, and he relaxed. Armed robbery would probably get him ten to life, while breaking and entering might only mean five years. I touched Fern's knee. "I like your friend."

"If a man's in trouble," Midge said, "you help him. Still on that pastel kick, Fern?"

That started her off, and for the next half hour they were off in a world of their own, arguing the respective merits of oils versus water colors. We hit the Hollywood Freeway and the Thunderbird was a silent arrow through the Friday night traffic. Then Wilshire, headed west. Behind us the Civic Center was a dazzling smear of light. Fern slowed. Those last two miles seemed like two hundred. Nobody spoke until we turned into the alley in back of a brownstone office building.

Fern got out first, staring tautly at the black Chrysler parked a dozen yards down the alley. Her fingers tightened around my wrist. "Tony, that's Castle's car!"

"What would he be doing here?"

"I don't know."

Midge murmured, "This mean a change in strategy?"

Fern shook her head, tight-lipped. We went around to the lobby entrance. The lobby was still and deserted, except for a tired janitor who glanced up briefly and went back to his squeegee and pail.

In the elevator Fern said quickly, "Tony, give Midge a hundred dollars."

Midge looked pained. "This trip's for free. Later, however, you may visit my garret to purchase a few minor masterpieces." I made a mental note to do just that.

As we left the elevator, Midge took out a pencil flashlight and large key ring. When we came to the chartreuse cork door at the end of the corridor, he examined the lock and smiled. He handed me the flashlight. I held it steady while he worked on the lock.

There was a soft snick and the door swung open. From inside came the indistinct blur of voices. Midge looked at us questioningly, putting his finger to his lips. I made motions for him to wait downstairs in the car. He nodded, and disappeared down the corridor. Fern and I went inside and softly closed the door.

The reception room was a jungle of inky shadows. Behind the Jacobean desk, the tapestries were a pale screen of light. A man's shadow appeared on the screen, as we knelt behind the Greek statuary.

"He *knows*, I tell you!" It was Wallquist's voice, bitter and defiant. "The way he grinned at me this afternoon when he asked about the Van Ryn. When the cops find him he'll spill his guts."

"And who's to believe him?" The other voice was cynical, yet soothing. "He's practically a convicted murderer. You're a respected art dealer—"

Wallquist cursed. "If only Juan weren't so damned greedy! He got me into this mess, Castle. And to you, it's amusing!"

Fern stared at me in chill realization.

"...relax," Castle was saying. "Ramos is still on the coast, Wally. The sooner he gets his end, the sooner he goes back to Venezuela. How much longer does he wait?"

"Two, three days. These things take time, Ronnie." There was a cunning note in Wallquist's voice. "If he would settle for thirty thousand tomorrow—"

Castle's flint laughter. "I promised him fifty thousand. And I always keep my word, Wally." The scrape of a moving chair. A distorted shadow shivering behind the tapestry. "By Monday noon, then?"

"Listen, it's a Canadian client. He's got millions. But he may have difficulty in transferring funds—"

"Monday noon, Wally?"

"All right." The art dealer's voice collapsed. "Why should you care? You've got what you want."

"Naturally," Castle said coldly. "But I want to pay Ramos off, get him out of the country. Understand?"

"Obviously. Did you tell him his wife is in town?"

"I told him. He's going to let her get tired of waiting for him. Ultimately she'll give up and go back to Caracas. As far as she's concerned, he's found another girl."

I had a picture of Consuela sitting in her lonely hotel suite, waiting for a phone call that would never come.

"Juan's a cold fish," Wallquist said slowly. "But why did he have to—"

"Stephen became greedy. You can learn from that." The tapestries parted. Castle appeared—a regal figure in blue serge. His creamy hair shone.

"One for the road?" The sound of a glass clinking.

"Not that stuff," Castle said with contempt. "And lay off it until Monday, will you?"

The tapestries closed. Castle walked past us in the dimness, so close I could almost touch him, opened the corridor door and went out.

From the inside office came a heavy sigh. Silence. Then the sound of a phone dialing. Wallquist's voice, moist, thick, "Thelma...? Wally, honey."

A pause. I'll be over in ten minutes, baby—what? Why not?" His voice turned harsh. "So you've got a migraine again. Take an aspirin. Sure, you can sleep in tomorrow morning—on one condition." He chuckled. "*If* you wear the blue negligee. That's right baby—ten minutes."

He hung up. "Bitch," he said. I thought about the blonde receptionist with the fine body and the tired eyes. The lights flicked out as Wallquist's shadow passed us. The outside door closed.

I stood up and stretched, helping Fern to her feet. She was trembling.

"Fern, I can't feature an operator like Castle mixed up in a phony art racket."

"He's not," she whispered. "All he ever wanted was the Lee Shore. The Shore's worth a million dollars a year, if you know how to run it. Castle knows how."

I thought about the private saturnalias in back rooms, fifty dollars admission. "Then Stephen was deliberately mismanaging the Shore to put Max in the red. He must have contacted Castle originally, with his scheme to steal the Rembrandt. Purpose: to strap Max, so he'd have to sell the Shore to Castle."

"But Ramos tricked Stephen, killed him. Why didn't Castle care?"

"Why should he? Let's find Ramos' office."

We went back of the Jacobean desk through the tapestries. I turned on the hall light and tried the door to Ramos' office. It was locked. I threw a shoulder against it. On the fourth try, wood splintered and gave. We went inside and turned on the lights.

It was more of a studio than office. I saw swathed canvases, an easel. Oil reproductions hung on the cork walls. Fern examined them.

"He's good," she said. "He's very good. Open the desk, Tony."

The rosewood desk was locked. I tried to pry the drawer open with a pallette knife. Finally I smashed it open with my heel.

My nerves were shrieking piano wire.

We found what we wanted, five minutes later.

It was a cracked lithograph reproduction of the Van Ryn in the bottom drawer of the desk, buried under several watercolors. With the lithograph was a short article clipped from a German art magazine, *Die Kunst Fer Aile*. The date of the magazine was June, 1936. In another drawer were two preliminary charcoal sketches. Fern compared them with the lithograph carefully.

"It's all we need, darling." Her eyes were shining as she put the sketches into a manila folder. "Max won't believe us, at first. But at least he'll question Wallquist. I've a hunch Wallquist will talk, once Lupo starts on him."

I had the same hunch. "Let's get out of here," I said.

We left, turning out the office lights. In the elevator I kissed Fern, long and hard. The elevator doors opened. As we stepped into the downstairs lobby there was a flicker of motion on my left. Then the darkness splintered apart in white pain.

I was down on the marble flooring on hands and knees, shaking the agony out of my head, trying to rise.

There were two of them. The one who stood over me was big, blond, neatly dressed. The other was lean and darkly immaculate. He had Fern backed into the corner alcove. She was holding the manila envelope in a death grip, staring at him like a snake-hypnotized bird.

"Give," he said patiently, holding out his hand.

Fern's eyes darted to mine. Her scream died stillborn as he slapped her, and took the envelope. I lunged erect and hit him. A weak, glancing blow. The other man spun me expertly and threw his knee into my groin. I went down, retching. He stood over me, amused.

"No more heroics, please. George?"

"Right here," George said, glancing into the art envelope. He paid no attention to Fern as he took out a silver cigarette lighter and set fire to the sketches. She gave a wordless cry and flew at him. George casually backhanded her against the brass elevator gates.

I tried to push the marble flooring away from me. The blond man kicked my elbow. I fell heavily on my side. The sketches were flaming brightly in the sand-topped cuspidor. Blondie grinned down at me in gentle reproof.

"We're helping him," he told George. "He doesn't appreciate it."

"His type never does." George poked at the burning sketches.

"Typical felon," Blondie said. "No gratitude. He steals someone else's property, then tries to stop us from destroying the evidence."

I cursed him. Fern huddled in the alcove corner, crying without sound. The alcove was secluded from the main lobby, beyond eyeshot of the glass entrance doors. I realized what had happened. Castle must have spotted Fern's Thunderbird in the outside alley.

"That does it," George said, poking at the embers. "I trust you've done your duty as a public citizen."

"Quite," Blondie said with comic righteousness. "I've already called the police."

"Let's go," George said, glancing at his watch. Side by side, they walked across the lobby, not looking back.

The entire thing had taken less than ninety seconds. Ninety seconds of deft violence by two men who resembled young corporation executives, and who did their jobs with expensive deadly precision. Two sleek hoods who had not even bothered to kill me because I was already cold meat for the gas chamber.

I was choking with a wild sick rage as Fern helped me wobble to my feet. My entire body felt like mush. "Hurry," she whispered through tears. "Please hurry, darling."

As we turned into the alley we saw the Chrysler purring down Wilshire. Castle sat in the back seat, looking almost bored. To him I was a minor organism, a gnat with its wings smashed, left to die. A potential threat that had been disposed of, nothing more.

When she saw the Thunderbird, Fern made a small broken sound. The air had been let out of two tires. Midge slumped motionless over the wheel, blood on his forehead. His breathing was thick, stertorous.

Then we heard it. The distant scream of a siren.

George and Blondie had timed it with loving care.

Midge stirred, moaned.

"Help me, Tony!" Fern's voice was a frantic sob as we slid Midge from behind the wheel. He stood erect, rubber-legged, shaking his head and wincing.

"Man skulled me," he grunted. "For why?"

"Later!" I grabbed his arm. "Can you walk, Midge?"

He couldn't. Half-dragging, half-carrying him, we made it to the street. Down the block I spotted a cruising cab. It moved toward us with agonizing slowness. The siren was a devil's shriek that died as the prowl car careened into the far alley entrance. The red spotlights impaled Fern's Thunderbird as we ran to meet the cab.

CHAPTER ELEVEN

"WHERE to?" The cabbie gave us a sharp glance to make sure we weren't drunk. All three of us were panting in the back seat.

"Western and Santa Monica." I blurted the first intersection that popped into my head. He shifted into second. As we passed the office building I saw the prowl car parked in the alley mouth. One cop was examining the Thunderbird and the other was cautiously entering the lobby. For a little time I was free. Not for long.

Two hours ago, I had beaten a law officer unconscious. The story would hit the big metropolitan dailies by morning. *Fleeing*

Killer Breaks Arrest. An hour, six hours, a day from now, someone would frown at me in quick recognition. They would walk to the nearest phone. And, within minutes, a hard-faced plainclothesman would come up behind me and say, "Let's go."

And I would go. All the way to that cyanide chamber at Quentin.

Midge fingered his scalp, wincing. "Just for nothing," he said plaintively. "Just because. Two men walk by the car. They look at me. Then—wham!"

"Castle likes to make sure," Fern whispered. "Let me look at that scalp, Midge."

The little Negro had an egg-sized lump, but there was no evidence of concussion. I told Midge what had happened. I spoke in guarded whispers, staring at the cabbie up front. Midge clucked sadly. "All my fault, children. It was very unprofessional of me to wait there."

Fern's hand found mine. "We shouldn't keep the cab too long, Tony."

I knew what she meant. We had left a warm trail. Within an hour the police would check out the trip tickets of all cabs operating along Wilshire. They could trace us easily. Already, the driver was eyeing us in the rear-view mirror.

"You need a car," Midge said softly.

"Brilliant," I grunted. "You can excrete one, maybe?"

"Maybe." He leaned forward and gave the cabbie a Sunset Strip address. Fern looked at me with a beaten hope.

"Last chance coming up, darling."

"Val?"

She nodded. Val was leaving Max, sometime tonight. Possibly she had grown tired of him. More possibly she had a rendezvous with someone else. Ramos? Castle?

Ten minutes later we were shooting past the glittering supper clubs on the strip. Midge said suddenly, "Next corner," and the cab pulled over to the curb I paid the driver and we got out. He gave us a long look before he drove away.

The place was a hundred yards back from the boulevard. For the strip, it was drab, unpretentious. A curved, brick walk, and dwarf pines festooned with Chinese lanterns. There was a blank white cement wall with a single Chinese hieroglyphic on it in blue neon.

"Friend works here," Midge said, leading us through the red lacquered doors.

The dining room was the ultimate in oriental decor. The tables were ebony, scarlet, and gold. We passed a long onyx bar with exquisitely carved stone Buddha's flanking the fireplace. The headwaiter was a stooped Chinese with a fixed smile and eyes like wounds.

"Reservations, sir?"

"Friends of Charlie Wong," Midge said. "Tell him it's Midge."

The headwaiter bowed. We waited at the bar while the bartender polished glasses in the discreet gloom and pointedly ignored us. In less than fifty seconds the headwaiter returned and beckoned. We followed him around the bar and down a long red-carpeted hall into a small sitting room with gold dragons limned on black drapes. The headwaiter vanished and Midge said, "Sit a while. It could be five minutes or an hour."

We sat. A faint surf of sound came from the dragon drapes. I got up and peered through. The adjoining room was a haze of cigarette smoke. Six men sat around a table, playing fan-tan. Midge clucked disapprovingly. I sat, fidgeting.

"They play no limit," Midge murmured. "Charlie owns a third interest in this place. He's the main attraction for that back room. Professionals come from as far as Frisco to see if they can beat him."

"Do they ever?"

"Sometimes," Midge said, as a giant walked through the drapes.

At first glance he looked like a living Buddha. The almond eyes were almost buried in rolls of yellow fat. He had a face like the full moon, and not a single hair on his massive skull. He weighed at least three hundred pounds. The gold earring was the final touch.

"Charlie," Midge said, standing. They shook hands. The giant regarded us briefly and turned back to Midge.

"Long time," he said. "Expected you a year ago." His voice was thin, astonishingly reed-like for so huge a frame.

"I'm proud," Midge said. "Bite the bullet and such jive."

"But now you're here." Wong's eyes swept Fern, myself.

"My friends wish a car," Midge said simply. "It will clear up an old obligation."

Wong's frown was a massive thing. "Your semantics are poor tonight, little man. I do believe you said obligation."

"Your hearing is flawless as your memory is poor." Midge stood like a frail bitter pygmy. "For your information, Charles, the hounds sweated me for days. I had but to name a name, and my five years in Quentin would have been reduced to one."

Unexpectedly, Wong smiled. "And you desire payment for keeping your white plume unsmirched? This is your pride, chappie?" Black man and yellow man, speaking their strange and terrible hyperbole. Yellow man regarding Fern as though she did not exist. I had the feeling Midge was bargaining for our lives. "I must make a phone call," Wong said heavily. "I take it your friend is hot."

"Exceptionally. His name is Tony Pearson. The girl is not involved."

Wong nodded curtly and left the room. "Amazing man," Midge told us. "Twenty years ago he took his master's degree in sociology at the Sorbonne. Five years ago he was a prominent fence for the syndicate. Today he is restaurateur and gambler."

The headwaiter came in with three drinks on a tray. Mine was a plum-colored brandy that tasted a thousand proof. Whatever Charlie Wong was, he had manners. I felt gratitude toward Midge, and faint wonder. He lived by an iron code of ethics. Part of that code meant helping a friend, regardless of danger or price. He could have squeezed the fat gambler for a job, for money. But he had sacrificed his pride to help me instead, because my girl, I supposed, had once done him a favor.

I reached into my pocket and touched Fern's five hundred dollars. As I moved past Midge to set my empty glass on the tray, I bumped into him. His drink splashed on the carpet. I was apologizing and picking up his glass, when Wong came back into the room. I had managed to slip two hundred-dollar bills into Midge's coat pocket.

Wong stood looking at me out of his tiny pig eyes. "Your friend is a walking sacrifice, Midge. He has offended certain ones in high places. May I suggest you disassociate yourself from him at once?"

"Where's the car?" Midge asked.

Wong closed his eyes as if in pain. "You are a quixotic fool. If the hounds do not find him by morning it becomes a job for the organization. Castle has offered five thousand dollars for him. A half hour ago he eluded the hounds on Wilshire. May I suggest—"

"The car, you fat hustler," Midge was implacable. "Before I obscenity on your honor."

Wong shrugged a gigantic shrug and tossed me a car key. "Parked two blocks down," he said. "A black fifty-four Pontiac." His chuckle was surf-breaking. "The car, friend, is hot as you are. Does it matter?"

I told him it did not matter. Midge accompanied us to the outside corridor. "Good luck, children. I'm staying. I plan to break Wong's game for him." We shook hands. I felt the rustle of bills and stared down at the money now in my hand. "I told you once," Midge said quietly, "buy one of my canvases some time. So long."

"Thanks, Midge," Fern kissed the little man's cheek. As we went outside he smiled after us like a small benign Uncle Remus.

We walked through the carnival glow of the strip holding hands, not talking. As I opened the Pontiac's door for Fern I felt a cold certainty that we were being observed.

Wong had the indefinable taint of the illicit about him. Hustlers can be a charming breed, but most of them would sell their sisters for the right price.

And Castle had offered five thousand for me.

I got behind the wheel and turned on the ignition. The Pontiac slid easily away from the curb. No one stared after us; there was no sudden blare of police sirens. I turned off on a dark side street and doubled back toward the civic center.

"It's eight-fifteen," Fern said tautly. "Johnny goes off duty at nine."

"You think Val's already flown?"

She shook her head. "Not this early. We've got a good hour."

An hour wasn't enough. I found the freeway but the Friday night traffic was thick. It was after nine by the time we hit Newport.

"Fern, what kind of woman is Val?"

"Pure bitch," she said with soft venom. "An ex-model who married money when she was twenty, and got divorced six months later. Her second marriage lasted almost a year. Max is her third. She makes a game of infidelity, but Max doesn't notice—or pretends not to."

I tried to picture Val as the scheming type. It was no use. Beautiful, pampered, with a female streak of viciousness. But not a calculating cold planner. Val and Ramos together simply did not jell.

Lupo? The little man had seemed fiercely loyal to Max. But it could have been simple jealousy that had maimed George Fair with that dart. Although Lupo was hardly Val's type.

It was nine-forty when we hit Point Rafael and turned up the winding hilly road. I parked in the dark cottonwoods two hundred yards from the house. Fern gave a small sob of relief when she saw the Buick station wagon parked in the drive.

"She's still here," she breathed. "I'm going in, Tony. I'll try to stampede her. I'll tell her I've just come back from the Shore and that Max is drunk and ugly. That he's been hinting about Val and Stephen, asking me questions. Then I shall yawn theatrically and hit the hay. You'll follow her?"

"Right," I said huskily, pulling her into my arms. "Kiss for luck?"

It became a long savage farewell kiss that left us both shaken. "Call me in an hour, Tony—no matter what. Promise?"

"Promise."

Fern touched my cheek with a wordless gesture, then hurried across the drive into the house. She disappeared in the veranda shadows and I felt very much alone.

Five, ten minutes. I lighted a cigarette. The poplars stood out like silver sentinels in the moonlight, and the landscape was a Goya canvas, dreamlike and unreal.

Twenty minutes later a dark figure emerged from the side door, carrying an overnight bag. Val. Before getting into the Buick she glanced back at the house. The Buick's headlights flared and its tires chewed gravel. She came up the winding road at forty miles an hour and I counted to a slow ten before following her.

I kept the Pontiac's lights off all the way down to the coast highway. Val had turned south, towards La Jolla. For the next ten miles I stayed a quarter-mile behind, cruising at seventy. All this time I had a strange preoccupation over my last chess game with Stephen.

I remembered a knight sacrifice he had made. An apparently premature move, which concealed a deadly rook mask. I had ignored the knight, and Stephen had announced mate in three.

I thought about Val finding Stephen's body in the cove five days after his death. Stephen making love to her a few days before he was murdered. I thought about Consuela Ramos' dark proud beauty. *"Juan has always come back to me, senor."*

It was like a floodlight being suddenly turned on inside my head. Stephen's long-range planning, his deal with Castle. His obvious seduction of Val. Ramos arranging with Wallquist to fence the Rembrandt through underground channels. All the jigsaw fragments twinkled into place at once. I felt contempt for Val, and pity.

Like me, she was a sacrifice pawn. Right now, I had suddenly realized, she was keeping a rendezvous with sudden death. Her own.

Ahead, the Buick slowed as we drove through Dana Point. I kept the Pontiac at thirty. On my right, the beach houses were thinning. Abruptly the Buick turned off on the cliff shoulder. Its headlights winked out. I drove a few hundred yards farther and pulled over to the edge of the highway. I made myself light a cigarette and wait two minutes before making a U-turn. I drove back and parked behind Val's Buick. The car was deserted. At the edge of the beach cliff was a picket fence, with a rickety stairway leading a hundred yards down to the sand. The nearest house was four blocks north, perched high on a bluff promontory.

A full moon played hide-and-seek among black, scudding clouds. Far south, you could see distant bonfires flickering on the strand. College kids, probably, waiting for the first grunion run of the season.

Nestled in the cliff hollow below, I saw the beach house. One of the windows was a yellow square of light. The moon went behind a cloud, and I started gingerly down the steps in darkness. Halfway down I heard voices and froze.

The night wind tasted of salt and there was only the distant boom of surf. I descended slowly. As I reached the bottom step the flashlight glare exploded in my face. Val's giggle was a hot knife in the stillness.

"The pose is fine, Tony. Hold it, please."

A man's voice. Light, amused. I had guessed right, but it was small consolation now. I stared blindly into the flashlight beam.

"Hello, Stephen," I said.

CHAPTER TWELVE

"WALK slowly, old man." Stephen shifted the flashlight to let me see the gun. "Toward the cottage, if you don't mind."

I walked toward the looming bulk of the beach cottage, hating myself, wondering how long it had taken Val to spot me tailing her. As if reading my mind, Stephen said patronizingly, "She wasn't sure until you doubled back and parked behind the Buick. Right, Val?"

"That's right, darling," she said.

Val opened the cottage door for me and I went in. The living room was a soft blend of pastel furniture and green tropicals, with one entire wall done in pale limestone. Stephen motioned Val to the pink chesterfield. "Nice place," I said.

"Belongs to Max," Stephen said. "Fern and I honeymooned here, six months ago. Sit down."

I sat. There was a subtle difference in him. His eyes were calm and dead. In repose his lean face was utterly devoid of expression, and it came to me that evil can be a functional thing. Stephen would kill me without passion or thought, because I was an obstacle not worthy of survival. In that moment I tasted hatred like a thick bile in my throat.

"That mustache," I said, looking at the embryo smudge his lip. "Did you reinforce it with grease paint last Monday, when you checked out of the Beverly Wilshire as Ramos?"

"Black crayon," Stephen smiled. "Very effective. For your information, I am Ramos. Since last Sunday, when you killed me."

The .32 in his fist came up, steadied on my chest. Val rose to her feet, suddenly pale. "You promised," she whispered. "We were only going to tie him up. Please, darling—"

"He's going to kill us both," I snapped. "Use your head. You're just excess baggage from here on out. All he ever needed you for was to find Ramos' body after the crabs had made it unrecognizable. By Monday night he gets a fifty-grand payoff from Castle, and probably a dummied passport. As Ramos, he flits. I suppose he told you to leave a farewell note for Max?"

"Y—yes. I—"

"The cops find us both dead, here in the beach cottage. Both of us half-naked, whiskey splashed around. A drunken lovers' quarrel, with the gun still in my hand—"

Almost casually, Stephen chopped the gun across my temple. Pain flamed in a scarlet explosion behind my eyes. I touched my cheek and felt warm stickiness. Stephen glanced at Val in tender mockery. "Do you believe him, darling?"

She shook her bright head wordlessly, staring at him. But in that moment, she knew. It was in Stephen's flat smile, the way he eyed her with remote pitying contempt. I had a feeling he would savor Val's last moments on earth. He would watch her face as he pulled the trigger.

"Complex," I said admiringly. "But clever."

I tried to touch his weakness, his vanity. Anything to stall him, to wipe that execution smile off his face. I spoke as an inferior chess player to a master. And I edged imperceptibly forward in my chair, my thigh muscles tensing, trying not to look at the gun.

Stephen frowned. "Complex? How?"

I moistened my lips. "Your planning was so long range. Was it Castle's idea for you to run the Shore into the red?"

"Mine," he said dryly. "It was the obvious way to pressure Max into selling the Rembrandt. Castle was delighted. All he wanted was the Lee Shore. He contacted Ramos through Wallquist, but Juan turned out to have certain—scruples."

"That's what I mean. Too complex. Too dangerous, even if it worked."

"Not at all. We simply got him into a big game. One of Castle's back rooms. Let him win at first." Stephen chuckled in recollection. "Then we clobbered him. Thirty thousand dollars. Poor frantic Latin. When we finally offered him a chance to get off the hook he painted that reproduction like an inspired man."

Val's breathing was harsh in the silence. Her gentian eyes did not waver from the muzzle of the .32.

"Then Val's scream that night was coincidence," I said. "You had already switched paintings a few days before."

"Certainly. My original plan was to disappear, making it look like an accident. But when I met you at Briarview—"

"You decided to give Max a real corpse instead. Ramos was ideal, wasn't he? It meant a bigger split all round, besides framing me for your death. Last Sunday night you followed Ramos outside and killed him. You stripped the body and mutilated it before planting it under the landing—"

"No!" Val's voice was a thin wail. "Darling, you said Tony killed him! That you needed me, you were in danger—"

Her voice trailed off. Stephen gave her a bored glance. I said, "He planned to wait a few days longer before telling you to find the body, Val. But I got out of jail soon."

"Not too soon," Stephen shrugged. "Both Val and Fern identified the body as mine."

"Wrong," I said. "Fern recognized it. But she played dumb. Who do you think told me to follow Val?"

His nostrils flared. The .32 was rock steady, pointed at my navel. "Go on," he said softly.

"Fern's waiting in my car on top of the cliff. If she hears a shot she goes for the cops. Stalemate, chum."

Stephen glanced questioningly at Val. She sat on the pink chesterfield, biting her fist. "I'm not—sure," she said miserably. "I thought Fern acted funny. I didn't actually see her go to bed. She could have joined him outside, after I left."

Stephen weighed it. It was a bluff he couldn't afford to call. "Val," he said gently. She looked up at him, and for the first time I saw his magic with women. His charm lighted up the entire room. His smile was a benediction, the essence of need. "I need you, darling," he said.

"Yes," Val said. "Yes."

"Stand up, Tony." The gun gestured. I stood, slowly.

"Now turn around." I turned. Then the quick swish of his shoes on the carpet. I braced myself, trying to gauge the second of impact, to roll with the blow. I didn't, quite. He almost caved in my skull.

When I came to, there were voices. The carpeting was soft and warm against my cheek. I wanted to burrow into it drowsily, to sleep for a very long time.

"Certainly he lied." It was Stephen's voice, vibrant, reassuring. "Tony's a psychopathic liar and murderer. You should feel sorry for him."

"I believe you," Val whispered. The sound of a kiss. My insides squirmed. He had bound her to him with chains of passion to make her believe black was white, he was that good. "I brought a gun in my handbag," Val said proudly. "Just in case. See?"

Stephen chuckled. "You call that a gun?" Another kiss. "Darling, he's dangerous. If he moves, shoot him. I'll be right back."

The kitchen door closed. Silence. I opened my eyes and saw the sheen of Val's nylons.

I turned over on my back. She almost shot me.

As I tried to get up, Val gave a startled gasp and raised the gun. It was a tiny pearl-handled boudoir special, a .22. "Don't you move," she breathed.

"You're a fool," I said. "He doesn't need you any more, understand? As soon as he comes back we both get it—"

"Be still!" Her face was chalk white, she was fighting hysteria. "I don't want to listen. You couldn't possibly understand. Stephen loves me."

"For your information, he still loves Fern." I managed a brutal grin. "Think about it a while."

It was a crude lie, but the only thing that might shatter the wall of emotion in which Stephen had enclosed her. In that fractional second her gun wavered, and I came up fast from the floor and slapped it out of her hand.

"It's not loaded," Val said. She looked at me with a tired smile, and unexpectedly burst into tears. I retrieved the .22 and checked the magazine. Empty. It was typical of Val.

Stephen would be at the top of the cliff by now, moving like a shadow in the darkness. I gave him thirty seconds to inspect the empty Pontiac and decide I had lied about Fern, another fifty seconds to descend the bluff steps four at a time. I grabbed Val's arm. "Come on!" To my surprise she did come, listlessly.

Outside, we headed south, toward the bonfires a half-mile down the beach. Tidal sand sucked at our shoes. We hugged the base of the cliff, moving slowly through inky shadows. It was a temptation to ambush Stephen when he returned to the cottage. But his gun was loaded. Val's wasn't. And it would have been childish to risk her life in the balance.

Val paused, panting. "I'm tired, Tony."

I shushed her. "Listen!"

The sharp slam of the cottage door. Stillness. I peered back at the cottage and saw nothing. Two hundred yards away, Stephen was coming after us in silence. Val and I were two errant pawns. Very unsporting of us. I pressed Val back into a deep niche between the rocks. Her body tensed, then relaxed against mine. Her breath was warm in my ear. "He's not bad, really. Don't hurt him. Promise me you won't hurt him—"

"Quiet!" I wanted to hit her.

The moon came out from under tattered clouds. Fifty yards of salt-white sand separated us from the ocean. Here the beach was a narrow crescent bounded by cliff and dunes, gradually widening as it stretched south. We were utterly alone. Stephen could take his time. No one would hear the shots.

I bent down and groped for a handful of rock shards. Val drew a quick convulsive breath and I squeezed her arm for silence. I threw the rocks back toward the cottage, aiming at the curve of cliff wall. They struck with a faint clatter.

We saw Stephen.

He had been waiting behind a grassy dune. Now he stood motionless, thirty yards away. The moonlight etched him with a terrible distinctness. Two-legged carnivore with a white smile. The .32 glinted in his fist as he moved to another dune.

"Oh, God," Val's nails dug into my wrist. "Look at his face!"

Stephen stood in a balanced crouch, studying the cliff minutely. Abruptly he vanished behind a rise of sand. At first, I didn't get it.

Then I stared south and felt a sick realization. Ahead, the boulders curved diagonally outward toward the surf, forming a wide angle against the sand. To go that way meant target exposure. We were boxed in.

Val stirred against me in the darkness. "Tony?" A ragged whisper.

"Hush!"

"I'm a fool, Tony." Her face was a dim oval, raising to mine. "He's going to kill us both, like you said."

"It's a standoff, Val," I put an arm around her shoulder. "He thinks your gun is loaded. He'll be cautious—for a while."

"And then?"

I said nothing. We listened to the crash of the surf. The tide was coming in. Unexpectedly, Val's body moved against mine.

"Tony?"

"Stop it," I said.

She made a sound that was half giggle, half sob. She kept on with what she was doing, and the thunder in my blood drowned out the waves. I groped for her hands, pinned them.

"Please." Her breath was a soft furnace against my ear. "Yes. I'm crazy. But you don't know what it's like. Stephen knows. He's rotten, but he understands. He—"

I clamped a hand over her mouth. She bit me. I swore.

"Please," she said.

"Haven't you ever been to a doctor?"

"Many times. They talk about basal insecurity and father fixation and usually wind up making a pass at me." Her bright head tossed restlessly. "Sometimes they complete the pass. Max suspects, but doesn't know. Still, Max doesn't need me. He doesn't need anybody. Poor Max."

"Poor Max," I said bitterly. "So you helped Stephen rob him blind. Didn't you know he killed Ramos?"

"No," she whimpered. "Stephen called me Tuesday, the day after he disappeared. He told me you were tied in with Castle's syndicate, that you had killed Ramos by mistake. That his life was in danger, he needed my help. Tony, you're not going out there!"

"No choice." I patted her hand. "No matter what happens, stay hidden."

I hit the sand flat on my belly, crawling toward the high dunes.

Five years ago it had been like this. Five years ago, in Korea, squinting through the dawn of Punchbowl Ridge and waiting for the impact of a sniper's bullet. Crawling through sand, with your belly muscles knotted in anticipation of sudden death.

Nothing stirred on the dunes. The beach grass was motionless. I crawled face down, moving from one shadowed depression to another, praying for the moon to stay behind the clouds another five minutes. In my right hand was Val's useless gun.

He could be a hundred yards down the beach by now. He could be watching me from the other side of the dune. Far to my right, the beach flats were churning in phosphorescent needle splashes. A school of grunion, spawning in the shallows. I huddled behind a tiny dune, looking back at the cliff. It was a gigantic wall of shadow. Then I saw Val and almost cursed aloud.

She had emerged from the depression. She was standing, silhouetted clearly in the moonlight, staring at me like a pale frightened doll. Much later I wondered if she had some wild idea of diverting Stephen's attention, of possibly pleading with him. I never found out.

He came up over the dune directly in front of me, ten feet away. His face was polished bone in the moonlight. He did not look quite human. Hardly pausing to aim he fired twice.

My shout was lost in the roar of his gun. From five feet, I hurled Val's automatic squarely into his face. He lurched sideways. The .32 slammed again and sand kicked up inches from my face. I hit him low and hard, knees driving, and we rolled down the slope in a thrashing tangle of arms and legs.

I couldn't hold him. He moved with a writhing steel strength that flung me clear as we hit the wet beach flats. Then we stood facing each other a yard apart, panting. The .32 glittered in the sand ten feet away. He ignored it. He came at me, lips peeled back over his teeth, fists driving like pistons. I tried for his groin and he took my knee easily on the outside of his thigh and knocked me down with a whistling left hook that almost tore my head off.

I was down on my back. Stephen leaped. I rolled, desperately, as he came down stiff-legged where my face had been. It was an utterly unequal fight. Take a ninety-pound collie, a brave, determined beast. Pit him against a forty-pound lynx. The lynx invariably tears the collie to shreds. And Stephen weighed a lot more than forty pounds.

I managed to roll to my feet, gasping, my whole body shaking. Stephen came in, measuring me for a right that would have broken my jaw. But I was holding a fistful of damp sand. I threw it in his face. As he clawed for his eyes I grabbed his shirt, slumping forward, and butted him in the face. I felt the crackle of breaking cartilage, and Stephen made an animal sound in his throat. I brought my right elbow down like a hammer into the side of his neck. He quivered, stumbling toward me. I dodged back from his hands, and scooped up the .32. Stephen hesitated, his face a devil's mask of blood. I fired from eight feet.

And missed.

He had moved with incredible speed, veering sideways behind a dune.

Killing lust clotted my vision. It was a madness, an obsession, to destroy this man who had stolen my woman, had beaten me, had framed me for murder. I ran after him, and he was a darting, fleeing shadow that vanished down the south slope of beach. I fired after him again, futilely.

My breath came in great racking sobs. I ran after him, and stumbled, falling to my knees. The impact brought back sanity. I got up slowly, and went to find Val.

She was lying in the sand, eyes closed. The front of her dress was soaked with blood that looked like black ink in the moonlight. I cradled her in my arms and started toward the bluff steps.

CHAPTER THIRTEEN

HALFWAY up the cliff steps I sat down, fighting to keep from passing out. In my arms Val moaned softly and stirred. "Tony?" A burbling sigh.

"Take it easy," I said. "I'll get you to a doctor."

"I'm—sorry, Tony." Her eyelids fluttered, closed.

It gave me strength to reach the top of the steps. I got her into the front seat of the Pontiac and slid behind the wheel. When I pressed the starter, nothing happened.

I got out and lifted the hood. In the darkness it was, impossible to see what he had done. It could have been the timing rotor, the distributor, or a disconnected battery. I didn't know. All I knew was that somebody was swearing in a cracked, hopeless monotone. Me.

Val was dying. I had to get her to a hospital. Later, I realized Stephen had counted on that. He had fled, realizing that Val was my only living witness. With her dead, the police would never believe me. Another murder charge, open and shut.

I looked at Val's Buick, and started back down the cliff steps. Fatigue was a twisting scalpel in my side. The moon was a great silver floodlight, bathing the still peacefulness of sand and sea. I tried to imagine Stephen lurking in the nearby shadows. But there was only the slap of the waves as I walked into the cottage. Val's handbag was lying on the pink leather chesterfield. In it were the ignition keys to the Buick.

It took me a gasping, staggering eternity to climb those steps a second time. But I finally fell into the Buick, fumbled with the ignition. The engine kicked over with a purr. Why hadn't Stephen disabled it, also? No time, maybe. Maybe he expected to make his own getaway in it. I didn't know. I sat, drawing long shuddering breaths of utter exhaustion before I went back and lifted Val out of the Pontiac, as gently as I could. She was heavy, flaccid. As I lifted her into the Buick she coughed weakly, spitting blood.

I drove into Dana Point at eighty miles an hour. The dash clock said almost eleven-thirty when I found an all-night diner and consulted its phone book. There was an emergency clinic a mile north, just off the coast highway.

The clinic turned out to be a sprawling Spanish stucco with a dim light in the foyer. I kept punching the door buzzer viciously, and it seemed like a very long time before the male nurse opened the stained glass door and stared at us.

We were something to stare at. I looked like a tramp, with my clothes torn and sandy, my battered face. Val looked like a pale beautiful corpse in my arms.

"Later!" I snapped as the nurse started to ask questions. "She's hemorrhaging badly. She's got two bullets in her. Is there a doctor?"

He nodded calmly and helped me get her down the hall to a sickroom. He was a blond stocky man with big hands surprisingly gentle as he stretched Val out on the emergency table.

"Go back to the desk and fill out an admittance form," he said crisply. "I'll call Doctor Slattery. He'll be here in five minutes."

"How—is she?"

"Bad. She needs plasma." His frown was coldly suspicious. "How did it happen?"

"Tell you when the doctor gets here." I went back down the hall to the reception desk. I was filling out the admittance form when I saw the newspaper lying on the desk. A late night final.

I picked it up and turned to the front page. The story was on page one. *Slayer Resists Arrest, Flees.* Reading the story I felt a weird sense of unreality. Only a few hours ago, and it was already in the newspapers. On the fourth page was a photograph of my face. A photo that had been taken three years before when I had won a local tournament. Stilch had probably found it in my room. The picture made me look very young, fatuous. The story said nothing about my hitting Officer Stilch with a coffeepot. Only that the police expected an arrest before morning.

In a few minutes the nurse came down the hall. Without looking at me he sat down at the desk, rubbing his temples.

"It's been almost ten minutes," I said harshly. "Where's the doctor?"

"He's coming."

He looked at me with tired gray eyes and lighted a cigarette. "But there's no hurry now. Pity you couldn't get here sooner."

"You mean she's—"

"She died while I was administering plasma."

Suddenly, all I could think of was Max. I had a vision of his big ugly face distorted in grief. Lament for an unfaithful wife. His rage would be a killing thing—if Max discovered Fern had been with me tonight...

"I called the police," the nurse said. "You'd better stick around—*hey, come back here*—"

Once again, I ran. Out to the foyer and through the stained glass door. I had to warn Fern, and quickly. I had to get her away from the house of Max Baird. I was outside, in the Buick, hitting the starter, when I heard the growing shriek of sirens. They were very close. On the coast highway, I wouldn't have a chance.

I jumped out of the Buick and ran back to the foyer. The nurse tried to bar my way. He set himself and swung clumsily. I straight-armed him. He was shouting as I ran down the hall. Those sirens were a soft moan outside, and there was the metallic slam of car doors. The nurse was in the foyer doorway, shouting incoherently. I dodged into one of the wards and closed the door behind me.

Lying on the hospital cot was an old man, sleeping. In the dimness, his face had a faint bluish pallor. I stepped gingerly past him to the washroom and stood rigid against the marble basin. From this angle I could not be seen from the doorway. My breathing was a harsh rasp in the silence.

Heavy footsteps sounded down the corridor. The deep authoritative voice of the law. The shrill explanations of the male nurse. The voices faded.

The bathroom window was about two feet square, slightly above my head. I grabbed the sill with my fingertips and hoisted myself up to eye level. From almost directly under the window I heard the thrashing of shrubbery. Voices:

"You say he ran out the back door?"

"Yes, sir. I tried to stop him and he slugged me." The male nurse's voice. "He must be out there."

"If he is, we'll find him." A gruff voice, edged with caution. "You say he had a gun?"

"I'm not sure. The girl was shot twice."

"But you can definitely identify him as Pearson."

"Yes, sir. He looked just like his picture in the newspaper. He even signed the admittance statement as Pearson.

"Cold son-of-a-bitch," the officer said. "You'd better go inside. We'll need a statement."

Silence. Distant door slam. By craning my neck I managed to peer outside. Below was a dimly lighted garden with a small Spanish courtyard. In the center of the courtyard was a stone fountain. The surrounding brick walls were lined with thick tropicals and shrubbery. I saw three indistinct figures with flashlights and drawn guns, methodically probing the bushes.

"Funny thing, him showing in Dana Point. We got a flash earlier that he'd been spotted in Los Angeles. With Mrs. Locke."

"So he's crazy. You can't figure them. Did you call Stilch?"

"Yes, sir. He should be here any minute."

"This bird must have an obsession for women. First, he kills Locke over his wife, then kills Mrs. Baird. Is Headquarters contacting Baird?"

"I believe so. Captain, I'm afraid he's not out here."

More thrashing of brush. "Strange," the captain said. "Delahanty's covering the outside area. You think he could be hiding in the clinic?"

"It's possible, sir. He damned well isn't down here."

A heavy grunt. "Come on."

I had perhaps three minutes. They would cover the clinic room by room. The footsteps died away and there was the slam of the back door. I loosed the screen catch. I pushed the screen outward and it gave on its hinges. I hoisted myself through the window, head and shoulders. I was some six feet above a bank of acanthus. I wriggled through the window and fell, landing heavily on my back and shoulders. The screen had swung back to position. After a while I shifted delicately. I moved to a thicker area of shrubbery in the corner of the courtyard. Above me was a lighted window. I heard muffled voices. They became suddenly clear. I was huddling under the reception-room window.

"Pearson's on foot?" Stilch's voice, calm and cold. He hadn't wasted any time getting here.

"That's right," the captain said. "We've got three squad cars blocking the south edge of the highway and two cars combing the immediate area. A mouse couldn't get through. How did Baird take it?"

"Hard. He's on his way here now to make identification. You've got the M.E.'s report?"

"Death at approximately eleven-thirty, confirmed by the nurse's statement. One bullet in the left side, the other near the lower right ventricle. But why should he bother to bring her to the clinic?"

"Probably a passion killing. Afterward he was scared. He figured maybe she had a chance to live if he got her here in time. Most of that type feel a superficial remorse—after it's too late."

"I'd like to get my hands on that bastard," the captain said thoughtfully. "Just for two minutes. I'd make him forget all about women. What's your theory with regard to Mrs. Locke?"

"The old triangle story. He was reported with her earlier tonight. He apparently had a later tryst with Mrs. Baird. I can't figure why. Did you pick up Mrs. Locke for questioning?"

"She disappeared from Baird's house earlier tonight. We've got her description on teletype. You figure her for accessory?"

"Probably. I've a hunch we'll find them together."

"I sure feel sorry for Mr. Baird," the captain said. A pause. "Baird's a pretty big man in Point Rafael, isn't he?"

Sharply: "How do you mean?"

"He owns the Lee Shore. Understand it's quite a place." A smirk in the captain's voice. "Of course, I've never been there. Out of my territory."

There was frost in Stilch's tone. "You'd have to talk to Jed Wells about that. I'm only his deputy."

The voices drifted beyond earshot. I huddled in the dank tropicals, listening to the small night sounds. I was beyond hope, beyond planning. Fern had vanished. And if the police didn't shoot me on sight, my predestined end was that little room with the bad smell at San Quentin.

I tried to sleep. It was no good. My teeth kept chattering.

It was four in the morning. The clinic was dark and quiet. The press members had come and gone. But there would still be patrol cars cruising the nearby darkness. I was a fish in a net.

With Val dead, Stephen had nothing to fear. Right now, he was contacting Castle. He needed money, a plane, a fast boat. By this time tomorrow, Stephen would be in Acapulco or somewhere.

A random thought jerked me erect. Castle didn't actually need Stephen anymore. And the lean, white-haired gangster was utterly amoral. His obvious payoff for Stephen would be a moonlight swim with concrete water wings.

Ergo, Stephen had some kind of hold over Castle. Wallquist? I didn't know. But it gave me an idea.

I flexed aching muscles, and moved. The courtyard was dark and still. The garden gate was unlocked. I opened it cautiously and peered outside. There was a highway patrol car still parked in front of the clinic. Nobody was in it.

Five minutes later I was walking rapidly down the palm-lined road towards the coast highway. Morning fog was rolling in from the Pacific, a thick gray curtain that could mean the difference between life and death. Once a cruising prowl car passed and I flattened myself against a palm.

Fifteen minutes later I reached the coast highway. On the southeast corner the neon sign of a Serve-Yourself gas station shone redly in the mist. I went around in back, to the men's room. The attendant sat in his lighted glass cubicle. He glanced up, yawning, then went back to his paper.

First, I stripped. I was blood and sand from head to foot. I used paper towels to dry myself, rubbing until the skin tingled. The face that stared out of the bathroom mirror looked incredibly tired. But rest was not what I wanted.

I replaced Stephen's .32 carefully inside my shirt, under the waistband. There was one cartridge left in the chamber.

I was going to find Wallquist.

Outside the washroom I found the phone booth, near the grease rack. I dialed an all-night cab agency and gave them the station's address. They promised to have a cab there within five minutes.

The attendant was no longer in his office cubicle. He was out by the pumps, wiping a customer's windshield. I walked boldly toward the corner. I was standing there seconds later when the red spotlights hit me and there was the sharp whip crack of a voice:

"Don't move, Pearson! Hands behind your head."

The prowl car had stopped abreast on the highway. Now it swerved into the station and two officers got out. They approached me with professional caution, guns drawn. One of them was tall, with a tanned hawk fare. He handcuffed me, and found Stephen's gun.

The station attendant came over. He had a slack, bucktoothed grin.

"Thought you'd never get here." He eyed me in fascination. "Is there any kind of reward?"

"We'll let you know," hawk-face said. "Appreciate your calling."

The cop saw the look on my face and added: "We've alerted every place in the surrounding area, mister. He called us while you were in the can."

I said nothing. They shoved me into the back seat of the squad car. We drove north, toward the county seat. In the east you could see the gray sickness of dawn.

CHAPTER FOURTEEN

I WAS officially booked on suspicion of murder, photographed, and fingerprinted. They took me down the asphalt tile corridor to a room adjacent to Stilch's office. It was a small room with three barred windows, four chairs, and a large oak table. They left me alone with a big, sunburned deputy. I asked for a cigarette and the deputy handed me a pack, and matches. My body was one vast throbbing ache. But oddly enough I did not feel the need for sleep. Not yet. That would come later, under the glare of bright lights and the stabbing questions.

A wide, hard-faced man came in and sat at the table. He looked about forty; rimless glasses and thinning sandy hair. His voice was a courtroom bell.

"My name's Golightly, Assistant County Prosecutor. Would you care to dictate a confession?"

"Am I entitled to a lawyer?"

A contemptuous frown. "You figure on pleading temporary insanity, something like that?"

"Not at all. Stephen Locke killed Valerie, and I can prove it! Bring in the recorder and I'll make a detailed statement."

Blood darkened his forehead. "You'll get a sanity hearing within two hours after you make such a statement. If our psychiatrists declare you sane we'll ask for—and get—an automatic death penalty. You killed Locke six days ago! We're giving you a chance to level—"

"There's a black fifty-four Pontiac hardtop a mile south of Dana Point. You'll find Locke's fingerprints on the hood where he put them earlier tonight."

The sunburned deputy stirred in his chair. Golightly sat motionless, looking at the table. Finally he said with repressed fury, "Bring in the recorder, Tom."

They let me tell it in my own words. I said nothing about Midge or Charlie Wong. I confessed to stealing the Pontiac from a lot on Sunset strip. Once, Golightly interrupted me. He called in another deputy and had me give him the location of the Pontiac. He let me tell the rest of my story without interruption. When I finished he turned off the recorder and leaned forward. His questions came like blows from a tack hammer.

"First, Deputy Stilch came to your apartment. You attacked him. Why?"

"I was scared. Free, I could clear myself—"

"And when you found these…ah…charcoal sketches in Ramos' office, you thought you had partial proof of your innocence. Right?"

"Yes. That's right."

"Then why didn't you call the police from Ramos' office?"

The question came like a whip, and left me with my mouth open, fumbling for words. I finally muttered something about giving the sketches to Max first, and Golightly grunted. His pale eyes were relentless on mine.

"You say two men attacked you and burned the sketches. You and Mrs. Locke fled in a cab, correct?"

I just nodded.

"And where did you steal this Pontiac?"

"In the parking lot of The Players." The Players was a nightclub two blocks from Charlie Wong's.

"Then you drove back to Point Rafael. You let off Mrs. Locke at Baird's house. You followed Mrs. Baird to a beach house south of Dana Point. There, Stephen Locke tried to kill both of you.

Valerie Baird was fatally wounded. Again, Pearson, why didn't you notify the police?"

The question was asked with a theatrical weariness. In Golightly's eyes was a growing disgust.

"Because I wanted to get her to a doctor," I said.

"Very laudable. Where is Mrs. Locke now?"

I just blinked. He leaned across the table and said savagely, "Baird arrived home a little after midnight. He found a Dear John note from his wife. Fern Locke was nowhere in the house. Her bed gave no evidence of occupancy. Where is she, Pearson?"

"How the hell should I know?" The implication hit me, and I stood up, shaking. So did the deputy. "Listen," I whispered, "I happen to be in love with her. Wherever she is, she's safe—"

"Is she, Pearson?"

I sat, limply. Fern had waited at Baird's house for my call. An hour later she had gone to some undesignated rendezvous by herself. Wallquist? The Lee Shore?

The door opened and a deputy motioned. Golightly left the room. He was gone almost ten minutes. I lit a cigarette. My fingers kept twitching from fatigue. My eyelids weighed a ton. The deputy sat watching me like a cat. Golightly returned with a faint smile.

"Getting back to that Pontiac you stole. It fascinates me. How come the lot attendant didn't stop you?"

I hesitated. "He was at the side door helping some lush into his Cad. He never noticed until we drove out of the lot past him."

"I see. Let's review the beach cottage incident. You left the side door unlocked, right?"

"That's right."

"And the Pontiac you left at the top of the bluff with an inoperative motor." He was relaxed, almost benign. "Do you recall leaving the ignition keys in the car?"

"I think so. Yes."

"You must have. They weren't among your personal effects." Suddenly he shifted attack. "Quite a devil with the ladies, aren't you, Pearson?"

"How do you mean?"

"Look at you. Six-one, blond hair, big handsome golf pro. I'll bet you could have just about any girl you wanted."

What got me was his patronizing smile. He was talking as to a small child.

"Quite a feat, keeping two women on the string at the same time, isn't it?"

I saw where he was leading, and how it would look to a jury. "Wrong route," I said. "I never even met Valerie Baird until last Sunday night."

"You can prove that, of course." Bland deadly voice, eyes like blue ice.

"You know damned well I can't prove it! What are you trying to build?"

"Simply that there was no black Pontiac. Deputy Carstairs just called in from Dana Point. He checked the beach cottage you describe and found the doors locked. There was no sign of disorder; no Pontiac parked at the top of the bluff."

"Stephen doubled back," I breathed. "He locked the cottage. He ungimmicked the car and drove it away."

"Right after Carstairs phoned in his report, I called The Players. Did you know they're closed down this week? Remodeling. Try again, Pearson."

He wasn't bluffing. It was in his eyes, his smile.

"Then it was King's," I said. "Or some other place. I don't remember."

"Damned right you don't! Because you never followed Valerie Baird anywhere. It was all prearranged for her to pick you up, wasn't it? Only Fern suspected. You tried to shake her and she became violently jealous. You had a fight with her. Perhaps you killed her. When Valerie found out she became afraid of you. She saw you for what you really are—an oversexed psycho, subject to killing rages when crossed. She backed out of her promise to run off with you. So you cracked, completely. You killed her with two shots from that .32 you were carrying when we picked you up."

I wiped sweat from my eyes. "Then afterward, why did I take her to the hospital?"

He shrugged. "Fear. Remorse. After she died you became panicky, and tried to run. Where's Fern Locke?"

"I don't know!"

"Look at me. You killed her, didn't you?"

I was getting groggy. "I want a lawyer."

"No lawyer in the world would touch your case with a ten-foot pole. Why'd you kill Valerie Baird?"

"Locke. It was Stephen Locke."

"Locke's dead. Dead. Like you're going to be if you don't come clean. Valerie left the house at approximately ten o'clock. Where did she pick you up?"

"It was Stephen."

"Was it Los Angeles? Laguna?"

"It was the beach house. Baird's beach house."

"You were with Fern at the time. The police found her car abandoned in an alley in Los Angeles about eight o'clock last night. They found blood on the steering wheel. It was Fern's, wasn't it?"

"No. It was Midge's—"

"Who's Midge?"

"Nobody. I don't know whose blood it was."

"Fern threatened to turn you over to the police. She was jealous. Is that why you killed her?"

"It was Baird's beach house."

"Is that where you hid Fern's body?"

"Fern's alive. I don't know where she is."

"Val became afraid of you, didn't she? She changed her mind. You felt furious, betrayed. So you shot her."

"It was the Rembrandt. Stephen and Ramos—"

"That Rembrandt angle is pure hogwash, and you know it! We've got the gun you killed Valerie with. We've got method, motive, and opportunity. I'm not making any kind of deal, Pearson. You might get off with life if you tell a straight story. No promises. Pearson, look at me!"

His words rattled at me like hail, without meaning. His face looked fuzzed, out of focus. Now his palm came down on the table like a gunshot, and I jumped.

"I want a lawyer," I mumbled.

His questions were spikes, nailing the lid down on my coffin. It went on and on, and after a time I could see yellow sunlight coming into the room. I was retching with fatigue when the questions finally stopped and they took me to my cell. I did not remember whether or not I had confessed. I did not care.

My cell was small and clean. Steel casement windows, a cot, a sink, a toilet. I lay on my bunk with the echo of Golightly's questions still going on in my brain like a mad metronome. The turnkey came down the corridor with breakfast on a tin tray. Oatmeal and black coffee. The coffee was weak and had tiny spots of oil floating on top of it, but it was the most delicious coffee I have ever drunk in my life. I broke my last cigarette in two, and smoked one of the halves. Then I slept.

They woke me late in the afternoon. Two strange deputies took me back to that little room with the oak table. It was just like the morning, only worse. Golightly ridiculed me. He did not shout or swear. He kept probing the weak points in my story with his soft courtroom deftness, and twice he made me contradict myself about the times I had followed Valerie. Finally he brought in the recorder.

"Last chance, Pearson. I sincerely believe none of the killings were premeditated. Tell it again in your own words, what really happened. Locke's death was an accident, wasn't it? After that you became panicky—"

I cursed him.

His smile turned glacial. "Have it your way. Just answer one question."

"Go ahead."

"Based on the testimony you've given so far, do you honestly believe even a jury of your own relatives would take less than thirty seconds to convict you?"

I thought about it. "I guess not."

"But it's the truth so you're stuck with it, right?" He was a tower of righteous contempt. I just nodded.

"You figure the wilder the story the more chance you'll have of a hung jury. It's poor strategy, boy. Tomorrow morning you're going up against two specialists. You'll receive comprehensive written and oral sanity tests. The results of those tests, plus your recorded statement, will send you to the gas chamber."

"All right," I said wearily. "Now can I have a lawyer?"

The door opened and Stilch came in. He looked tired. "Come on back to your cell, Pearson."

Golightly gave him a queer frown, but said nothing. Another deputy took me back to my cell. Fifteen minutes later Stilch came along the corridor. The turnkey unlocked the cell door and let him in.

"Cigarette?" He extended a pack.

"Thanks," I said.

I inhaled greedily. The big deputy leaned against the bars, his smile quizzical. He had a small white bandage on the crown of his head.

"You swing a pretty mean coffeepot, dad."

"I'm sorry," I said, and I was. "I was scared."

"You lied to Golightly about that black Pontiac," Stilch said gently. "Want to tell me about it, off the record?"

"A friend helped me. The friend has a record and isn't involved in any of this. The same friend helped me sneak into Wallquist's office. I wouldn't tell you where he is now, even if I knew."

"I see," Stilch nodded. "Do you know what I did yesterday evening, after you crowned me?"

"What?"

"First, I called the county seat and had them put out a general fugitive alert on you. Then I had four stitches taken in my scalp. It hurt like hell."

His face got that stony Indian look. "Next, I did something no self-respecting cop would do. I asked the M.E. to go over Steve Locke's corpse with a fine tooth comb. Know what he found?"

I shook my head, not daring to hope. Stilch said, "A portion of the right thumb was still intact, enough for a print. Last night I had it checked with Sacramento. We got the call back ten minutes ago. This particular corpse has a different thumbprint than shows on Locke's driver's license. Ergo, it's not Steve Locke."

When it sank in, I almost choked with relief. "You mean I'm free?"

His smile was brutal. "Hardly. Ballistic tests show Valerie Baird was killed with two bullets from the same gun the arresting officers found in your shirt—"

"Stephen's hiding out within fifteen miles of here! He's probably in one of Castle's back rooms at the Shore. Castle will probably sneak him out of the state by tonight. For God's sake—"

"Take it easy. I believe you."

"You do?" I blinked. This was a switch. "Then how about questioning Wallquist? You could pull Castle in, sweat him—"

"And he'd be out in fifteen minutes," Stilch grunted. "We've got nothing to hold him on. What I should do is wait for Jed to get back. Monday, let him worry about the whole mess."

"By then Stephen will be out of the country! And Fern—"

I choked off as I realized where Fern was, where she had to be. Last night I had kissed her goodbye. She had poked at me with a shaken intensity. *Call me back in an hour, Tony. Please.*

Stilch read it in my face. "You know where she is?"

"At the Shore," I said. "She must have gone there last night when I didn't call her back. Castle's got her."

"Tough."

I was on my feet, yelling at him. "You callous bastard, you know I'm innocent! You can't sit by and let them kill her—"

The back of his hand felt like sheet iron. The slap came without warning, knocking me down.

"Four stitches," Stilch said with a tearing bitterness. "You stupid bastards who think you're clever enough to break ordinances—withholding evidence, resisting arrest. Who think a cop is some kind of fumbling parasite on the civic payroll. If you hadn't fought me last night Valerie Baird would be alive right now. We could have questioned her. She might have told us where Locke was hiding. "I'm sorry, Pearson. You're a day late and a dollar short."

The cell door clanged behind him. After a time I got up. I sat listlessly on the bunk.

Ten minutes later Stilch returned to my cell. The turnkey opened the door and he said, "Come on." I did not ask questions. We went down the corridor to his office. He shut the door and sat down. His jaw muscles were knotted and his eyes held a hard wet shine.

"I'm just an ordinary cop," he said softly. "That's why I'll never be county sheriff. Baird backed Jed in the last election because he can handle him. Nobody handles me. Understand?"

"I understand."

"Officially, I've no right to go after Castle, to raid him. The Shore is Jed's business. He's paid to look the other way. Two weeks after I shut them down they'd be wide open again. And inside of a month Jed would find some excuse to lift my badge. You've got just one chance to clear yourself, Tony. If it fails—you stand trial for Val's murder, and I'm an ex-cop."

He went over it, step by step. His plan was excellent. It had only one flaw.

If it failed, I wouldn't have to worry about the gas chamber. They don't execute corpses.

CHAPTER FIFTEEN

FIRST, Stilch had me repeat descriptions of the two men who had slugged me outside of Wallquist's office. He left the room and returned with a handful of mug shots. I leafed through them. One of the photographs looked familiar. "Blondie," I said.

Stilch nodded. "His name's Donlevy. Two years in Quentin on a narcotics rap. Arrested a few times on morals violations, once for assault. He works for Castle. Let's go."

Within the next fifteen minutes Stilch cut red tape with amazing efficiency. I was officially released in his custody for the purpose of securing additional evidence. Outside, it was blue dusk and the stars were earning out.

"Seven o'clock," Stilch said. "You've got two hours. Where's your car?"

"At the Hidaway, in Laguna. Would it be better if I took a cab?"

"Your car's better." He hesitated, looking at my clothes. "You've got time for a shave and shower at my place, if you wish."

It brought a sudden lump to my throat. As we drove toward Stilch's Newport apartment, I decided this unpredictable giant was one of the nicest guys I had ever met.

It was seven-thirty when I stepped out of Stilch's shower. I shaved, and found a clothes brush in his towel closet. It helped little. My suit was still a mess. I found Stilch in the kitchenette, brooding at the phone.

"I just called Baird," he said. "He doesn't like any part of it. He thinks you killed Valerie. But he'll go along."

I felt sympathy for Max. A big tough Greek with the heart of a child. He would accept Val's death with a surface fatalism but his inner anguish would be unspeakable. I was glad, in that moment, that I was not Stephen Locke.

Our next stop was Laguna. Stilch dropped me off at the Hidaway. Miraculously, my Ford was still parked in the back lot. Nobody had bothered to steal it. "You get ten minutes' start," Stilch said bleakly. "Then I call headquarters; tell them you escaped from my custody. The Highway Patrol might shoot you on sight. Feel like backing out?"

"No."

He grinned. We shook hands and he drove away.

I walked across the street and got into the Ford. I drove slowly down the coast highway and passed two drive-ins before I found one that looked busy enough. Dinner was a beef sandwich, soggy fries, and black coffee. I ate like a starved wolf. The carhop hardly glanced at me as I paid the check. It was twenty minutes after eight.

Driving toward Point Rafael, I tried to analyze the tension gripping my insides. It had been like this during the big tournaments—the avid hush of the gallery as you concentrated on a delicate approach shot. But now there was something added. A sense of destiny, a hard core of anger. It might be interesting to take such a mental attitude into a golf tourney some time—if I lived.

At nine o'clock I pulled into the parking lot of the Lee Shore. Mauve spotlights bathed the facade in shifting colors as I walked boldly toward the doorway arch. The doorman was a gigantic Negro-Gargantua in silver pants and vest. He looked impassively at my seedy flannels, but did not try to stop me.

The lobby was a plush cathedral of marble pillars and sea-green carpeting. Giant tropicals exploded from flagstone planters and you could see the outside pools through a wall of glass. Your first impression was of sedate, carefully tailored splendor.

Then you heard the laughter from the bar. You saw the faces in the lobby, male and female, the glazed anticipation. Ahead of me, a woman in cerise slacks and gilt sandals was walking into the bar. She had brightly hennaed hair and looked at least seventy years old. I followed her.

The bar was a murk of red light and cigarette smoke. The erotic sob of invisible violins counterpointed hushed giggles from the booths. It was like a hall of mirrors, the garish light distorting expressions, accenting the slyness, the moist smiles, the shamed hunger.

The bartender drifted over, soundless as smoke. He looked like the doorman's twin brother.

"Pernod," I said.

He gave me a half-moon grin and moved down the bar. That order had just branded me as one of the boys. I belonged. The woman on the adjacent stool stirred, looked at me. She was the hennaed crone I had seen in the lobby.

"Are you from Paris?"

"Not lately," I said.

"I knew it." She leaned breathlessly over. "I lived there for twenty years. Spotting continental types gets to be a hobby. Is this your first time?"

I hesitated. She flashed a withered, intimate smile. "Try the amethyst room if it's your first time. You'll feel so *cleansed* afterward, know what I mean?"

The bartender brought my pernod. As I paid him, there was a furtive burst of titters from one of the booths. I did not turn my head.

"Poor things," said the hennaed grandmother, looking. "Sick people with money. Dykes and queens, groping for expression. You're different. I can tell." She glanced at her watch and slid off the stool. "I'm going upstairs, dear. The amethyst room, don't forget."

I promised not to forget. She left the bar raptly. Four other couples were also leaving. I watched them cross the lobby to a private elevator near the reception desk. All on their way to cloud seven. I felt soiled, ashamed of being a member of the human race.

Then I saw Blondie.

He came into the bar wearing a midnight blue jacket and white slacks. He sat two stools away. The bartender poured him a cup of coffee.

"Hi, Donlevy," I said.

He looked over and spilled his coffee. Carefully, set the cup down. His eyes were bemused.

"Where's Castle?"

"Upstairs. In the Cinnabar Room." He said it almost diffidently. For him the situation must have been without precedent. I should have been safely behind cell bars, not sitting here in this bar, calmly sipping a pernod.

"I'm supposed to see him." I stood up, decisively. "It's about the Rembrandt. He'll understand."

"Fine." Blondie moistened his lips. "Sure."

We went out of the bar together. He seemed dazed, but grateful to me for taking the decision out of his hands. We went into an ivory elevator with blue leather lining. On the way up neither of us spoke. Then his face changed and he snapped, "Hands over your head."

I stood meekly while he patted my clothes for weapons. "You won't find it," I said, deadpan. "It's a midget cobalt bomb concealed behind my left wisdom tooth."

"Wise," he spat out. "Cute."

The elevator door opened. We walked down a hall of rose-colored carpeting, past picture windows framing the Pacific. In front of us a green leather door opened and a fat man in tuxedo came out. His face was pearled with sweat. He stared blindly at us, retching. Blondie ignored him.

Two doors down we went into a small dark alcove. Two quietly dressed men looked at me without recognition. "Identification, sir?"

"He's with it," Blondie said nervously. "Castle wants him."

"Right now?"

Blondie's thought processes were tortuously clear. Whatever Castle wanted could certainly wait until this particular floorshow was over. While he was deciding, I shoved hard on the swinging gilt door on my right. They grabbed at me, too late.

I was in the Cinnabar Room.

The first confused thought was that I had blundered into a ballet recital chamber. About fifty people sat in tiered seat rows, looking at the brilliantly lighted stage dais. Five girls in crimson leotards pirouetted to the raw throb of drums. Unnoticed, I sank into the back row of seats.

Castle sat four rows down, regal in dinner jacket, intent on the dancers. A few seats away, I recognized a fading movie queen who had gone through four husbands and was still big box office. Near her sat a once-famous bandleader who had dropped out of sight a few years back, after some unsavory publicity resulting from morals charges. Sick people with money.

The drumbeats quickened. The stage lights turned dusky purple. I stared at the dais. Five flawless bodies, moving in primitive abandon.

Their leotards were painted on.

Once I had been to a stag show. In the middle of it I had left with sick revulsion. But what was happening onstage made stag shows seem stilted and Victorian.

Two men came onstage. They wore loincloths and were muscled like Hercules. They advanced with tantalizing slowness, silhouetted in gigantic shadow against the drapes. Their movements were stylized as a Japanese frieze. The music sank to a raw demanding whisper. The dancers were completely preoccupied. It did not seem as if they could possibly be doing what they were obviously doing. Yet their movements were perfectly synchronized to the music. Choreography by Dante.

It was beyond paganism, beyond black mass. The stage was a nexus in time drawing you back three thousand years to the wild fertility rites of Carthage in the temple of Tanit. One of the dancers raised her head. Her scream blended with the harsh dissonance of brass.

Simultaneously, someone nudged my elbow. I turned, as in a dream. Castle sat next to me.

I stood up. Castle motioned me toward the door. Once I looked back. A woman in the audience was crying out incoherently. She was stumbling toward the dais, ripping off her clothes.

We were outside, in the alcove. "Move," Castle said. He held a gun steady, a short-barreled .38. We walked along the corridor. Those dancers curled in a slow pinwheel like slime in my brain. I wanted badly to vomit. At the end of the corridor we turned down a short flight of steps to an oak door. Castle opened it, and we went in.

It was a large room with parquet flooring and fireplace. French windows framed the dark slope of beach. Fern sat in a white womb chair by the fireplace. Across from her, on a leather chesterfield by the french windows, sat Stephen.

CHAPTER SIXTEEN

THE ROOM was choked with a harsh dry tension. My first emotion was wild relief. They had not harmed Fern. Not yet.

"I'm sorry, Tony." She looked up at me with a tragic smile. "When you didn't call me last night, I became panicky—"

"And came snooping here to see if I was safe," Stephen grinned. "Obviously, she still loves me. We're married, remember?"

One of Stephen's cheeks was darkly swollen, and his broken nose was bound with adhesive, yet he sat cool and deadly amused. Castle beckoned with the .38. "Sit down, Tony."

I sat on the chesterfield opposite Fern.

"How did you get out of jail?" Castle asked.

"Bail," I said. I had rehearsed this twice with Stilch. "Valerie talked before she died. There's a fugitive warrant out for Stephen right now."

It had all the potential of a hand grenade.

Stephen sat motionless. Castle rocked easily on the balls of his feet, studying Stephen like a lean, white-haired cat. "So you had it all wrapped up," he murmured. "No loose ends—"

"He's lying!" Stephen's eyes flicked mine in chill appraisal. "I've played chess with him, and he's lying."

"We'll see. Here..."

Castle tossed Stephen the gun. I tensed on the chesterfield, and relaxed. Stephen was too fast. "Soon enough." He tasted the words. "Very soon, now, Tony."

From the adjoining room came the sound of a phone dialing. Castle's curt voice. I glanced at my watch. Nine thirty-five. I had to stall, desperately, for all possible time. But time was running out. Stephen leaned back with a faint smile.

"An interesting gambit," he said. "But it's over, Tony. Your mistake was letting Fern help you. Because, deep down inside, she still happens to be in love with me. See? She's blushing."

Fern gazed at him steadily, her lips tremulous. She was fighting to keep from going to pieces and I wondered, with a pang, how strong his basic attraction still was. Stephen read my face and chuckled.

"You're right; our love life was a cold war. Yet if I died right now, she'd grieve, terribly. Right, darling?"

Killing him had become a necessity elemental as breathing. I moved delicately on the chesterfield, gauging the split seconds that would mean grappling for the gun, or writhing on the parquet with my guts torn out by .38 slugs.

"Don't, Tony," Fern whispered. My chance was gone.

Castle came back into the room. He stared at me with sardonic perplexity. "You fool," he said. "Just what did you hope to gain?"

I said nothing. Castle turned to Stephen. "Val died without talking. Pearson escaped an hour ago. They're combing the entire county for him."

"Well," Stephen's smile turned dreamy. "Stand up, Tony."

I saw it in his eyes. He had never been able to break Fern's spirit while they were married, but now he was going to break her completely and forever. By killing me.

"Stephen," Fern said.

"Yes?" The gun steadied on my chest. He did not look at her.

"I'll go with you," Fern said in a carefully controlled voice. "Like you wanted me to. I swear it, darling. He can't hurt you—"

"But it's necessary," Stephen said seriously. "Don't you see how necessary it is?"

He was no longer quite sane. The pressure of hiding had finally cracked his brilliant instability. Castle saw it, and stopped smiling. He said, "Wait. Not here."

"Why not here?"

"Because it stinks. His being here stinks. Alive or dead, I don't want him near the Shore. Supposing you leave tonight—"

"I told you earlier, I'm staying. I leave Monday night after we've settled up."

"You're being glandular again," Castle said coldly. "Wallquist doesn't collect until Monday. Ask them, they were both eavesdropping."

"He's right," Fern said. "It's a Canadian client. He's paying four hundred thousand for the Van Ryn."

I wanted to kiss her. Stephen sat with a curious rigidity. "Four hundred—"

"Don't be a fool!" Castle took two furious steps toward Fern. "Isn't it obvious? She's playing cute."

Stephen frowned at Fern, reading her. "It's true," I said. "He's holding out on you. Why not call Wallquist, ask him?"

Almost, it worked. For a moment the .38 wavered, and I saw uncertainty in Stephen's eyes. Then Castle laughed with shriveling contempt. "Go ahead, call Wallquist. You're dead, remember?"

Stephen sighed. "Ronnie, if this is a holdout—"

"It's not, but I'll still up the ante, you suspicious clown. I'll make your share a hundred thousand—provided you stay on my yacht until Monday night. The Shore's too risky."

It was like a clash of wills between father and son. Stephen, with a jungle wariness, examined Castle's soft lethal logic.

"I was planning a Catalina cruise this weekend," Castle said patiently. "The yacht's anchored two miles out. My cabin cruiser's at the landing on the other side of the jetty. You can run the cruiser out to the yacht, and dispose of these two on the way. A year from now, the police will still be looking for them."

Fern stirred, her dark eyes fixed on Castle. Her smile was the prelude to hysteria.

"You're wrong!" I fought to keep my voice hard. "When both of us vanish, Stilch starts wondering. So does Max. They pull Wallquist in, start grilling him. He'll crack like a walnut—"

"Jed Wells comes back from vacation tomorrow," Castle breathed. "A smart sheriff, Jed. Too smart to interrogate innocent bystanders."

It was cut and dried. Wells would smother any sideline investigation. Ultimately it would be one of those cases that gather dust in the sheriff's unsolved file.

"Not bad." Stephen stood up, handed the gun to Castle. I had no chance to jump him. "Only one exception, Ronnie. Fern goes on board the yacht with me. We can have a brief, second honeymoon. Objections?"

Castle seemed oddly relieved. "As long as she doesn't talk."

"She won't." Stephen stood over me, hands loose at his sides. "Just so Tony doesn't prove too troublesome beyond the breakwater—"

His palm whipped at my throat. A quick, killing blow.

But I was already in motion, rolling backward across the chesterfield.

As I hit the floor Stephen kicked me in the temple. A glancing blow, but it turned my muscles to water. Fern screamed. Stephen's heel drove down to crush my windpipe; and Castle shouted, "Listen!"

We heard it. Distant, frightened shouts. The muffled pounding of many feet. "A raid," Castle said incredulously. "How—"

The door flew open. Blondie stared glassily at us. His face had been battered almost beyond recognition. Someone shoved from behind and he staggered and fell. Stilch came into the room. Behind him were Max and Lupo.

For one incredible second no one moved. Max stared at Castle, at Stephen. His dark face was expressionless, cast in stone.

Then the room exploded in a crescendo of movement and sound.

Max roared incoherently and charged at Stephen. Castle shot from ten feet and Max went down like an eyelid. Stephen was a blur, moving diagonally across the room as Lupo went after him. Stephen's fist struck; it seemed a tapping backhanded blow. But Lupo went sideways like a thrown stone. Glass shattered as Stephen knifed through the french doors. Stilch was on his knees behind the overturned chesterfield, shooting methodically at Castle.

The shots blended into a drumfire of continuous sound. Castle collapsed in a writhing coil on the parquet.

I was on my feet, running across the room. Fern divined my intention and got in my way. I pushed her aside and went through the french doors, slashing my hands on the glass shards. I sprawled on my knees on hard-packed beach sand. Fifty yards down the strand Stephen was running fleetly toward the stone jetty.

I got up and pounded after him. Then someone tripped me from behind and I sprawled on my face. It was Fern. She was sobbing, her face bright with tears in the moonlight, and she was trying to tell me something. I struck at her savagely, turning after Stephen, and damned if she didn't trip me again.

I got up. She had her arms around me, her damned lying arms around me, and I tore them away. Did she love him that much? I was sobbing, deep in my throat. It had taken this to bring it out, the thing I had feared. I had known it was inside her, and Stephen had known it; known that he had left his bright corrosion forever on her soul, and years from now he would think about it and he would laugh, remembering.

I shoved Fern so hard she fell, and I ran down the beach after Stephen. He had too good a start. I reached the jetty in time to hear the cough of the cruiser's motor as it moved away from the landing. I hurdled the jetty, splashing knee-deep in water, and I was too late.

The launch was fifty yards beyond the surf, gathering speed. Stephen waved me a mocking goodbye from the helm.

It was all over.

I felt drained, empty. On the other side of the jetty my legs gave out and I sat down on the sand.

I sat there for what seemed a very long time, watching the confusion in the Shore parking lot. Protesting figures in evening dress were being herded into paddy wagons. I counted four squad cars. Stilch was making a clean sweep. I thought about the headlines and wondered if they would indict Jed Wells when he came back Monday, or if he would simply resign because of ill health, the way they do.

Two figures came down the beach. Fern and Stilch.

"We won," Stilch said somberly. "Finding Stephen justified the raid. An hour ago they picked up Consuela Ramos and brought her down from Los Angeles. She definitely identified her husband's body."

I said that was fine.

"Castle's dead," Stilch continued. "He talked before he died. A sketchy confession, but we had Max and Lupo for witnesses. Max got a superficial scalp wound."

Fern's eyes were pleading, but I would not look at her. "He got away," I said tiredly. "In Castle's launch. He'll head for Newport harbor, somewhere down the coast. They'll never catch him."

Stilch winked at Fern. He seemed remarkably unconcerned. "Pearson, you're a fool."

Looking at Fern, I agreed.

"For a while we were afraid Donlevy wouldn't tell us where you were," Stilch said. "Lupo worked on him. He came around very quickly. Lupo, incidentally, has a broken collar bone."

Fern knelt in the sand. Her voice was a clear whisper, "Remember when Midge mentioned Castle had rented his yacht to some friends for a La Paz cruise last week? Remember, Tony?"

I looked at her without understanding. Stilch lighted a cigarette. "Castle never had the slightest intention of splitting with Steve," he said. "Yet he couldn't risk any violence at the Shore. Fern suspected it when he lied about his yacht being offshore."

His words were meaningless. But Fern looked so lovely and pitiful that I put my arms around her. She gave a choked sob. "Forget it," I said tiredly. "You were married to him. You couldn't help it."

"It's not what you think, Tony—"

"Sure." I patted her head. "Of course not."

We started back down the beach. I said, "We might at least notify the coast guard."

"Forget it." Stilch squinted out to sea. Both he and Fern seemed tensed, waiting for something. "Castle told us something else before he died. There's no honor among thieves."

Then it came.

It came in an orange sheet of flame illuminating the entire ocean a half-mile out. The explosion followed seconds later, a giant cough. Scattered red sparks glowed distantly, then winked out.

"No point in bothering the coast guard," Stilch said cheerfully. "Come on, let's go down to the county seat."

It was two in the morning. We were drinking coffee in Stilch's office at the county seat—Max, Fern, myself. Max sat chewing a dead cigar, a bandage around his forehead. He had seemed utterly withdrawn from the entire proceedings, the recorded statements, the flash of newspaper cameras, the questions. Stilch came in, calm and tired.

"Downtown Los Angeles just called in. They've had Wallquist in the station house for the past two hours. When they threatened to throw a murder accessory charge at him, he confessed. They'll probably charge him with grand theft. We're contacting the Canadian authorities first thing in the morning to recover the Rembrandt."

Max said, "So where does that leave me?"

Stilch shrugged. "Ultimately, the Dutch government gets their Rembrandt back. It's out of my hands. You might even catch a fine for illegal possession."

Suddenly Max seemed shriveled, old. In the end they had all turned on him. Adopted son, faithless wife, treacherous business partner.

"I've lost the Shore." Max was speaking to himself, not to us. "The Rembrandt. Val's gone. Stephen's gone. I've still got me a big house, a country club. I've got Lupo." He shivered. "I'm sorry, Tony."

"Forget it."

Max sat stiffly erect. "I want to make it up to you. Yesterday I fired my new pro. He tried to change my stance."

Fern's finger tightened in mine.

"I'll give you a five-year contract," Max said huskily. "A piece of the club. What say?"

Big, lonely, vulnerable Greek, pleading for something I could never give him. Fern looked at me, her eyes soft. A year ago we had fought about this. I had wanted the tournament gamble, she had craved security. I loved her. It was no choice.

"Thanks," I said, trying to smile. "Thanks, Max…"

"We're sorry," Fern interrupted gently, "but let us take a rain check on it, Max. First, Tony and I are following the sun for awhile."

It was like gold, and I stared at her, afraid to believe it, and her smile was all the reassurance I needed.

"The Phoenix Open starts next week," Fern said shyly. "It still gives us time for a honeymoon."

Max was saying something else, something about staking me to the summer circuit if I'd sign with him. But I wasn't listening.

I was kissing my girl.

THE END

If you've enjoyed this book, you will not want to miss these terrific titles…

ARMCHAIR SCI-FI & MYSTERY CLASSICS, $12.95 each

C-40   **MODEL FOR MURDER**
by Stephen Marlowe

C-41   **PRELUDE TO MURDER**
by Sterling Noel

C-42   **DEAD WEIGHT**
by Frank Kane

C-43   **A DAME CALLED MURDER**
by Milton Ozaki

C-44   **THE GREATEST ADVENTURE**
by John Taine

C-45   **THE EXILE OF TIME**
by Ray Cummings

C-46   **STORM OVER WARLOCK**
by Andre Norton

C-47   **MAN OF MANY MINDS**
by E. Everett Evans

C-48   **THE GODS OF MARS**
by Edgar Rice Burroughs

C-49   **BRIGANDS OF THE MOON**
by Ray Cummings

C-50   **SPACE HOUNDS OF IPC**
by E. E. "Doc" Smith

C-51   **THE LANI PEOPLE**
J. F. Bone

C-52   **THE MOON POOL**
by A. Merritt

C-53   **IN THE DAYS OF THE COMET**
by H. G. Wells

C-54   **TRIPLANETARY**
C. C. Doc Smith

If you've enjoyed this book, you will not want to miss these terrific titles…

ARMCHAIR SCI-FI & HORROR DOUBLE NOVELS, $12.95 each

D-141   **ALL HEROES ARE HATED** by Milton Lesser
            AND THE STARS REMAIN by Bryan Berry

D-142   **LAST CALL FOR DOOMSDAY** by Edmond Hamilton
            HUNTRESS OF AKKAN by Robert Moore Williams

D-143   **THE MOON PIRATES** by Neil R. Jones
            CALLISTO AT WAR by Harl Vincent

D-144   **THUNDER IN THE DAWN** by Henry Kuttner
            THE UNCANNY EXPERIMENTS OF DR. VARSAG by David V. Reed

D-145   **A PATTERN FOR MONSTERS** by Randall Garrett
            STAR SURGEON by Alan E Nourse

D-146   **THE ATOM CURTAIN** by Nick Boddie Williams
            WARLOCK OF SHARRADOR by Gardner F. Fox

D-148   **SECRET OF THE LOST PLANET** by David Wright O'Brien
            TELEVISION HILL by George McLociard

D-147   **INTO THE GREEN PRISM** by A Hyatt Verrill
            WANDERERS OF THE WOLF-MOON by Nelson S. Bond

D-149   **MINIONS OF THE TIGER** by Chester S. Geier
            FOUNDING FATHER by J. F. Bone

D-150   **THE INVISIBLE MAN** by H. G. Wells
            THE ISLAND OF DR. MOREAU by H. G. Wells

ARMCHAIR SCIENCE FICTION CLASSICS, $12.95 each

C-61   **THE SHAVER MYSTERY, Book Six**
          by Richard. S. Shaver

C-62   **CADUCEUS WILD**
          by Ward Moore & Robert Bradford

ARMCHAIR MYSTERY-CRIME DOUBLE NOVELS, $12.95 each

B-1   **THE DEADLY PICK-UP** by Milton K. Ozaki
          KILLER TAKE ALL by James O. Causey

B-2   **THE VIOLENT ONES** by E. Howard Hunt
          HIGH HEEL HOMICIDE by Frederick C. Davis

B-3   **FURY ON SUNDAY** by Richard Matheson
          THE AGONY COLUMN by Earl Derr Biggers

If you've enjoyed this book, you will not want to miss these terrific titles...

ARMCHAIR SCI-FI & HORROR DOUBLE NOVELS, $12.95 each

D-131   **COSMIC KILL** by Robert Silverberg
BEYOND THE END OF SPACE by John W. Campbell

D-132   **THE DARK OTHER** by Stanley Weinbaum)
WITCH OF THE DEMON SEAS by Poul Anderson

D-133   **PLANET OF THE SMALL MEN** by Murray Leinster
MASTERS OF SPACE by E. E. "Doc" Smith & E. Everett Evans

D-134   **BEFORE THE ASTEROIDS** by Harl Vincent
SIXTH GLACIER, THE by Marius

D-135   **AFTER WORLD'S END** by Jack Williamson
THE FLOATING ROBOT by David Wright O'Brien

D-136   **NINE WORLDS WEST** by Paul W. Fairman
FRONTIERS BEYOND THE SUN by Rog Phillips

D-137   **THE COSMIC KINGS** by Edmond Hamilton
LONE STAR PLANET by H. Beam Piper & John J. McGuire

D-138   **BEYOND THE DARKNESS** by S. J. Byrne
THE FIRELESS AGE by David H. Keller, M. D.

D-139   **FLAME JEWEL OF THE ANCIENTS** by Edwin L. Graber
THE PIRATE PLANET by Charles W. Diffin

D-140   **ADDRESS: CENTAURI** by F. L. Wallace
IF THESE BE GODS by Algis Budrys

ARMCHAIR SCIENCE FICTION CLASSICS, $12.95 each

C-58   **THE WITCHING NIGHT**
by Leslie Waller

C-59   **SEARCH THE SKY**
by Frederick Pohl and C. M. Kornbluth

C-60   **INTRIGUE ON THE UPPER LEVEL**
by Thomas Temple Hoyne

ARMCHAIR SCI-FI & HORROR GEMS SERIES, $12.95 each

G-15   **SCIENCE FICTION GEMS, Vol. Eight**
Keith Laumer and others

G-16   **HORROR GEMS, Vol. Eight**
Algernon Blackwood and others

:

Made in the USA
Middletown, DE
27 February 2023

25386168R00144